郑州大学外语系

宋运田

Dep. of Foreign languages
    of Zhengzhou University
    Zhengzhou, Henan
People's Republic of China

    Song Yun-tian

Contemporary
Chinese Short Stories

Panda Books

Panda Books

First edition, 1983

Copyright 1983 by CHINESE LITERATURE

ISBN 0-8351-1076-1

Published by CHINESE LITERATURE, Beijing (37), China

Distributed by China Publications Centre (GUOJI SHUDIAN)

P.O. Box 399, Beijing, China

Printed in the People's Republic of China

CONTENTS

A Herdsman's Story

Zhang Xianliang

IT had never occurred to Xu Lingjun that he would ever meet his father again.

Now, he was talking with him in a luxuriously furnished room on the seventh floor of a smart hotel. Here, outside the window, there was only a sheet of blue sky dotted with a few floating clouds. But there, far away on his farm on the loess plateau, the scene was entirely different with stretch after stretch of green and yellow fields, broad and flourishing. Sitting in this room, wreathed in mist-like smoke from his father's pipe, he found himself flying up and up above the clouds and everything before him transformed into an unfathomable illusion. Yet, the familiar, almost coffee-like fragrance of his father's tobacco, the one with the Red Indian chief on the label which he'd known from early childhood, proved to him that he was not in some fairyland in the sky but very firmly in the real world.

"Let bygones be bygones," his father said, waving his hand. Ever since obtaining his bachelor's degree at Harvard in the 30s, he'd kept the airs of his student days. Now, sitting on a sofa cross-legged in his fine suit, he continued, "The moment I set foot on the mainland, I learned the current political term 'look forward'. So you'd better get ready to go abroad."

All at once, Xu felt a sort of nameless depression brought on by his father's appearance as well as by the room's decoration. He said to himself, "It's true that bygones are bygones, but how could I possibly forget all that's happened?"

Thirty years ago, on an autumn day much like this, Xu, clutching a note addressed by his mother, had found his way to a western-style villa on Avenue Joffre in the French Concession of Shanghai. The yellow leaves looked even more withered after the shower and raindrops dripped relentlessly from the parasol trees outside the barbed-wire-topped wall. The iron gate of the villa had been painted an intimidating grey. Only after repeated pressings of the bell did a small hatch in the gate open and the doorkeeper appear. It was the man who often sent letters to his father and the two recognized one another. Presently, the boy was ushered along a cement path flanked by two rows of ilex trees and soon arrived at the sitting room of a two-storey building.

Of course, his father had been much younger then. Wearing a cream-coloured woollen vest, he was smoking his pipe, his head bent, one elbow resting on the mantlepiece. On the sofa in front of the fireplace sat the woman Xu's mother cursed and damned all day long.

"Is this your son?" Xu heard her ask his father. "Doesn't he look like you! Come over here, child!"

Motionless, Xu shot her a glance. He had seen, he remembered now, a pair of shining eyes and heavily rouged lips.

"What's the matter?" Father looked up.

"Mum is ill. She wants you to come back right away."

"She is always sick," Father growled, leaving the fireplace and pacing to and fro furiously on the green-

and-white-striped carpet. Xu fixed his stare on his father's step, trying to hold back his tears.

"Tell your mother I'll be back soon." His father finally stopped in front of him. His mother had heard this time and again over the telephone and Xu knew that it was not to be relied upon. Timid but obstinate, he ventured again, "Mum wants you to go home right now."

"I know, I know. . . ." With that, Father placed a hand on the boy's shoulder, and encouraged him gently towards the door. "You go ahead and take my car. I'll come along in a while. If your mother's condition takes a turn for the worse, urge her to go to hospital first." Leading his son into the front hall, he patted the boy's head affectionately and suddenly continued in a low voice, "If only you were a bit more grown up, you'd know that your mother is a difficult woman to get along with, she's so . . . so. . . ."

Looking up, Xu saw how weak and bitter his father was and felt sorry for him.

But no sooner had the automobile in which Xu sat started along the leaf-carpeted street in the French Concession than the tears coursed down his cheeks and a wave of humiliation, self-pity and loneliness suddenly seized him. He felt that nobody else except he alone was really to be pitied. In truth, he got little affection from his mother. Her fingers touched mahjong more often than they did his hair. And neither had he ever received much guidance from his father. Whenever he did come home, he invariably looked gloomy and bored, and then usually the endless quarrelling would break out between the two of them.

As his father had said, if he had been a bit more

grown up, he would have been able to understand. In fact, even at the age of eleven, the boy had long had a vague sense of things anyway. What his mother wanted was her husband's affection, while his father wanted badly to discard such an ill-tempered wife. And neither of them had ever needed him. Xu was fully aware of the fact that he was nothing more than the product of an arranged marriage between a student returned from the United States and a young woman from a landlord family.

That night, as usual, his father didn't come home. Before long, it was learned that he had left China with his mistress, and eventually his mother died in a German-run hospital.

It was at that time that the People's Liberation Army entered Shanghai.

And now, thirty years had passed. After all of these unprecedentedly eventful and changing years, his father had suddenly turned up, claiming to want his son to go abroad with him. All of this seemed mysterious and inconceivable. He could hardly believe that his own father was now sitting in front of him, and neither could he believe that it was really he himself who sat opposite.

When Miss Song, his father's secretary, opened the wardrobe door, he happened to catch a glimpse of several suitcases pasted with colourful labels from hotels in Los Angeles, Tokyo, Bangkok and Hong Kong, as well as the oval trademark of Universal Airlines. The small wardrobe symbolized a whole new world. For Xu Lingjun, however, coming here all the way from his farm had meant travelling by bus and train for two full days after being notified only three days previously. Squashed into a corner of the sofa, his grey artificial leather handbag, regarded as quite fashionable on the farm, now looked crumpled and pitiful in this magnificent room. On the top of the bag was a knitted nylon pouch containing his toothbrush, towel and several tea-brewed eggs that he hadn't finished on the road. The crushed and dried eggs, which seemed strangely out of place here, reminded him of the evening of his departure when Xiuzhi, his wife, asked him to take some more for his father. Thinking of this, Xu couldn't help but smile bitterly.

The day before yesterday, Xiuzhi had insisted on taking Qingqing, their five-year-old daughter, to see him off at the county's bus station. It was the first time he had left the farm since their marriage and this trip had thus become a grand occasion in his small family.

"Daddy, where's Beijing?" asked Qingqing.

"It's northeast of our county."

"Is Beijing much bigger than a county town?"

"Yes, of course."

"And are there irises in Beijing?"

"No, there are no such flowers there."

"Are there any oleasters?" she persisted.

"Oh, no. There are no such wild fruits."

"Oh, what a pity!" Qinqing heaved a long grown-up sigh. Cupping her chin in her hands, she appeared thoroughly disappointed. To her, all good places ought to have both irises and oleasters.

"You silly girl!" Old Zhao, the cart driver, teased. "Beijing is a very big place. But this time, your daddy might go very, very far away. Why, he might even go abroad with your grandpa. Isn't that right, Teacher Xu?"

Xiuzhi, crouched behind the driver, gave her husband a gentle smile but said nothing.   In the same way that Qingqing couldn't envisage the size of Beijing, she couldn't imagine that he would ever go to other countries.

The horse cart bumped along the dirt road.   On the north side of the road stretched a neatly tended field, on the south, pasture land extended far off into the morning mist, off to where he used to tend horses.   This place had a magnetic quality all its own and so, looking at the grass or at a particular tree, endless memories would well up his mind.   And this morning especially, he found everything on this grassland more precious and attractive than ever.

Knowing that a big oleaster tree stood directly behind a nearby trio of poplars, he hopped off the cart and returned shortly with some fresh fruit which everyone promptly set about eating.   Oleasters were a local wild fruit with a bitter-sweet flavour and grew mostly in the northwest.   They had served as his staple diet during the famine years in the 60s and it had been a long time since he ate them last. Now, tasting them again, he was seized with nostalgia.   No wonder Qingqing had wanted to know whether there was such fruit in Beijing or not.

"Her grandpa has probably never tasted them," Xiuzhi remarked smiling, spitting out the pit.   It was the most she had ever exercised her imagination to try and picture what her father-in-law from afar would be like.

As a matter of fact, it was not difficult to imagine, for father and son bore such a close resemblance to one another that Xiuzhi could easily have recognized her father-in-law had she just run across him in the street. Both had long and narrow eyes, straight noses and full lips, and even their gestures betrayed their common blood. The father, however, did not look his age. Instead of being wan and sallow, his complexion was as brown as his son's, having been tanned on the beaches of Los Angeles and Hong Kong. He still paid great attention to his appearance. His hair, though silver, was always neatly combed and his fingernails well-manicured despite the age spots which had long since appeared on his hands. Around the exquisite coffee cup on the side-table lay scattered the Three B brand pipe, a tobacco pouch made of Moroccan sheepskin, a gilt lighter and a diamond-inlaid necktie pin.

It seemed highly unlikely that he would enjoy eating oleasters!

2

"Why, how strange, you even get the latest songs here!" exclaimed Miss Song in fluent Chinese. Tall and well-proportioned, her long, black hair bound with a scarlet satin ribbon, she was enveloped in a delicate jasmine fragrance.

"Look, Director Xu, how familiar Beijing people are with disco dancing. It's even more frenetic than in Hong Kong. I guess they're really modernized now!"

"Surely it's hard to withstand the temptation to enjoy yourself." With that, Director Xu smiled enigmatically like an ancient sage. "They don't think of themselves as ascetics any more."

Directly after supper, Father and Miss Song took him to the ballroom. He would never have imagined such a place, even in Beijing. When he was a child he had been taken by his parents to the famous dance halls of Shanghai, places with names like the "D.D.S.", the "Paramount", "The French Night Club" and so on, and it seemed now that he was revisiting these once familiar haunts again. However, seeing the effeminate men and masculine women loitering like ghosts in the pale, ghastly-white light, he felt at once extremely uneasy, and like someone in an audience suddenly dragged on to the stage to act, failed to enter into his role. His glimpse in the hotel restaurant just a moment ago of numerous elaborate dishes which had only been pecked at increased his strong sense of disgust. On his farm, people were used to putting the leftovers into a lunch box, which they brought along whenever they went to the county town to have a meal in a state restaurant.

All of a sudden, the music sounded again in the main hall and several couples began to dance frantically. Instead of linking arms, they leaned first forwards then backwards, teasing each other face to face, just like cock-fighting. And this was how they got rid of their excess energy! It reminded him of the peasants who were now labouring barefoot in the hot rice-paddies. Swinging their arms from right to left and vice versa, they would lean over to cut the rice. Sometimes they raised their heads, shouting in hoarse voices to the peasant standing in the distance, two buckets at either end of his shoulder pole: "Hey, hello! Water, water!..." How good it would be if he could lie down under the shade of a tree near the irrigation ditch with its muddy yellow water, and inhale the fragrance of rice straw and alfalfa on the breeze. . . .

"Can you dance, Mr Xu?" asked Miss Song standing next to him, jolting him out of his pleasant reverie.

Turning around, he glanced at her: She too had shining eyes and heavily rouged lips.

"Oh, no, I can't," he replied absent-mindedly, smiling. He could graze horses, till land with a plough, cut rice and winnow wheat.... Why should he learn to dance like this?

"Don't put him on the spot!" his father said to Miss Song with a grin. "Look, Manager Wang is coming to ask you to dance."

A handsome young man in a grey suit approached them and after he'd made a low bow to Miss Song, the young couple left for the dance floor.

"Was there something else you still wanted to think about?" Father demanded, lighting his pipe again. "Of course, you know better than I do, it's easy to get a visa at the moment but no one knows what may happen in the future."

"There's still something here I can't bear to leave." Turning around, he looked directly into his father's eyes.

"Including all those bitter experiences?" his father asked sombrely.

"Yes, precisely because of those, this happiness is all the more precious to us."

His father shrugged his shoulders and gave him a puzzled stare.

A wave of melancholy swept over him. It was then that he realized that his father belonged to a world utterly unfamiliar and incomprehensible to him. Their physical resemblance could never balance their spiritual estrangement. They stared at each other in the same way, but neither could see into the deep reservoir of the other's experience.

"Is it that . . . that you still hold a grudge against me?" He lowered his head.

"Oh, no, not at all!" The son waved his hand, using a gesture of his father's. "As you've said, 'Let bygones be bygones.' No, it's something else entirely. . . ."

By then, the music had changed, the light in the hall seemed to have become even more dim than before, and he could no longer make out the shadows of people moving about on the dance floor. Lowering his head again, his father constantly mopped his brow with his right hand, and the expression of weakness and bitterness once again appeared on his face.

"It's true that what's past is past. Still, the bitterness remains when one recalls. . . ." The old man heaved a sigh and went on, "But, I've missed you very much, and now. . . ."

"Yes, I believe you." His father's low-pitched murmur and the pensive music in the background moved him. "And at times I've missed you too."

"Honestly?" his father raised his head.

Yes he had. He remembered in particular an autumn night twenty years earlier. Streaming through lattice paper torn by a heavy rain, the moonlight fell on a group of shabbily-dressed herdsmen lying in the earthen shed. On the ground next to the wall was Xu Lingjun. Shivering all over with the cold, he suddenly rose from the damp rice straw. Outside, the muddy ground, lit brightly by the moon, glistened like pieces of broken glass. There were puddles everywhere and the air stank. Finally, he found a stable, which, with the heat given off by the horses' droppings, was comparatively warm and dry. Horses, mules and donkeys were chewing hay. Finding a vacant trough, he climbed on to it, and lay down at once.

The stable was dimly lit by a small sliver of light reflected on to one of its earthen walls and each of the animals had its head lowered over its trough as though paying homage to the moon. He suddenly felt extremely sad. The whole scene somehow symbolized his complete solitude. Abandoned by people, he was now forced to associate with horses and cattle.

He wept bitterly and curled up on the narrow trough, remembering how in his life he'd tried to defend himself from pressures from all directions. At first, he had been forsaken by his own father and later on, after his mother's death, his uncle had taken away all of her things, leaving him alone. He had been obliged to move into his school dormitory and to study on a people's grant. It had been the Communist Party that had taken him in and a people's school that had brought him up.

In those bright days during the 50s, though sensitive and reticent as a result of his early years, Xu gradually became absorbed in collective life and, like most middle school students at the time, he cherished a beautiful dream. And before long after his graduation it had come true. Wearing a dark blue uniform, notebook tucked under his arm and carrying some chalk, he had entered the classroom as a primary school teacher. From then on, he had a new direction in life, a direction of his own.

But not long afterwards the leaders at the school had to fulfil the quota of Rightists set by their superiors and he was suddenly put in the same category as his father. In his past, the bourgeoisie had forsaken him, leaving him nothing but the "immovable estate" of his heritage, and now others forsook him, labelling him a Rightist. In the end he had been deserted by all and banished to this remote farm to be re-educated through labour.

Having eaten its hay, one of the horses walked along beside the wooden trough towards him. Standing as close as its tether would reach, it stretched out its head and he felt a gust of hot breath on his face. Opening his eyes, he saw its brown head nuzzling out grain next to him. It slowly became aware of his presence but instead of being startled, the animal sniffed with its moist nose and brushed across his face with its soft velvet muzzle. Moved greatly by this soothing gesture, he embraced its long, haggard head and wept bitterly, his tears rolling down its brown mane. Then, kneeling on the trough, he carefully scraped together the scattered grain and placed them in a pile before his animal companion.

And Father, where were you then?

3

Now, he had finally come back.

It wasn't a dream. His father was lying on a bed in the next room and he was sleeping on a soft spring bed. Feeling the mattress, Xu Lingjun thought how different it was from that hard wooden trough. Over the carpet, sofa and bed spread many small squares, reflections of the moonlight pouring through the curtain. In that hazy moonlight, the day's impressions surfaced clearly in his mind and over and over again he saw how completely incapable he was of adapting himself to everything here. His father had come back, but they were now strangers to one another. His return had only evoked bitter memories and disturbed his peace of mind.

Although it was already autumn the room seemed hot and close. He lifted the woollen blanket, sat up and propped himself against the headboard. Then, switching on the bedside lamp, he indifferently scrutinized the whole room until his gaze at last fell on his own body. As he stared at the muscular arms, the veined calves, the splayed toes of his two large feet and at his calloused palms and heels, he recalled the conversation with his father that afternoon.

Soon after finishing his coffee, Father had let Miss Song go, and had then started to tell his son about recent developments in his company, about the ineptness of Lingjun's half-brothers and his own longing for his native land.

"... At last, with you by my side, I may have a bit of consolation," he said with a smile. "What happened thirty years ago has upset me more and more. I know that family origin is much stressed here and that as a result your life won't have been an easy one. I even thought that you might not still be alive. But I have been concerned about you all along. Every now and then I'd see you as you were when you were small, especially how you lay in the arms of your wet nurse the day your grandpa held a huge feast in Nanjing. I remember it as clearly as if it had just happened yesterday. There were so many guests from Shanghai that day. You know, you were the first grandson in the family...."

And now, in the soft light of the green-shaded bedside lamp, he suddenly experienced a strange sensation, looking at his own strong physique. Hearing the story of his own childhood for the first time from his father made him sharply contrast his life in the past with his life now. He suddenly discovered the real cause of the estrangement between his father and himself: This boy who was the first son of the eldest branch of a wealthy family held in high regard by the Shanghai magnates and their wives had now become a veritable labourer! And mixed into this transformation process had been so much bitterness as well as so much joyful hard work.

Because of his homelessness, it was arranged that Xu Lingjun should become a herdsman on the farm after his release from education through labour.

In the early morning, when the sun had just risen over the poplar grove and the silver dewdrops were still glistening on the grass, he would unbolt the stable and in a great rush, horses and cattle would tumble out, vying with each other in racing to the pasture. Startled, the larks and pheasants would flee from the thick grass with cries of alarm. Flapping their wings, they skimmed over the herd, darting towards the poplar woods like arrows. Mounted on his horse, he galloped along the well-trampled path as though throwing himself into the very bosom of nature itself.

There was a large swamp overgrown with reeds and, scattered at random amongst them, the horses and cattle began to graze, with only the sporadic noise of their breathing and splashing breaking the silence. Lying on the earthen slope, the young herdsman used to stare up at the sky, at the snow-white clouds which seemed as changeable as life itself. By then, sweeping across the tips of the grass and the swamp's surface, a light breeze gently brushed over his whole body and he felt lulled by the fresh air laden with the mixed aroma of moist earth and horses' sweat. In this contented state, he would catch the odour of his own sweat and realize how closely his own life had been tied to that of nature. It was a state that would arouse in him an endless series of reveries, as if he himself had melted entirely into this wilderness wind. He existed everywhere, yet lost his own individual nature. As a result, his dejection disappeared instantly, both his sadness as well as his bitterness at his unlucky fate, and in their place emerged a love of life and a love of nature.

At noon, their bellies full and round, the horses paced out of the thick reeds one after the other, some shaking their manes, others switching their tails to drive away the gadfly and botfly. Then, gathering around closely, they would look at him with their big, kind eyes. Sometimes, No. 7, a white piebald, would stealthily skirt round several companions to play tricks on lame No. 100. Not to be outdone, the latter would turn and give the former a good kick with its game leg. Quickly dodging aside, No. 7 would circle the herd with its head raised high, silver drops of water flying in all directions. Whenever that happened, Xu Lingjun would pick up his long whip and shout at them fiercely. Promptly pricking up their ears, the other horses and cattle would turn about to shoot reproachful stares at the troublemaker. And finally contrite, like a mischievous upbraided schoolboy, No. 7 would stand in the knee-deep water, quietly moistening its muzzle. Seeing this, the young herdsman felt that although he was living among animals, he had simply become a fairy-tale prince surrounded by a host of spirits.

Under the scorching sun, the cloud shadow moved slowly along the foot of the distant hill. Waterfowl, prompted by the swamp's warmth, began to cry out among the reeds. The place was not only vast, it was beautiful. Here, even the abstract idea of a "motherland" took on definition and became concrete. He felt satisfied and at peace. Life was, after all, beautiful. Both nature and labour had offered him things he couldn't get within classroom walls.

At times, there would be a rain shower in the pasture. At first, it appeared in the form of a screen of black threads suspended over the hill slopes in the far distance and then, buffeted by the wind, would draw nearer and nearer. In a twinkling, the rain would pour down and the whole grassland would be totally enveloped in a white mist. As the shower approached, Xu Lingjun had to drive his flock to the strip of forest for cover. Long whip in hand, he would get on his horse and gallop round the scattered herd, hollering loudly at them. In moments like those, he felt a sense of vitality and strength, no longer insignificant and useless. And it was through this hard battle against the wind, the rain and the mosquitoes and gnats that he gradually restored his faith in life.

Only when it rained could herdsmen from different teams get together under the small canopy which, built as a shelter, looked just like a tiny boat anchored in a vast sea of mist. It was cool and wet beneath the canopy, and generally permeated with the strong scent of low-grade tobacco. Listening attentively to his friends' merry conversations and bawdy jokes, he would now and then be taken aback by the fact that they didn't invest their labour and their lives with so many complex emotions. He was delighted at this new understanding. Honest and simple, these herdsmen were happy, though their lives were hard. He began to admire them.

"They say that you're a Rightist. What does that actually mean then?" an old herdsman of about sixty or so asked one day.

"It means. . . ." He hesitated, hanging his head in shame. "A Rightist is one who has made a mistake in the past."

"No, not at all," put in a herdsman from the Seventh Team. "The Rightists are those who spoke the truth in 1957. That year, the intellectuals were under attack." Frank and outspoken by nature, he was fond of making jokes, and people had nicknamed him "Glib Tongue".

"Why is speaking the truth regarded as making a mistake? If all of us fail to speak the truth, everything will be in a mess." The old herdsman kept on smoking his pipe and continued, "Well, in my opinion, one is better off as a labourer than as a cadre. Look, I'll soon turn seventy, yet I'm still neither hard of hearing, nor dim-sighted, nor stooped, and my teeth are good. Why, I can even still eat roasted soyabeans —"

"And precisely because of that, you'll be a labourer again in the next life!" Glib Tongue interrupted him laughing.

"Well, none the worse for that!" the old herdsman retorted earnestly. "Anyway, without our labouring day and night, the cadres wouldn't be able to keep their positions and the intellectuals couldn't go on with their reading and writing. . . ."

This simple, frank and sometimes sporadic kind of dialogue would occasionally arouse strong emotions in him. Just like seeing a rainbow after a shower, he felt refreshed. It made him long for a return to the simple and honest life, to take pleasure from the present as they did.

Over the course of his long-term physical labour, he became used to a fixed way of life and this new pattern stubbornly moulded him in its own image. As time passed, everything that had gone before eventually seemed like a dim dream, or like a story about someone else he'd read in a book. At the same time, his memory was divided into two separate parts by this new way of life so entirely different from that of the past. As a result, his former big city life grew more and more illusory and only the events of the present were real and true. In the end he had been converted into one who was not only fit but also able to live on this terrain. He had become a herdsman both in name and in reality.

In the early years of the "cultural revolution", people all forgot about his past, but then someone recalled that he had originally been classed as a Rightist and it was felt necessary to parade him through the streets. Just at that critical point, however, having consulted one another under the canopy, the herdsmen of all the different teams declared unanimously that there was no more good grazing in this pasture, and, after orally notifying the administrative office of the farm, they all decided to move on to another pasture on the hill slopes. Of course, Xu Lingjun had to go with them. Once up into the hills, one couldn't return home for at least two or three months. None of the "revolutionary clique", therefore, was inclined to follow suit. In this way, Xu Lingjun put his simple baggage on the back of a horse and rode away together with them, finally leaving the chaos behind. As soon as they set foot on the highway, all the herdsmen shouted cheerfully: "Hell! Now, we've more or less gone up into the hills. Who cares whose mother's going to marry whom?" Whistling loudly, they brandished their long whips to urge on the horses and cattle, raising a cloud of yellow dust as they went. In the distance ahead he could see a grazing area on the slope, glistening in the sunshine like a vast piece of green jadeite. . . . That day remained etched in Xu Lingjun's mind, something he treasured for ever with a special affection.

His memories were a mixture of the bitterness and happiness experienced in different stages and aspects of his life. But he felt that, without the bitter times as a contrast, his happiness now would surely be a pallid and valueless thing.

Then, in spring last year, he had suddenly been summoned back to the administrative office from the pastures on the slope. Anxious and fearful, he entered the office of the farm's political department. Having read a document to him, Deputy Head Dong then informed him that it had been wrong to label him a Rightist in 1957 and that, as well as having his name entirely cleared, it would soon be arranged for him to be a teacher again at the farm-run school. A newly hatched fly was buzzing to and fro in the office, landing now on the wall, now on the filing cabinet. Carefully following the fly's every move, Deputy Head Dong picked up a magazine, itching to swat it. "Well, you can go and get your transfer order from Secretary Pang next door. Report for duty at the school tomorrow." Finally, the fly landed on his desk, but craftily fled before the magazine was slapped down. Greatly disappointed, Deputy Head Dong sank back into his armchair again. After a while, he advised sombrely, "Listen, from now on you must work hard and don't make any more mistakes."

Xu Lingjun was completely taken aback by this unexpected event, almost numbed, as if hit by an electric current. It was hard to grasp the significance of this correction in the political life of the country as well as the radical change it would make to his own life in the future. In fact, he hadn't even dared think of such a day. Nevertheless a great happiness began to seize him. The emotion filtered through his body like alcohol, making him dizzy. At first, he felt a dryness in his throat, then trembled slightly all over and at last burst into sobs, tears running unrestrainedly down his cheeks. Even Deputy Head Dong, who always affected a solemn manner, was deeply moved by the scene, and quickly stretched out a hand to him. Not until this moment, with Deputy Head Dong's hand grasping his own, had he begun to have even a dim hope for his future.

And, once again he entered the classroom in a dark blue uniform, notebook under his arm and chalk in hand, resuming finally the radiant dream he had cherished twenty years ago. This was not a well-off farm. The children were all dressed in rags and the classroom permanently filled with the intermingled smells of sweat, dust and hay. Sitting motionless behind rough desks with their eyes wide open, the pupils all stared at the newcomer, wondering why this herdsman had suddenly become a teacher. But soon, they placed their trust in him. He didn't think he was making any special contribution, and dared not even imagine that he was serving the socialist cause and the "four modernizations" of his country, which he thought of as marvellous deeds accomplished only by heroes. He thought that what he did was nothing more than conscientiously fulfilling his duty. But even so, he was respected by all his pupils. On the morning he left for Beijing, he noticed that these pupils, standing in twos and threes on either side of the path they took to school every day, fixed their eyes on the horse cart. Probably they too had heard that, having found his rich father, he would soon go abroad. Controlling a desire to express reluctance at his departure, they watched the cart move off until it rolled across the stone bridge, through the poplar woods and finally disappeared at the far end of an uncultivated field.

Sometimes, herdsmen from other teams would come to call on him from more than ten *li* away. The old herdsman was already over eighty, yet he still moved smartly. Sitting on the brick *kang*, he would pick up a Chinese dictionary and caress it, saying, "How clever he is. He fully deserves to be called a scholar. Look, what a thick book. It would probably take a whole lifetime to read it all!"

"No, it's a dictionary, which you use for looking up new words," Glib Tongue explained to his older companion. "How foolish you are! The longer you live, the more muddle-headed you become!"

"That's true. Here I am over eighty, and still illiterate. Whenever I go to see a film, I can't even make out what the title is, and can only see figures moving around on the screen."

"Well, whatever we do we must learn to read. A few days back, while I was preparing medicine for my cattle, I nearly fed them something that was for external use only," said Glib Tongue. "Well, Xu, you are one of us. Now, we're too old to learn any more, so we'll leave the education of our children in your good hands."

"Good!" the old herdsman took up the cue. "If, Xu, you succeed in teaching my grandsons to read thick books like this, it shows that you really care about your poor friends who have shared the same lot with you on the grassland."

The simple words drove home to him the value of his work, gave him further hope for the future. From all of them he had again smelt the odour of horses' sweat, the flavour of grass and hay as well as the breath of nature itself, something he felt he knew, something quite different from the depression he'd experienced with his father and Miss Song.

In the eyes of these herdsmen, in the eyes of his pupils and of the old colleagues who once again worked together with him, he had seen his own worth. Was there anything more precious and pleasing than this?

4

In the morning, he and Miss Song accompanied his father along Wangfujing Street and he found himself unused any more to city life. Here, unlike the countryside, the ground was covered with asphalt or tarmac, not moist and spongy to the step. People streamed along the street, noisy but apathetic. Engulfed in this great commotion, he felt a tension which soon exhausted him.

In the arts and crafts store, the father wrote a cheque for six hundred yuan and ordered an exquisite blue and white porcelain dinner service from the famous Jingdezhen kilns. In a porcelain shop, the son picked up an earthenware jar for two yuan. The delicate little pot with its brown and yellow antique-style decoration could almost pass as a relic excavated from a Han tomb. He had never seen such things in his little country town in the northwest. Xiuzhi had often praised the pickles from her home town and had long wanted a really fine pot. The one she had now had been brought by some- one from Shaanxi and for it she had traded five pairs of cloth shoe soles, which had taken her several nights to make. But it was ugly now, its surface laced with white salt stains.

"Your wife must be a real beauty!" said Miss Song coquettishly when they got back to the hotel. "Your love for her is admirable. It makes a person jealous!" She wore a new red-and-black-striped silk blouse un- derneath her light purple cardigan and a thin gray wool skirt. In the hot autumn sun, her jasmine perfume was even more pungent.

"Well, marriage is a kind of bond and duty after all." Slowly stirring his coffee, Father heaved a sigh, and then picked over the words carefully as if savouring the meaning. Perhaps he was thinking of his own case. "Whether you love your wife or not, you must keep your promise to the very end of your life or you'll feel guilt, anguish and remorse. I want you to go abroad, but not alone. You must bring your wife and daughter too."

"Would you tell us about your romance?" Miss Song said. "Your love affair must have been rather special. I'm sure there will have been lots of young women run- ning after a handsome man like you!"

"My love affair?" He smiled apologetically. "I didn't

even know my wife when I married her, let alone have a courtship."

"Oh?" Miss Song feigned exaggerated surprise, while his father shrugged his shoulders.

He wanted to tell them how he and Xiuzhi had married. But their abnormal marriage had been overshadowed by a national disaster, a humiliation for the whole nation. He was ambivalent about whether or not he should tell them the whole story in case they made fun of what he regarded as sacred. Unable to decide, he silently sipped the coffee. There was sweetness in the bitter drink. Sweetness blended with bitterness. Only a mixture of the two could produce such a special, exciting aroma. Father and Miss Song might be able to appreciate its particular taste, but would they be able to understand the meaning of his complex life? In those chaotic years, marriage, like everything else, had been thrown off course. Theirs had been more like a blind combination. Both Xiuzhi and he had found it absurd and had never anticipated the unexpected happiness which befell them. So, the more difficult the circumstances then, the more precious this happiness was now. Whenever they recalled their abnormal marriage, mixed feelings of grief and warmth rose in their hearts, something incomprehensible to anyone but themselves.

It all started one spring afternoon in 1972. As usual, after watering the horses and bolting the corral, he returned to his small hut. He had hardly put down his whip when Glib Tongue broke into the room.

"Hey, Old Xu, want a wife?" he declared. "You just say the word and I'll send her here tonight!"

"Send her here then," he said smiling, thinking it was a joke.

"Great! No going back on your word! The woman's got her certificate to prove she's single. As for you, I've had a word with the farm leader. He said as long as you had no objections, he would give you your certificate at once so I'll go and pick it up for you and give it to the admin people on my way back. Then I'll bring the girl here and we'll have the wedding tonight!"

It was just getting dark and he was sitting on a stool reading when he heard children outside chorus: "Old Xu's wife's coming! Old Xu's wife's coming!" The door was thrown open and in dashed Glib Tongue as he had that afternoon.

"It's all settled and done! I won't drink a drop of your wine but at least offer me some water! Hard work, you know. I almost ran my legs off this afternoon going thirty *li* and back." With that, he ladled some cold water from a pot and gulped it down. Drying his whiskered lips, he heaved a long sigh of relief. "Hey!" he cried out. "Why don't you come in? This is your home now! Let me introduce the two of you. This is the Old Xu I mentioned. His full name's Xu Lingjun. A nice fellow except he's a little poor. But nowadays, the poorer he is, the more honour he gets!"

Only then did he notice a strange girl standing at the head of a group of children outside the door. She wore a gray, badly creased tunic and held a white bundle in her hand. She scrutinized the dusty, sooty hut coldly as if she really was preparing to live in it.

"What's going on?" He was shocked. "What kind of a joke is this?"

"Why, it's not a joke at all!" Glib Tongue fished out some paper, and slapped the edge of the brick bed. "All the documents're here! It's official. Understand?

I told the man in the political department that you were out grazing horses and had asked me to get all the necessary documents together. If you go back on your word, you'll put me in a fix. Do you hear me, Old Xu?"

"What are we going to do?" he asked Glib Tongue, throwing his hands in the air. The girl walked in and quietly sat down on the small stool he had just vacated. She seemed perfectly at ease, as though their conversation had nothing to do with her.

"What's to be done? It's a matter between husband and wife now. How can you ask me?" Glib Tongue placed all of the "official documents" on the brick bed. "Now then, have a happy life together. Next year you'll have a nice chubby baby. You must give me a special treat then." He went to the door and waved his hands, shooing the children away as though they were little chicks. "What's there to look at? If you haven't seen your parents' wedding ceremony, you can at least ask them about it. Now clear off, all of you!"

With that, Glib Tongue took his leave.

In the dim yellow light, he stealthily sized up the girl. Not very pretty, she had a small retroussé nose surrounded by tiny freckles, a head of lustreless brown hair, and looked haggard and wan. He felt sorry for her and poured out a glass of water. "Have a drink, you've walked a long way...."

She looked up and her eyes met his earnest stare. Silently she gulped the water down. Her appearance improved as her strength returned. Moving over to the brick bed she folded up the quilts. Then she took a pair of trousers and smoothed out the worn patch at the knee on her lap, untied a little white bundle she had brought with her, picked a piece of blue cloth, a needle and some thread and began sewing, her head lowered. Her movements were deft and unhurried. She seemed to have a refined vitality which manifested itself in her movements rather than in her appearance. And then this wretched looking girl made the hut spotless with a little tidying here and there. She seemed to be playing a piano with the quilts, the cotton-padded mattress and the clothes as keys. To him it seemed as if there was music in this shabby little hut.

Then suddenly, he remembered the brown horse and his heart ached. He felt that not only had he known her but that he'd been waiting for her all these years. Seized by a sudden wave of passion, he unthinkingly sat down beside her on the edge of the bed. He covered his face with his hands, afraid to let himself believe that happiness had at last come to him, worried that this unexpected joy might only bring him new misfortunes. His hands still covering his eyes, he relished this strange new feeling. The girl stopped her sewing. Her intuition told her that this was a man you could rely on all your life. She did not see him as a total stranger at all and placed a hand on his slightly hunched shoulder. So the two sat on the cloth-covered edge of the brick bed and talked till dawn.

Xiuzhi was from Sichuan. In those years, the people in a province known for its abundance could not get enough to eat, not even sweet potatoes, and starving peasants had to leave their homes to save their lives. Girls who could marry themselves off to someone in another place fared better. Once a girl got settled outside, then she would introduce other girls in her village as wives there too. In this way groups of girls left home with their possessions in little bundles, went beyond

Yangping Pass, crossed the Qinling Mountains, and travelled through countless railroad tunnels, short and long, in the direction of Shaanxi, of Gansu, of Qinghai, Ningxia and Xinjiang. If the parents could afford it they would buy their daughter a train ticket. Otherwise the girl had to slip surreptitiously on to a train and try to travel unnoticed, stop by stop. In her little bundle would be some patched clothes, a small round mirror and a comb. Armed with these few small things, she gambled with her youth, perhaps even her life. She might win happiness or she might lose completely.

At the farms in this district, this kind of marriage was popularly known as an "eight-*fen* marriage".* Younger men and older bachelors too poor to buy wedding presents for local girls would turn to those from Sichuan. The Sichuan women here would, if asked, offer a name almost as if they had a catalogue of unmarried girls. Then a letter would be posted. Based on this summons, a girl would arrive and a marriage would take place. Xiuzhi was one of these. Originally, she had come to marry a tractor driver in the Seventh Production Team. But unfortunately, after hitchhiking with identification issued by her village authorities, she arrived to find he had died in an accident three days earlier. She did not go to the crematorium. It was not necessary since she had never set eyes on him. And she was too shy to go to the go-between because she knew the woman was in dire straits too, with a disabled husband and a small child. All she could do was sit in front of the corral of the Seventh Team, gazing blankly

---

* Eight *fen* is the postage for a letter.

at her shadow as it described a slow arc on the ground around her.

Glib Tongue had learned of all this at noon when he had gone, kettle in hand, to fetch some hot water at the corral. Leaving his horses behind, he went from door to door trying to find a way out for the girl. Now there were only three single men left in the team and all three came to the corral to have a look at her, but thought her too scrawny and too small. Finally Glib Tongue remembered Xu Lingjun, then already thirty-five or thirty-six.

And so he had got married. That had been his romance!

"Old Xu's got married!" It had been quite an event in the village. Even those who were engrossed in factional feuds temporarily forgot their squabbling and came to congratulate him, a man impartial to disputes, a man who was harmless and worked hard. Human beings are human beings after all, and the villagers felt warmed themselves by offering their warmth to others, realizing their humanity had not been entirely lost during those turbulent years. Someone gave him a cauldron, others several catties of rice, cloth coupons and so on. A young vet started a collection, and each household offered fifty *fen*, to be used for starting a family. The leading body of the farm decided that he should be given a three-day honeymoon just like anyone else. Even in those dark days, the villagers had all been very kind.

So with those charitable donations as a foundation, they started a new life.

Xiuzhi was optimistic and hard-working. With only two years' schooling behind her, she couldn't, of course, express her feelings in a cultured way. But after seeing the film *Lenin in 1918* at the village square the day after her arrival, she repeated a line spoken by Lenin's body-guard, "There'll be bread, and milk too," and soon this became her pet saying, always causing her to giggle. Her eyebrows were thin, her eyes were small, and when she smiled they turned virtually into slits like crescent moons. With her dimpled cheeks as well, she had a charm of her own.

While Xu Lingjun grazed the horses during the day, she made adobe bricks in the scorching noon sun. After-wards, she carted the bricks back and began to build a wall around her hut. And so on a land of 9,600,000 square kilometres, she marked out eighteen square metres for herself. "At home," she said, "there are always trees in front of each house. You can't see the sky for their branches." So she rooted out two bowl-thick poplar trees from the field and, with surprising strength, dragged them back and planted them on either side of her little courtyard. When the walls were completed she began raising poultry. And as well as the chickens, ducks and geese, she kept rabbits and doves, a pastime which earned her the nickname "Com-mander of Three Armies". But what made her most unhappy at this state-owned farm was that pig-raising was not allowed. In bed at night she often told Xu Lingjun how she had dreamed of having her own fat pigs.

This remote farm was like a stagnant pond and the leaders were slow about carrying out policies, correct or incorrect, from above. Though there was the risk of being crushed as a "remnant of capitalism", Xiuzhi, like hardy grass growing through the cracks in a rock, stuck to her own ideas and the number of small animals grew rapidly, as though from the hands of a magician. "There'll be bread, and milk too." And sure enough, after one year's hard work, their life was much improved. Despite their meagre wages, they had all that they needed. Xiuzhi had the tenacity even to go against the social current. On her way back from the fields every evening, she carried Qingqing on her back, followed by a crowd of chickens, ducks and geese, while doves perched on her shoulders. Then firewood would be burning merrily in the stove beneath a cauldron of water. Like a Thousand-armed Buddha, she could put everything in its rightful order.

This woman, raised on sweet potatoes, had not only brought him a warm hearth but also had made him strike roots in this land. They nourished the roots with their own labour and their union strengthened his affection for the land, enabling him to see more clearly that a life of work was simple, pure and just. He was suffused with a happiness he had sought so many years before.

And then the day came when Deputy Head Dong announced that his name and reputation had been officially cleared, and he was given five hundred yuan as compensation in accordance with the policies of the financial office. When he told his wife what had happened, she was delighted and her face lit up. Having wiped her hands on her apron, she started to count the brand-new notes.

"Hey, Xiuzhi, from now on we're just as equal as anyone else," he shouted cheerfully in the direction of the little kitchen while washing his face. "Did you hear me, Xiuzhi? What are you doing in there?"

"I've counted this several times but I just can't work it out! What a pile!"

"*Aiya*! You're really.... What does the money matter? What's worth celebrating is that I'm politically exonerated!"

"What do you mean by 'politically exonerated'? To me, you're still yourself. They said you were a Rightist in the past. Now after all this time they say it was a mistake. But if that's true, why on earth should they warn you not to make a mistake again? Heaven only knows what they're doing! Who should be careful not to make mistakes again? We'll still live the way we always have. Now we've got money, we'll have a peaceful life. Don't disturb me, let me count it again."

True, Xiuzhi, who was fifteen years younger, had never thought of the two of them as inferior. She was simple, honest and provincial. What was a Rightist? The question had never entered her small head. All she knew was that her husband was a good man, an honest man, and that was enough for her. Often when working together with the other women she would say, "Qingqing's father's really just a simple and honest man. He wouldn't make a sound even if you kicked him, and he'd move at the same pace if he had a wolf chasing him. It's a sin to bully somebody like him. Whoever has will have to pay for it in the next life!"

It was true that she liked money and was quite frugal and the five hundred yuan delighted her enormously. Her hands trembled, her eyes were brimming with tears of joy. But when she learned that his father was in business abroad, she said nothing about money, but instead asked him to take the old man some tea-brewed eggs. She often said to her seven-year-old daughter, "You can only feel at case if you spend money you've earned yourself. When I buy salt, I know that it's with money I've earned selling eggs. When I buy chilli, I know that it's with money I earned harvesting rice. When I buy you exercise books, I know I earned the money from working overtime threshing and winnowing. . . ." She had no abstract theories, no profound philosophies, but her simple, clear words made the small girl understand that work was a noble thing. Only the rewards of one's own labour could make a person feel good. It would be a humiliation to earn money through exploitation or through dependence on others.

Xiuzhi could not sing. When Qingqing was one month old, the three of them climbed on to a truck and went to the county seat to have a photo taken in the county's only studio. On the streets of that little town, an ice lolly vendor sang out, "Lo — lly — Lo —lly —" and that had become her lullaby. While rocking her baby, she would sing, softly imitating the northwest accent, "Lo — lly — Lo — lly —" This monotonous, remote, sweet singing not only hypnotized Qingqing but also soothed her husband who, sitting beside them reading, felt a simple, fundamental kind of happiness.

There were lolly vendors at Wangfujing too. But they never sang, sitting instead behind counters with long faces. It was dull, uninteresting. He missed her sweet lullabies, her pet sayings, her optimistic smile.

He could not stay here. He must go back. There were friends who had helped him when he was in difficulty and who now needed his help.   There was the land which he had watered with his own sweat, which even now seemed to glisten in the fields after harvest. There was his beloved wife and daughter.   His whole world was there, even the very roots of his existence.

5

And now he was back at last, back to the familiar little county town. The county's only asphalt road stretched in front of the bus terminal still covered with a thin layer of brownish dust which, when the wind blew, whirled around the small stores, the bank and the post office. The cotton fluffer across the road was still working monotonously as though it had not stopped once since he left.   The bus terminal entrance was crowded with peasants selling sweet rice, fried pancakes and sunflower seeds.   Flanking either side of the terminal were dilapidated old houses, on some of which the original engraved lintels could still be seen.   The new theatre, still under construction, was enveloped now in scaffolding, on which bricklayers moved about busily.

Getting off the bus he felt as if he had been dropped from a parachute.   Now, at last, he was back on solid ground.   He loved everything about the place, even its flaws, just as in his own life he now cherished even the bitter memories of the past.

He thumbed a ride on a horse cart and reached his village at dusk.   Over the hills to the west, the setting sun cast its oblique rays, bathing the village and its inhabitants in a rosy glow.   Xiuzhi's two poplars towered over their house, quiet and still, as if looking at him from the very depths of their souls.

The horses and cattle were tramping home. As they crossed the dirt road they halted, eyes wide, as if recognizing him. Only when the cart was far off in the distance did they turn their heads and continue on their journey, languidly heading for their barns.

A wave of warmth rose within him. He thought again of the conversation with his father before leaving. That evening, the two men had sat in armchairs, face to face. The despondent old man, wearing silk pajamas, was hunched over and smoking.

"Leaving so soon?" he asked.

"Yes. The school's preparing the mid-term examination."

After a brief silence, he said again, "I'm so happy to have seen you." Despite his attempts to control his emotions, his lips trembled. "You're a very mature man, I can see that. Probably because of your firm faith in things. That's good. What a man looks for is faith. To be frank, in the past I looked for it too. But religion couldn't satisfy me...." He paused, waved a hand as if brushing away something in disgust and then suddenly changed his topic. "Last year I read an English version of the *Selected Stories of Maupassant* in Paris. There was a story about a deputy finally meeting the son he had left long ago and the son turned out to be an idiot. I couldn't fall asleep after I'd read it. And later on I often had visions of you, thinking you were in trouble. But now I feel at ease. Almost beyond my wildest expectations, you've become...a...." He couldn't find the right word. The son however saw a satisfaction, a kind of consolation, in his eyes. He knew that both he and his father were happy about this reunion since each had got what it was that he needed. His father's guilty conscience had been assuaged. And at a crucial moment, he had reviewed his own past and come, to some extent, to understand the meaning of his life.

The sun had now sunk behind the hill and was shooting its last golden beams at the clouds above. In the reflection from the glowing clouds, the hillside pastures, the fields and village were covered in a gentle dusk light. He was approaching his school, the playground already in sight. From a distance it looked like a still lake surrounded by brown-patched grassland. Caressed by the evening breeze, he was swept by a wave of tenderness. In the end, he thought, his father had not really understood, although he had said that he himself had had a firm faith too. Intellectual knowledge without a basis in emotional experience was an empty thing. At some times and in some ways feelings were more important than ideas. What he had now acquired after more than twenty years of hardship, were the feelings and the understanding of a labourer. This was his treasure. Profoundly moved, he felt his eyes watering. In the end, he hadn't wasted all of those hard years trudging along that difficult road.

He saw the school at last. A few people in front of his house were turned in his direction. The white apron Xiuzhi wore sparkled like a star twinkling in the gathering dusk. The crowd grew rapidly and, recognizing him, ran towards the road. A little girl in a red jacket raced towards him like a leaping flame. She was nearer and nearer, her steps faster and faster....

Translated by Hu Zhihui and Wang Mingjie

Zhang Xianliang, a native of Xuyi in Jiangsu Province, was born in 1936. After graduating from senior middle school, he worked as a teacher in Beijing and Ningxia. In the early fifties, he published 60 poems in newspapers and magazines. Wrongly labelled a Rightist, he stopped writing for 22 years until he was cleared in 1979. Since 1980 he has been on the editorial staff of the magazine **Shuofang** (The North) and has published more than a dozen short stories, three novelettes and a collection of stories entitled **Soul and Flesh.** "A Herdsman's Story" was named one of the best short stories of 1980 and was made into a successful film.

Zhang joined the Chinese Writers' Association in 1980 and is a council member of its Ningxia branch.

A Corner Forsaken by Love

Zhang Xian

ALTHOUGH it was already the last year of the seventies of this century, to the youths of Tian Tang Commune, the word "love" was still unfamiliar, mysterious and unspoken. Hence, when the new League committee secretary delivered a report at a mass meeting opposing "mercenary marriages" and spoke out this word loudly, his audience was rather surprised. The young men winked roguishly at each other and laughed outright, while the girls hurriedly bent down their heads, their faces flushed, giggling and exchanging bashful glances.

There was only one person who did not smile — a pretty girl sitting near a window in a corner of the hall, named Shen Huangmei. She was the Youth League group leader of the ninth team of Tian Tang Brigade. Her face was pale, and her large melancholy eyes stared perplexedly out of the window. She seemed to have heard nothing, as if the speech did not concern her. Yet suddenly her eyelashes blinked, and she forced herself to shake off the tears that moistened them. "Love", this word which she failed to understand, was now violently disturbing the youthful heart of this nineteen-year-old girl. She felt ashamed, sad and terribly afraid. She remembered her elder sister Cunni, the sister whom she always blamed and always thought about. Alas! If only Xiaobaozi had not entered her life, if that event had not happened, how wonderful everything would have been! Her sister would now be sitting beside her laughing unreservedly like the boys. Then, after the meeting, her sister would go arm-in-arm with her to buy some skeins of orange-red silk thread from the store to embroider their new pillowcases. . . .

Among the five sisters, Cunni was the luckiest one. She was born in 1955 at the time of a bumper harvest. When she was one month old, her parents had no difficulty in preparing a dinner for their guests. Her young father, Shen Shanwang, holding in his hand his little treasure wrapped up in a flowery quilt, said excitedly, "After I had taken Linhua to the midwife I went and put my savings into the credit co-op. When I returned the baby was already born. No one imagined that a first child could be born so easily. Somebody said that we should name her 'Shunni',* but I thought that as this was the first time since the beginning of the world that a poor peasant like me could put money into the bank I should name her 'Cunni'.** When she grows up, she'll have a wonderful life."

His jubilance affected everyone who came to congratulate him. At that time he was the deputy head of Kao Shan Zhuang Producers' Cooperative. He was optimistic, capable and full of courage and strength. The pear orchard that he grafted on a slope produced a good yield with its first crop. The wheat and corn he harvested were more than enough for his family after pay-

---

* The Chinese character *shun* means "easy, smooth", *ni* means "girl".

** The Chinese character *cun* means "saving up money".

ing the agricultural tax. In the small village of some twenty families, everyone was as happy as he, confidently looking forward to a bright future.

But five years later, when Huangmei came into the world, conditions had changed. Kao Shan Zhuang Producers' Cooperative had been converted into the ninth brigade of Tian Tang Commune. The auspicious name of the commune, "Tian Tang",* was chosen by the county Party committee secretary himself, taken from the saying: "Communism is our heaven, and the people's commune is the bridge leading to it." At that time, all the commune members, including Shen Shanwang, the brigade leader, were convinced that it would take only one step for them to walk into paradise. Unselfishly they had all felled their collective pear trees and the gingko and chestnut trees around their houses and sent the timber to the steel smelting factory. They believed that once the brilliant molten metal flowed out of the red hot crude furnace, they could softly cross the bridge to the communist heaven. But the only result was a pile of shapeless pig iron that had cost them ten thousand loads of firewood. This huge dump had no use aside from securely occupying a piece of farm land. That year, on account of drought, no seeds were obtained from the wheat and corn crops. The sweet potatoes sown in place of the pear trees yielded tiny potatoes only as big as Cunni's fingers. Linhua, her mother, big with child, had returned home after begging for help in a distant place. Shen Shanwang had been dismissed from his post for "attacking the movement to produce steel". He looked at his newly born, undernourished, second

---

* The Chinese characters *tian tang* mean "heaven".

daughter and, with a forced smile on his puffy face, said, "Who asked you to be born in a famine year? You certainly are a Huangmei!..."*

Due probably to sufficient nourishment in the womb and her mother's milk, Cunni, however, grew lustily. She put on weight even if fed with grass, and seemed to gain strength by drinking cold water. Still not quite sixteen, she was a strong, well-developed girl. She took over the carrying-pole from her sickly mother (who in the meantime had given birth to three more younger sisters) to help her father shoulder the heavy burden of supporting the family. The toughest job was carrying the state forest's pine branches downhill, and the work-points she obtained for this ranked the third of those of her own sex. Every day she went to the fields before daybreak and returned home after dark. She gulped down a bowl of sweet potatoes or corn gruel and fell asleep as soon as her head touched the pillow. At the annual distribution of profits, the overdraft of her family increased year after year, and she could not get even one cent for herself. But she was always bubbling with joy and never depressed. When she was most happy, she would even cradle her weak younger sister to her full breast and softly sing a few folk songs sung by her mother in her younger days.

Xiaobaozi, the only son of Uncle Jiagui, lived in the eastern part of the village. His real name was Xiaobao, and he was of the same age as Cunni. A strong boy, he had enormous energy when working. Once, when Aunt Jiagui slipped and fell down in a winter rainstorm

---

* The Chinese characters *huang mei* mean "a girl born in a famine".

when they were transporting pine branches, Xiaobao helped his mother up, put the two loads together and carried them both downhill. When the load was weighed, it was found to be over three hundred catties. All the people exclaimed, "Xiaobaozi's amazing, a real leopard cub!"* The nickname stuck.

In the early spring of 1974, the brigade cadres had gone at daybreak to the commune office to criticize "Old Confucius".** All the young labourers were sent to work at the site of the reservoir being constructed.   Uncle Xiang, the storekeeper, asked Cunni to stay behind and help him tidy up the storeroom.   As the old man told the girl to do this and that, he complained, "The cadres appeared and had a look around, then pointed at something. Then we were kept busy for a whole year blasting the mountains and breaking rocks.   When the mountain flood came, everything was quickly washed away. The next year, the cadres came again and pointed at something else.   The same thing happened.   What do they know about farming?"

"But aren't we supposed to learn from 'the foolish old man who moved mountains'?"*** Cunni asked unconcernedly.

"If we could fill our bellies by removing mountains, that would be fine!... Come here, sift this heap first. Slowly! Don't scatter the grain!..." Then he grumbled about the corn seeds, "Look at this corn.   It was grown

---

* The Chinese characters *xiao bao zi* mean "leopard cub".

** At that time there was a political campaign against Confucius stirred up by the "gang of four".

***A well-known old Chinese fable advocating perseverance in doing one's work.

in the soil where the pear tree roots still remain. The seeds are so small, perhaps they won't even sprout!"

"But aren't we supposed to 'take grain production as the key link'?" Cunni again replied offhandedly. She thought that although working with this old man was easy, she'd prefer carrying earth together with her chums at the construction site.

Then, the shape of a strong young man appeared on the doorstep of the storeroom. "Give me some work to do, Uncle Xiang!" he said.

"Xiaobaozi!" Cunni exclaimed joyfully. "How's your sprained ankle?"

"Go home and take a rest!" said Uncle Xiang.

"I feel bad resting," Xiaobaozi said with a naive smile. "As long as I don't carry heavy loads, I can do some light work." So saying, he picked up a wooden shovel and helped Cunni to sift the corn.

Uncle Xiang squatted down beside them, smoking a cigarette. Then he remembered that he had to ask the carpenter to repair the plough. After giving the two youngsters more instructions, he went away. In the hands of the two agile nineteen-year-olds, the work of tidying up the storeroom and sifting the corn was effortless. In no time the seeds were in the gunny sacks and the sweet potato slices were outside drying in the yard. "Let's rest a while," said Xiaobaozi, and he placed his cotton-padded jacket on a gunny sack and lay down.

Cunni wiped off the sweat from her face and sat down on the bags opposite him. She had also taken off her padded jacket, and was wearing a yellow-green woollen sweater, which had been her mother's dowry. Although it had been darned with different coloured wool and was already too small for her, it was nevertheless considered a great luxury by the young girls of the ninth brigade.

Xiaobaozi gazed at Cunni's face, which appeared unusually flushed in the bright sunshine, and at her full round breasts. A peculiar tickling sensation, which he had never experienced before, rose in his heart, exciting him, yet making him afraid. He searched for a topic of conversation.

"You didn't go to Wu Zhuang the day before yesterday to see the film show?" he asked.

"It's so far away, I couldn't be bothered," she replied, lowering her head to avoid meeting his scorching glance, while at the same time tearing off a dangling thread from the cuff of her sweater.

Wu Zhuang was a brigade in a neighbouring county. One had to climb over two mountain ranges to reach there. Even for such a young man as Xiaobaozi, the trip would take more than an hour. It was not a rich brigade; last year the pay for each workpoint was only thirty-eight *fen*. But even that small sum was the envy of the members of Tian Tang Commune. Less than thirty *li* along the road west of Wu Zhuang, there was a railway which the young people found particularly fascinating. During the Spring Festival the previous year, Xiaobaozi had gone there with several companions to have a look at a train. They spent half a day getting there and back, waited two hours at the station and were finally rewarded with the sight of a grass-green passenger train speeding past. Almost all of the members of the ninth brigade had never had the luck to see one. As for travelling in one, only the accountant Xu, nicknamed Blindman Xu, had had such an opportunity.

Xiaobaozi straightened his back languidly and sighed,

"I didn't want to go either! Films like *Tunnel Warfare* and *Land Mine Warfare* I've seen about umpteen times and can recite almost every line. But it's so boring to stay behind. Our pack of playing cards is practically in shreds. We asked someone to buy a new pack for us from the store, but so far we haven't yet got it!"

Besides going to see films and playing "a hundred points", the youths in this village had nothing else to do in their leisure time. The brigade subscribed to a newspaper published locally in the province, but it was only for the use of Blindman Xu at meetings. He always misread the characters *Kongzi yue* (Confucius said) as *Kongzi ri* (Confucius' sun), but, of course, no one dared correct the only intellectual in the whole brigade. Formerly they also used to sing folk songs, but now these were considered indecent and had been banned.

Suddenly, Xiaobaozi sat up and said, "I say, Blindman Xu told me he had seen some foreign films that were very interesting!" Then, with his mouth partly closed and smirking, he added, "In those films there are some scenes of...."

"Of what?" asked Cunni, catching the nuance in his voice.

"Ooch!... I won't tell you." Xiaobaozi, blushing, grinned to himself.

"Of what? Tell me!"

"Then don't blame me if I do!"

"Out with it!"

"There are...." He again sniggered, doubled over. Suspecting that he was going to say something improper, Cunni stretched out her hand and grabbed a handful of sand. As she expected, Xiaobaozi plucked up his courage and exclaimed, "There are scenes of men and women embracing and kissing each other!"

"Yuck! That's dirty!" Cunni's face grew red immediately and she chucked the sand at him.

Xiaobaozi dodged, saying, "It's true! Blindman Xu said so!"

"It's shameful!" Another handful. The sand mixed with the corn husks fell on to his neck and shoulders. He retaliated, and threw a handful of sand accurately at Cunni's open neck. The girl looked angry and cried, "Damn it! You ass!..."

Xiaobaozi smiled awkwardly. Baring his back he wiped his hard chest muscles with his shirt. Pouting, Cunni began to take off her jumper and shake off the sand clinging to her.... All of a sudden, Xiaobaozi was dazed, as if he had received an electric shock. He stared, his breath stopped and a gush of hot blood rushed to his head. While removing her sweater, Cunni had raised her blouse and exposed half of her white, full, soft breasts....

Like a wild leopard coming out of a ravine, Xiaobaozi pounced on her and clasped her tightly in his arms. The girl was terrified, lifting her arms to resist. But when his hot trembling lips touched her own moist ones, she felt a mysterious fit of giddiness. She closed her eyes, and her arms hung limply. All attempts at resistance were at once dispersed like clouds or smoke. Primitive passion raged in the blood of these two poor, uneducated, but very healthy youths. Traditional ethics, the dignity of reason, the danger of breaking the law and a girl's sense of shame were all burned to ashes.

2

After the first hoeing following the sprouting of the corn, Huangmei began to realize that her elder sister had changed. She was no longer carefree and she seldom laughed. When anyone spoke to her, she seemed deaf. Sometimes she wiped away tears from her pale face, while at other times she smiled to herself, her face glowing.... What was still stranger was that one night when Huangmei woke up, she found that her elder sister's bed was empty. Next morning, when questioned, she flushed and declared that Huangmei was dreaming.

During those few days, their mother had a relapse of her kidney disease, and their father hurried to borrow some money for a doctor from an uncle in Wu Zhuang. The whole family was in confusion, and no one had time to take notice of the change in Cunni. Huangmei alone had a presentiment that some calamity was about to strike her elder sister.

Inevitably it came, more terrible than anything Huangmei could have imagined.

It was at the time when the corn had grown waist-high. After supper, the tired commune members gathered in the brigade office to listen to Blindman Xu reading out the news by oil lamp. Huangmei left before the meeting was over, and returned home to put her three younger sisters to bed. Then she herself went to sleep. Shortly after, she was awakened by an uproar of crying and cursing mixed with the barking of dogs echoing from the hills. Never had there been such a turmoil. Huangmei lit the lamp in surprise. The dreadful din came nearer and nearer, until it approached the door of her home. Suddenly Cunni rushed indoors, her clothes in disarray, her hair dishevelled, and threw herself on the bed weeping hysterically. Then a bare-chested Xiaobaozi, his hands tied behind his back, was escorted into the house by the militia commander. From the glare of several torches, Huangmei saw that he had been beaten with switches and was covered in blood. He was kneeling upright, very ashamed, while his furious father slapped him. His mother sat paralysed on a stool sobbing, her face covered by her hands. Outside the door, a dense crowd of almost all the adults and children in the village had gathered. They hurled abuse and ridicule at him. Huangmei, terrified and trembling, was finally made aware that her elder sister had committed the most heinous crime in the world! She suddenly cried bitterly. Her dearest elder sister had brought catastrophe to the whole family and herself. The tender feelings of feminine self-respect, which had not yet taken root in her young heart, were especially sensitive and easily bruised. She sobbed loudly, sad tears pouring from her eyes. At the same time she mumbled words which were indistinct even to herself: "Shameless! Disgrace to the whole family!... Disgusting! Disgrace to the whole brigade!... Shameless! Shameless!..."

The turmoil did not abate until midnight.

Then Huangmei fell half asleep again. Drowsily, she heard the brigade leader dispersing the crowd, heard the voices of Uncle and Aunt Jiagui expressing their deep regret to her father and mother, and that of Uncle Xiang comforting and cautioning them not to be too hard on Cunni and warning them to be careful in case she did something foolish to herself. Her mother's grief was gradually changed into soft words of consolation. Huangmei finally fell asleep on her wet pillow, but her sleep was frequently interrupted by violent nightmares. In the last terrible dream, she suddenly heard two urgent cries coming from afar, "Help! Help!..."

Huangmei hurriedly sprang up from her bed. It was already broad daylight. Cunni was not in her bed, nor was her mother who was sleeping with her. Huangmei leapt up, rushed outside in her bare feet and followed the crowd to San Mu Pond at the edge of the village. Alas, Cunni had already been retrieved from the water and was lying stiffly on the ground. She had ended her life so quickly, so easily.

Huangmei's mother, hugging Cunni's body, was weeping hysterically and madly calling out her name. She was pulled away by her neighbours many times, but quickly she threw herself back on the ground. Her father sat quietly by the side of the pond, staring dazedly at the calm water. He was so still that people could have mistaken him for a tree stump.

The morning clouds shed light on Cunni's wet face and restored some ruddiness to her ashen complexion. She looked unusually quiet, unusually calm, without the slightest appearance of pain, protest or complaint against injustice. She had paid the highest price for her own blind impulse, and had cleansed herself of shame and culpability. Of course, her death was a terrible waste. But, to her, what remained in life worth caring about? Before jumping down into the valley of death, the only thing she could think of was to remove her old yellow-green woollen jumper and hang it on a tree. She bequeathed the only wealth life had bestowed on her, together with the warmth and fragrance of her young body, as a legacy to her younger sister. . . .

But that was not the end of the affair. About half a month later, a mournful wailing was heard coming from Uncle Jiagui's home. Two policemen were taking Xiaobaozi away. The whole village suffered a second shock, as people came running from the fields to stand at the roadsides and silently gaze at the pair of shining handcuffs on Xiaobaozi's wrists. Only Uncle and Aunt Jiagui, with tear-stained faces, followed their son.

"Comrades, Comrades!" Shen Shanwang dropped his hoe and came up. Although the death of his daughter had aged him ten years and made him more indifferent to life, yet his sense of duty stirred him. He therefore said to the policemen, "Comrades, we didn't file any charge against him!"

The policemen stared at him and answered contemptuously, "Get away! Move on! We're arresting a rapist who was responsible for a girl's death! What does it matter whether a charge has been filed or not! . . ."

Xiaobaozi, however, was quite composed. He held his head up, looking blankly around. All of a sudden, he stopped a minute and then ran quickly towards the desolate slope opposite him.

"Stop! Where are you going?" the policemen shouted chasing after him.

Xiaobaozi ran on, his frantic steps crushing the wild grass and brambles. Finally, he threw himself upon Cunni's new grave, sobbing bitterly and clawing the damp yellow earth with both hands. The policemen came up and shouted at him. Only then did he stop his tears, and, kneeling down before the grave, kowtow respectfully three times.

3

At the conclusion of the meeting, Huangmei left the hall with a heavy heart. Tian Tang Commune was in a corner of the county, and the ninth brigade was in a corner of that corner. She looked once at the setting sun hung low above the pine grove in the west. Fearing that she might be unable to reach home before dark, she abandoned her plan of going to the store and half ran along the footpath directly from the back street through the wheat fields uphill.

"Shen Huangmei, wait a minute! Let's go together!" The voice of the League committee secretary Xu Rongshu was heard behind her. His home was in the eighth brigade, which was separated from the ninth only by San Mu Pond. Huangmei, of course, was glad to have someone accompany her. In winter evenings, it was quite desolate. But she hadn't thought of walking together with a young man, especially Xu Rongshu. After a slight hesitation, she quickened her steps. When Rongshu caught up with her at the end of the wheat field, she moved away from him cautiously, keeping a distance of over four paces between them.

The death of her sister Cunni had left in her heart indelible shame and fear. She had taken over her elder sister's mulberry carrying-pole at too early an age. The burden of supporting her family was too heavy for her slender body. The spiritual burden was also too much for her young, tender heart. Fearing and hating all young men, she never talked with them when she chanced to meet them, but held herself aloof. She looked down upon her girlfriends who did not fear or hate boys. She had turned into a strained, unapproachable young woman.

But maturity inevitably came to her. The yellowish dryness disappeared from her face, giving place to a shiny, soft glow. Her eyebrows became thick while her once dull eyes were bright, clear and limpid. She felt her breasts swelling, as her shoulders and back grew fuller, and the yellow-green woollen sweater left by her elder sister became much too tight for her. In her heart there frequently rose a new, secret and strange feeling of happiness. On seeing some newly opened blossoms, she could not help plucking one and wearing it in her hair. On hearing birds' twitter, she found their songs so pleasing that she could not help standing still and listening to them for a while. Everything was so beautiful and good: the leaves on the trees, the crops, the wild flowers and the dew drops on them.... All things around her excited her. She often secretly looked at herself in her mother's broken mirror. When carrying water from the pond, she even cast a smile of satisfaction at the reflection of her own slender body. She began to chat with her companions. At New Year's Eve and other festivals, she also went with them hand-in-hand to the commune's store. Although she was wary of young men, she gradually found them less abhorrent.... At this juncture, Xu Rongshu entered her life.

She had known Rongshu since her first year in the primary school of the eighth brigade. Some boys bullied her. A boy in a higher class about the same age as Cunni came up and defended her. That was Rongshu. Later when her mother gave birth to her youngest sister, she had to quit school before she had finished her second year. When she was cutting green fodder for the pigs near San Mu Pond with her youngest sister on her back, Rongshu often secretly left his companions, took the sickle from her hand and quickly cut a large bunch and threw it into her basket. Just as quickly he left. Not long after, a burst of gonging and drumming was heard in the eighth brigade. Huangmei went to have a look with her younger sisters. She saw Rongshu in a new army uniform, which was too large for him, a large red paper flower on his breast, marching along the footpath beside San Mu Pond. He was going to join the People's Liberation Army.

At a League committee meeting the previous year, she had seen Rongshu again. He had been demobilized some days before. On entering the brigade meeting room, he glanced at the gathering shyly and, just like Huangmei and the other girls who had recently joined the League, sat down quietly in a corner of the room. Then several active members, who knew him well, came over, urging him to say something about his life in the army. He felt embarrassed, and, blushing, refused. "I served in peacetime. I didn't fight any battles. What have I to say? . . ." He had none of the confidence supposed to be characteristic of a revolutionary soldier. But for some reason this won the goodwill of Huangmei. When the election of a League committee member was put to the vote and the name of Xu Rongshu was read out, she boldly held up her hand to express her true regard for him.

At the next League committee gathering, Rongshu, the newly elected committee secretary, expressed a conflicting opinion and thus annoyed the Party committee deputy secretary, a former militia commander.

In the past, the activities of the League members of Tian Tang Commune consisted only of one kind apart from holding meetings. This was heavy manual labour, such as collecting manure or carrying stones. After a meeting, the League members had to do this gratuitously until late at night in order to "set an example as Communist League members". Rongshu, however, opposed this. He said, "Youngsters have their own ideas. I propose that we see a film tonight!" On hearing this, everyone laughed and clapped their hands. He was so thoughtful that he had already ordered some tickets beforehand from a factory in the neighbourhood of Tian Tang Commune. After a short meeting, he led them all there. On the way the boys and girls, in groups of threes and fives, joked and talked excitedly. Some of them even went so far as to sing folk songs. It was just as if they were celebrating a festival. Huangmei, for the first time in her life, sat comfortably in a soft chair and enjoyed the show. That night, also for the first time in her life, a young man appeared in her sweet dreams. He resembled a little the hero of the film who led the youths to build a water reservoir, but he was even more like her Youth League committee secretary. He laughed honestly and said something to her, when she was very near to him. On awakening, the moon was shining by her bed, soft and clear. For the first time in her life, a sweet, tender sensation arose in her heart. But instantly she felt ashamed and afraid. "What was it all about?" she wondered miserably. "Oh, dear! Thank goodness it was only a dream!..."

After she became a Youth League group leader, Rongshu often called on her. Huangmei's attitude towards him was just as before, cold and serious. She never asked him into her home. They discussed only official business matters such as the calling of a meeting or the distribution of work. Rongshu would stand outside the door, while Huangmei remained inside maintaining a distance of more than four feet, the one asking questions and the other replying. As soon as their conversation finished, Rongshu left. Huangmei, however, pretending to have something to do, often went out of doors and stealthily watched him depart. How she wished he would enter her house and sit and chat with her about some other subjects. With their increased contact, her contradictory moods grew stronger. One day, Huangmei returned home somewhat later than usual. Her eleven-year-old sister told her, "Rongshu called!"

Her mother, who had also just returned home, asked, "What did he come here again for?"

"He called on me to ask about grafting pear trees." replied Father. "He wanted to know how many years it takes a newly grafted tree to bear fruit, and how much one *mu* of mountain land can produce? I asked if that wasn't following the capitalist road. He said, no, it wasn't capitalism, and then he read me a newspaper article. That boy! ..."

Father shook his head as if disagreeing with Rongshu, but Huangmei could see that he had a good opinion of him. She was therefore secretly glad. Her mother, however, looked most displeased. She frowned and said, "He, he's always breaking the rules! ..."

Huangmei had already heard about Rongshu's quarrel with his uncle, the leader of the eighth brigade, over the question of not allowing commune members to rear chickens. People said that he was rash disobeying his leaders. Huangmei had ignored this. On hearing her mother, however, she felt angry and thought of defending him. Then, seeing her mother's inquisitive eyes boring into her, she lowered her head and ate in silence, pretending not to mind anything. After supper, her mother remained, whispering something to her father in her room. Huangmei heard through a chink in the door these words: "There is already some gossip about her! We must guard against her going the same way as Cunni! . . ."

Huangmei felt as if a knife had been thrust into her heart, and she collapsed weeping on her bed. She blamed her elder sister for having committed such a dreadful sin that even death could not expiate; she blamed herself for having been attracted to a young man! It was so wrong, so disgusting! "Revolting! Falling in love with a man! . . . Shameful!" She hated herself, burying her head deep in her quilt to prevent her weeping from being heard.

She made up her mind not to talk to Rongshu starting from the next morning. Should there be a need to discuss something, let him go to the assistant group leader! Wouldn't he feel strange, feel hurt? Let him! Why was he a man? . . ."

Soon after, she began to hate Rongshu. She overheard Blindman Xu saying in the brigade headquarters, "That boy, Rongshu, doesn't know how high the sky is and how thick the earth. He's quarrelled again with the brigade deputy secretary!" Someone asked, "Over what?"

"Hell! He says he wants to right the wrong done to Xiaobaozi!" replied Blindman Xu.

What?! Huangmei was greatly agitated. She almost cried out aloud. Xiaobaozi's being penalized was entirely his own fault; the punishment meted out to him was quite just. It was not wrong or unjust, or based on false evidence. He deserved no remission. This was practically the consensus of all the villagers. Huangmei did not differ. The death of her elder sister only made her resent Xiaobaozi more. Yet, how could Rongshu, a member of the Chinese Communist Party and a Youth League branch committee secretary respected by her, plead on behalf of such a bad lot as Xiaobaozi? How could he sympathize with him? Had Rongshu got some favour from Uncle and Aunt Jiagui? Huangmei trembled with anger. She considered confronting Rongshu directly, but when she saw him coming towards her with an honest smile on his face along the side of San Mu Pond, her resolve weakened. How could she speak about such a matter to him? She therefore turned round, pretending to go in some other direction, and returned home by a lengthy roundabout way. Afterwards, she regretted her action.

She felt furious with him, hated him, ignored him, feared him, and yet unwillingly thought about him. . . . These contradictory moods seized her alternately. Such was the mental state of this nineteen-year-old peasant girl.

If this can be described as "love", boys and girls living in other places will find it hard to understand. But Huangmei was living in the corner of the county, in the ninth brigade of Tian Tang Commune. Most of the girls there, at about Huangmei's age, had similar experiences of a secret passion, contradictions and anguish like Huangmei and Rongshu. Yet, after a while, the turmoil completely subsided, and everything became quiet and peaceful again. A relative or some other person would show up, offering a present of a yellow-green or rose-red woollen jumper, and, after similar rounds of bargaining, would reach an agreement. Then, on a certain day, this relative or some other person would bring a young man, and would accompany the boy and girl, who dared not look each other in the face, to have a photograph taken in Wu Zhuang or some other place. On a fixed day, the girl would then leave her father and mother, leave this corner. . . .

This was the customary way, generally acknowledged as the correct one by the villagers. Yet this was described as a "mercenary marriage" by the League committee secretary, who made a report at the mass meeting. He also spoke about "love"! What had occurred between Cunni and Xiaobaozi? Could that be called "love"? No, no! That was a disgusting and unlawful deed! Then, was there another way? — Huangmei felt it was all far beyond her comprehension. She could not help thinking about Rongshu, who was now behind her and silently accompanying her. Her companions, who came to the meeting with her, had all gone to the store. On the quiet mountain path there were only the two of them. She could hear her heart thumping loudly. . . .

Suddenly, Rongshu stood still, looked round and in a sonorous voice sang:

I love this blue ocean,
How long is the coast of our motherland! . . .

Huangmei was alarmed. Then, after hearing him sing

for a while, she was touched by the warmth of his song and could not stop herself from turning round to smile approvingly.

"Seeing this pine forest on the mountain, I remembered the ocean! I thought of the days when I served on a battleship! . . ." Rongshu said, smiling as if to himself. "It broadens your vision, if all our neighbours could have a look at the ocean, how wonderful that would be!"

"Huangmei, have you been to the main street? Don't you know that no one now will drive away peasants selling eggs and vegetables at the market? The Party's agricultural policy will soon be changed! All the slopes and hills will be returned to us and we can plant them again with pear trees. Uncle Shanwang, who's such a clever farmer, will again be called on to use his skills. As a first step, plant saplings in your family's private plot! . . ." He spoke freely and eagerly. "Aunt Shanwang's health isn't too good. She can cut branches and weave baskets at home to get some pocket money. Your third sister can begin regular work next year! The two younger ones can tend some sheep! . . . I have an army friend who is now a cadre in our commune. He told me that our Party Central Committee will soon issue a document to encourage us peasants to become wealthier! . . . It's true! You don't believe it?"

His eyes shone with hope. His voice was as musical as the babbling stream water and very appealing. Huangmei didn't believe what he said. As for getting richer, she had neither hoped nor even thought about it. Ever since she had begun to understand the world, the idea of getting rich had always been criticized as capitalist. What touched her was Rongshu's knowing so much about her family's problems and being so concerned about them. This was how he answered her coldness, wariness and hatred of him! She felt regret, her face burning. . . .

"Yes! If we don't get wealthier but remain poor all our lives, there's no use in talking about anything!" He shook his head feelingly. "Take Xiaobaozi as an example. Should we blame him alone? What about poverty, backwardness, ignorance, foolishness? Plus feudalism! And so an honest young man was clapped in jail. And your elder sister, she suffered an even greater injustice! . . ."

Hearing him say this, Huangmei at once felt insulted. She glared at him angrily and shouted, "I won't allow you to speak about that! I won't allow you to say anything about my elder sister! . . ."

She tried to control the tears that had begun to fall. She rushed towards the top of the hill and then raced down. Rongshu was baffled.

4

Nearing home Huangmei gradually calmed down. It was already dark. Her youngest sister greeted her from afar and rushed towards her. Soon, her mother also came out to meet her, her face wreathed in smiles. This made Huangmei suspicious. Her poor, overworked, ill mother had grown old and feeble before her time. Since the death of Cunni her face registered, apart from anxiety, only a blank, distracted expression. What had happened to make her feel so happy?

"Quick, hurry and look at what's on your bed!" she told her daughter.

There on the bed was a brand-new sky-blue woollen sweater, soft and with a captivating sheen under the feeble light of the oil lamp.

Huangmei picked it up in her hands, and, before she had felt its softness and warmth, threw it away as if she had been stung. She cried out, "Whose is it?"

"Yours!" said her mother, with an elated glance at her daughter, while scooping out a bowlful of hot corn gruel from the pot. "Your aunt brought it here."

"My aunt!..." Huangmei shuddered, her legs trembled and she sat down on her bed stupefied. Her aunt had visited her home not long ago. She had talked in whispers with her mother for a full half day, while steadily eyeing Huangmei. At that time Huangmei had guessed the mysterious intention in her look. Just as she had suspected, her aunt had now brought her this woollen sweater.

Her mother sat down beside her, and with an un- usually tender voice explained, "The young man is in Second Uncle's third brigade at Wu Zhuang. He's three years older than you. His elder brother is a worker at Bei Guan Railway Station with a monthly salary of over fifty yuan!..."

Huangmei felt a stream of cold sweat trickling slowly down her back. Her whole body shook, her ears buzz- ed, and she could not hear anything clearly.

"I don't want him!" she screamed. "No! I won't!"

She threw the woollen sweater at her mother, who, however, still smiled and held her hand saying, "They aren't asking you to go over to their home just now! He'll come to meet you at the Dragon Boat Festival and bring you your clothes. Sixteen suits!... After the engagement, they'll give us five hundred yuan in cash!"

"No! No! No!" The realization she was being insulted suddenly flashed into Huangmei's mind. She experienced a choking terror. She didn't know what to do, and could only let her tears fall quietly. Then, she went to run outside.

Near the door stood her miserable father and her three younger sisters staring blankly at her. Huangmei rushed out, covering her face with her hands. She stopped in the courtyard, leaned against the half-demolished earthen wall of the pigsty and sobbed loudly.

"What's the matter?" asked her mother, who had quickly followed her out of doors and who took her hand in hers. "Huangmei, you're a sensible child. Look at us! My health is poor. Your three younger sisters go hungry. We haven't any swill for the pigs. After rearing them more than half a year, we couldn't even get back the money we spent on them! If I take the eggs we've saved to sell in the street, I risk being driven from one place to another. I'll feel as scared as if I were stealing. Last year, when the profits were divided, we again had an overdraft and didn't receive one cent. I thought of buying a pair of socks for you, but. . . ."

Her mother also began to weep, while she continued complaining, "Your elder sister failed to live up to our expectations. Who else is there to depend on? We won't be able to live in our house if it isn't repaired next year. We're in debt. Where's the money for that? Your aunt said that when we got the five hundred yuan, we could. . . ."

"Money, money!" yelled the girl. "You're selling your daughter like some merchandise! . . ."

Her mother at once became speechless. She felt she

had no more strength, and holding on to the low earthen wall, she sat down slowly on the ground. "Selling your daughter like some merchandise!" These words that had deeply wounded her were, nevertheless, familiar to her. Who was it who at around Huangmei's age, and with the same outraged vehemence had uttered those very words? Who was it? — Who! None other than herself! . . .

It was one winter when the land reform team had come to Wu Zhuang. One night, when Linhua went to see the opera *The White-haired Girl,* she became acquainted with a good-natured, good-looking young farmhand called Shen Shanwang. From that moment, she suddenly understood the meaning of the word "lover" as it was sung in the folk songs. Nineteen-year-old Linhua not only bravely participated in the mass meetings to struggle against the landlords, but also went courageously to the corn field to meet her lover at night. But her parents had already arranged her engagement to the young proprietor of a store in Bei Guan Village. On hearing the gossip about Linhua, her fiancé's parents sent fifty silver dollars to her parents, demanding that the marriage take place that year. Linhua wept and raised hell, and was quite beside herself. She openly acknowledged that she had fallen in love with a poor young man from Kao Shan Zhuang Cooperative, declaring that she would follow him and suffer with him in the mountains rather than return to her feudal home. Her parents were enraged. They cursed and beat her in a locked room. She wept, shouted, rolled on the ground and threw the silver dollars all about her. She angrily yelled, "You, you want to sell your daughter like some merchandise!"

That was a time when the anti-feudalist blaze had burnt "the orders of parents and the contracts made by go-betweens"* together with the title deeds and loan receipts held by landlords. Pictures advocating the new marriage laws were pasted on the wall outside the gate of the village government. The heroine Liu Qiao'er** in the play and the child daughters-in-law in her village were both clear examples for Linhua. The good-natured, good-looking Shen Shanwang held in his hand the promise of the splendid future awaiting her. Linhua had more than enough courage to break out of the prison of feudalism!

"They want to sell their daughter like some merchandise!" The next day, in the newly whitewashed village public affairs office,*** acting upon this charge from Linhua, the land reform team with encouraging smiles issued both to her and Shanwang a marriage certificate bearing a photo of Chairman Mao. . . .

She had never imagined that today her own daughter would use the same words to accuse her as she had used thirty years ago!

"Why is it like this? Can time go backwards? . . ." She was shocked and puzzled. Lifting her head slowly, she gazed at the late winter night sky. Some cold stars shed their gloomy, dim light upon her, as if winking sarcastically. She seemed suddenly to have received some revelation that disturbed her, for she beat her breast and stamped her feet, and began to weep bitterly. At the same time she whispered to herself, "Retribution, retribution! This is what is called retribution!"

---

* The Chinese traditional slogan for mercenary marriages.
** The name of the heroine in the opera of the same title.
*** Another name for the village government.

From her mother's eyes, which had long been dry, tears flowed, saturated with the sullen hatred she felt in the depths of her heart. She hated Huangmei, Cunni and their father. She hated her own unlucky fate, hated the land to which she had come in her youth dreaming of a joyful future, and which had given her nothing but sadness and worry in return for the arduous labour she had expended on it for most of her life! . . .

Huangmei, in contrast, became more composed. She comforted her mother, saying, "Mama! Now no one will drive away people selling eggs and vegetables at the market! You can cut some branches and weave baskets to sell. My younger sisters can tend sheep. The slopes can be reconstructed and planted with fruit trees. Dad's a skilled farmer. Rongshu told me, our Party Central Committee has issued a document! . . . It urges us peasants to get richer! . . ."

"Document, document! One document today, another tomorrow! I've had my fill of them! Aren't we still as poor as before? Huangmei, I'm not willing to let you waste your life as I did!" Still tearful she began to calm down. "My child, you're a sensible girl. I know that Rongshu is fond of you, as you are of him. But you should think it over. What will you do if you're starving? . . ."

The storm had blown over. Her mother's feeble body leaned against Huangmei. Mother and daughter sat motionless and in silence, each immersed in her own thoughts.

"Mama, you must go in!" Huangmei urged in a low voice. Her eyes gazed at a cluster of houses of the eighth brigade, trying to locate one of them. "I have something to do! . . ."

Then, she stubbornly walked in the direction of San

Mu Pond. The events that had just happened had suddenly made her wiser; she was now more mature. All her prejudices, including her opposition to the idea of redressing the wrong done to Xiaobaozi, were now found to be unwarranted. She was confident that Rongshu had good reason for whatever he suggested. He knew a lot, he had even seen the world! How could Huangmei still doubt the document encouraging peasants to get richer? He might also give her some good ideas, tell her what she should do!

A soft warm breeze, the harbinger of spring in this remote area, wafted over the surface of San Mu Pond. It silently caressed the withered grass at the edge of the pond, silently wiped away the tears of the girl who had hurried there. Had spring finally come at last to this corner forsaken by love?

Translated by Hu Zhihui

Zhang Xian, was born in Shanghai in 1935 and in 1953 graduated from the mechanical engineering department of Beijing's Qinghua University. He began to publish his work in 1956 while working at the Iron and Steel Industry Institute of Engineering.

His stories "Memories" and "A Corner Forsaken by Love" were awarded prizes in 1979 and 1980. The film vesion of the latter was given a Golden Rooster Award in 1981. Zhang Xian is a member of the Chinese Writers' Association.

The Log Cabin Overgrown with Creepers

Gu Hua

FOR many years the story of a Yao girl has been told in the forests of the Wujie Hills, a young woman called Pan Qingqing, or Azure, who was a tree warden deep in those ancient and mysterious forests. She was born, grew up and married in the hills, and in all her life she only once went to the forestry station, which was itself remote enough. The young men there had only heard of this marvellous woman but had never set eyes on her. Her family had lived in Green Hollow for generations in a log cabin overgrown with creepers, a cabin built of fir trunks so strong that no axe would make an impression on them or wild boar shake them. The parts of the trunks that were sunk into the ground had long since turned black and grown layer upon layer of wavy mushrooms in lace-like patterns. Behind the cabin a mountain stream ran clear throughout the year.

The cabin's links with the outside world were a narrow track and a telephone line that had been put up before the "cultural revolution" to carry fire reports but had been cut by a heavy fall of snow one winter. Since the beginning of the "cultural revolution" there had been a never-ending succession of bosses at the forestry

station, and they had all been too busy cooking their
political pies to send anyone to reconnect the line, so
that this symbol of modern civilization no longer reached this ancient forest. But for the occasional sound
of a hen, a dog or a baby from the cabin and the column
of light blue smoke rising from its stove the thousands
of acres of woodland around Green Hollow would have
been peacefully sleeping day and night. Not all the
songs of the birds in the hills and all the blossoms opening and falling on them would ever have woken it.

Azure had lost both her parents early. Her husband
was a Han Chinese called Wang Mutong, a tall, power-
fully built man strong enough to kill a tiger. Husband
and wife were both forest wardens. Mutong liked a
couple of cups of Azure's corn wine before his meals,
and except that he got drunk occasionally and beat her
black and blue he was not a bad husband. He cared for
his wife, never sending her up the hills to fetch firewood, of which he always kept plenty ready cut in
stacks. He did not make her cut and clear firebreaks
through the trees, and for over ten years there had never
been a forest fire in Green Hollow. Nor did he expect
her to till the soil and plant the crops. He saw to it
that their big plot of land by the stream always had
more onions, pumpkins and other fresh vegetables than
the four of them could eat. All that Azure had to
do was to feed the pigs, suckle the babies, wash, make
and mend the clothes, and look after the house. At
twenty-six or twenty-seven she was still as lively and
fresh as an unmarried girl. Mutong could not read a
word but he was bursting with self-confidence and he
knew everything. He felt that he was the real master of
Green Hollow: the woman was his, the children were

his, and the cabin and the hills were his, though of course he did come under the forestry station. As the leadership had sent him to look after this part of the forest, that made him like a minor vassal in charge of his own fief. Before she'd had the babies Azure had often asked to visit the forestry station that was some 45 kilometres away but he had never let her go, sometimes hitting her savagely or even forcing her to kneel for long periods as a punishment. He was afraid that if his beautiful wife had her eyes opened by that lively, bustling place she would start getting fancy ideas. She might have been led astray by those smooth and pushy young men at the station. He only stopped worrying after she had given him the babies, first the boy and then the girl, which left her firmly tied to his belt and truly his woman. It was now the turn of the younger generation to be hit and forced to kneel. He ran the whole household by strict rules. The places of husband and wife, as of father and children, were all clearly set out in Green Hollow. Differences of status counted for a lot in this miniature society.

Mutong and Azure lived in virtual isolation from the world. It would be an exaggeration to say that she followed him in everything, but they were both used to each other and they got along without any trouble. Mutong would go to the forestry station once a month to collect their wages and bring back the rice, oil and salt for the family. Every time he came back he would tell her what had been happening at the station and the news he had heard there. Azure would listen with her dark and gleaming eyes opened wide and her mind filled with amazement. It was as if her husband were describing some foreign country on the other side of the world. In the last few years her husband had been telling her a lot about young students rebelling and making trouble. Teachers who wore glasses were being dragged around the hills with placards on them like performing monkeys. The forestry expert who had studied for half a lifetime was supposed to have drowned himself in a little pond so shallow that he had not even got his back wet. "We're better off as we are in Green Hollow. The gleaming black earth here is ever so fertile. You just have to stick a piece of firewood into the ground for it to grow and come into leaf. We're not educated. We bother nobody and nobody bothers us."

Some of what her husband said Azure understood and some she didn't. She was thoroughly confused, and was worried for those learned scholars who lived beyond their hills. Book-learning was a disaster, and she found herself thinking that she and her husband were lucky to have avoided it. She had so often heard him saying, "We're better off as we are in Green Hollow," that she came to believe it herself. She did not ask much of her husband, but simply wished that he would not hit her too hard when he lost his temper and started laying about him. Every evening at nightfall they shut the door of their cabin and went to bed. Half a pint of paraffin that he brought back from the station was enough to keep that lamp burning six months. Only when the moon and the stars happened to shine in through the wooden-framed windows set high in the walls could they spy on how the couple spent their nights.

"Azure, I want you to give me more babies."

"We've got Little Tong and Little Qing. You told

me the forestry station won't let people have big families any more. Don't women have to be sterilized?"

"Never mind that. Five more wouldn't be too many."

"Don't you care about how I'll have to suffer?"

"Suffer? Women don't mind a bit of suffering at child-birth."

"I'm scared of the people at the station telling us off."

"To hell with that. The worst they can do is refuse to give us extra grain rations. We've got soil and water here in Green Hollow. Just look at my hands: they're as big as rice-measures. Do you think I couldn't raise a few more kids? I'll clear a cotton field next winter, and you can fetch the spinning wheel and handloom your mum left you and clean them up."

"Get on with you. You think I'm a pheasant that you can keep in these hills."

"You're mine."

Azure said no more as her husband held her tucked under his armpit that smelled so sharply of sweat. She was very docile. She belonged to him. If he wanted to beat or swear at her that was only as it should be. She was in the bloom of youth, and could bear children as painlessly as a tree bearing fruit. When she fed the babies the milk flowed endlessly like sap from her white breasts. Her husband was young and strong. He could kill a tiger or catch a wild boar. When he embraced her, his arms were like a ring of iron; they did what husbands and wives probably do in other places, and he had so much strength it was as if he did not know what to do with it.

In the summer of 1975 the One-hander came to

Green Hollow. Let there be no confusion: he was not a man in authority but a city youngster who had come to settle on the forestry station in 1964. His real name was Li Xingfu and they said he had been born in the year of Liberation, 1949. He was tall, slender and rather elegant, and quick at selecting seeds and looking after saplings. He knew how to get on with any of the forestry workers or officials he met. But he had been carried away by his enthusiasm for travelling around the country exchanging revolutionary experience as a Red Guard in 1966, and had left a perfectly good hand lying by the railway track when hitching a ride on a train. From then on one of his sleeves had hung empty. After a few years hanging around in the city he had come back to the forestry station and this was when the workers there had nicknamed him the One-hander. From then on the station's leadership had been down on him. They had telephoned each of the felling districts and forest management teams but they had all refused to take him. Apart from the fact that the One-hander could no longer do heavy manual work he had been one of the "young revolutionary warriors". If he started exchanging revolutionary experience in some mountain hollow he would be as useless as a piece of wet beancurd dropped in a pile of ash that you couldn't either blow or wipe clean. One day, while Wang Mutong, the warden of Green Hollow, came to the station to fetch the grain for his family the station's political director bumped into him. Slapping himself on the back of the neck the political director thought: Yes! Why not send Li Xingfu off to Green Hollow to be a forest warden with Wang Mutong and his wife? The work was not too light or too heavy but just right, and on top of that there was nobody else for dozens of miles around apart from the very reliable and straightforward Wang Mutong and his wife. There was no one Li Xingfu could exchange revolutionary experiences with but monkeys and pheasants. Wang Mutong's first reaction to being given someone to work under his leadership was delight, which turned to disgust when he realized that this subordinate Li Xingfu was the One-hander. "Wang, my friend, you've been wanting to join the Party for years, haven't you? This is a test that our organization is setting you," said the political director, slapping him on the shoulder. "You'll have no problem keeping him in order — he's only got one hand. I'll have a word with him myself in a moment and make him agree to three conditions: in Green Hollow he'll have to obey your instructions in everything, he'll have to report everything to you, and he'll have to get your permission if he wants to leave the hollow. Show a bit of spirit. Try to reform this educated youngster who's gone wrong." Only then had Wang nodded his assent and decided to take the test that the organization was setting him by shouldering the burden of "education and reform".

Thus the One-hander had come to Green Hollow and become an important new member of the little society headed by Wang Mutong. Some twenty or thirty paces from their own ancient log cabin Wang Mutong and his wife built him a little, low cabin with walls of upright logs and a roof of fir bark on the bank of the jade-clear mountain stream. The new cabin and the old, the little one and the big, became neighbours. At first Wang Mutong had felt no hostility towards the

One-hander and liked being called Elder Brother Wang by him.

The One-hander was captivated from the very first by the beauty and peace of Green Hollow. Every day Wang Mutong would send him to sit in the watchtower on the ridge, so that each morning he would climb the narrow path that snaked through the mists of the great forest. It was like walking in a very hazy dream. The milky-white mist that covered the mountain and filled the valley was so thick it seemed to be a liquid on which you could float. When the sun showed through and the mists began to disperse at nine or ten in the morning he felt he was in another, enchanted world as he sat in the watchtower on the ridge with the brilliant greens of the foliage above him and below his feet clumps of tall Guangdong pines and Chinese hemlock trees rising through the rolling mist. But the One-hander knew the woods and the valley were no fairyland. He was aware that Wang Mutong and his wife were both young, and that she was tender and beautiful, with big, dark eyes that could talk and sing, although she tactfully kept a proper distance between them. But young people cannot bear loneliness. Was he destined to exchange experiences and make friends only with the golden monkeys, the thrushes and the grouse in this green valley?

Wang Mutong's boy Little Tong was seven and his daughter, Little Qing, five. At first the children had been rather afraid of "one-arm", but the situation had changed after the One-hander caught Little Tong some birds, brought Little Qing back some blossoms from the mountains to wear in her hair and let her look at herself in a little mirror. The children started to call him "Uncle Li" or "elder brother". A few days later Little

Tong insisted on going to sleep in the One-hander's cabin and refused to go back when his mother called for him. Mountain children are lovable in their own special way. When a snake slithered into the little cabin, making the One-hander shake with terror, Little Tong told him that snakes never bit people unless they were trodden on. Little Tong went on to tell him with graphic imitations about the three kinds of snakes in Green Hollow. "Green bamboo snakes are very lazy. They usually lie coiled up in the bamboo without moving." He put his head back, closed his eyes, and pursed his lips as he went on, "They spit their poison out like this" — he blew through his lips — "to lure birds, and as soon as the bird comes close they pounce and get a good grip on it. Then they coil round the bamboo again and take their time eating it up. The shouting snake is different. Its skin's the same colour as mud. It looks terrific going through the grass. It rears up about waist high, pushing the grass aside, like this." He made his eyes bulge, opened his mouth wide, and kept stretching his head forward. "It goes 'hoo, hoo', and it's really scary. There's another sort that's thick as a chopper handle and as long as a carrying-pole. Dad calls it a forty-eighter, and when it goes along it shakes its head all over the place. You'd think it was crazy." The One-hander, afraid that Little Tong was going to do another imitation, put his hand on the boy's head and asked, "How do you know all that?" "I've seen green bamboo snakes myself and dad told me about the shouting snakes and the forty-eighters. Dad catches snakes and sells them outside the mountains." The One-hander looked at the boy, of an age to be going to school, imitating the snakes, thought of that long, cold thing slithering out of the cabin, and felt miserably sad.

Adults observe children and children observe adults. The One-hander brushed his teeth and rinsed his mouth out every morning. Little Qing always poked half of her face out of the door of their cabin to gaze wide-eyed at this amazing sight. One morning she came timidly over and asked, "Uncle, does your mouth smell bad?" The One-hander, whose mouth was full of toothpaste, did not understand what she meant.

"If your mouth doesn't smell bad, why do you rub it with that brush every day?"

The One-hander had to laugh. When he had finished washing his face he said to Little Qing, "Ask your mum to buy you and Little Tong a toothbrush one day and brush your teeth every morning. Then they'll be lovely and white."

Little Qing was not convinced. "Mum never uses a brush, and her teeth are lovely and white."

"Does your mum's mouth ever have a nasty smell?" the One-hander asked, trying to press home his argument.

"She loves kissing me, and her mouth smells ever so nice. If you don't believe me kiss her yourself and see."

"Stop talking such nonsense, you little devil. Come back at once," Little Qing's mother called from inside their cabin.

The One-hander's face felt hot and his heart pounded as if he had just done something wicked. He shot back into his own little cabin.

It was a trivial incident, but Wang Mutong had heard. He dragged Little Qing to the doorway of their cabin and made her kneel there as a punishment. It was obvious that he wanted the One-hander to see. Although nothing suspicious had happened he now had eyes in the back of his head and was on his guard.

The life of the two households in Green Hollow flowed as calmly as the jade-green mountain brook behind the cabins. Although the deep places only came up to your calves and the shallow parts just covered your heel it could reflect the dancing trees, the clear blue sky and the leisurely floating clouds. It now reflected something new, a tall fir pole that the One-hander had put up outside his wooden cabin: a radio aerial.

This was to stir up trouble. The little black box in the One-hander's cabin could talk and sing. It broke the immemorial silence of the night among the ancient mountain forests. At first only the children took their courage in their hands to go to listen to it in the little cabin after nightfall, but after a while Azure herself began to drop in for a while on the pretext of fetching them home to bed. Of course, the next thing every evening was for Wang Mutong to appear to take his wife and children back to bed. Once his tone of voice was a little rough and "it's too early", Azure answered back with something like petulance. "If we go to bed the moment it gets dark I hate having to wait so long for daybreak." When Wang Mutong heard his wife say that she hated the long wait in bed till dawn a dark cloud fell over his heart. The tall and strongly built forester never went to listen to the devilish voices singing in the black box. He was going to preserve his inviolable dignity as a man and watch closely to stop things from developing any further.

Soon afterwards the One-hander organized Azure and the children to tidy up the piece of ground between the two cabins and make neat stacks of firewood and other things by the doors. The muddy and uneven ground that used to be filthy with dogshit and pig's urine was now level and clean. The One-hander said that he wanted to plant flowers there and teach Azure and the children to read and do the radio exercises. The thought made Azure's face all smiles. The children followed the One-hander round all day, and it was always "uncle says this" or "uncle says that's wrong". Anyone would think he was closer to them than their own father. This upset Wang Mutong, who did not like what he saw. Although the One-hander had only one arm he was gradually changing life in Green Hollow, like a worm silently turning the earth over. "Bloody show-off. He wants to impress us all in Green Hollow with his education. Anyone would think he's better than me."

He was not surprised when the One-hander made four suggestions about the work. The first was that the forestry station should be asked to repair the telephone line that had been out of action for years and to install a loudspeaker for cable radio between the two cabins. The second was that they should put up painted wooden notices on all the mountain paths into Green Hollow with the Forestry Code on them. The third was that he and Wang Mutong should have a system for patrolling the mountains and fire-watching with two eight-hour shifts a day; when on duty they should not make traps with bent saplings, dig up oriental bamboo rats, or do any other work on their own account. The fourth was that there should be a politics and literacy class that the

children could join in. When Azure heard this suggestion she smiled and gave her husband a wordless look
with her big, bright eyes that obviously said, "Look how
educated he is. He has such clever ideas — they sound
wonderful."

Wang Mutong saw all this at once. It was very pain-
ful. His face went hard, he tightened his lips, and his
eyes spat fury. "You smell good, don't you, just like a
brand-new latrine," they seemed to say. "You can keep
your fancy nonsense." He glared savagely at his wife
then said to the One-hander very bluntly, "City boy!
They always used to say that a stranger should follow
the local customs, and the guest does what suits the host.
You may not be a guest, but you're certainly not the
host. There hasn't been a forest fire here in fifteen or
twenty years. All the leaders we've had in the forests of
the Wujie Hills have always said my work's good. I've
been a model worker every year. I don't need any wires
or boards or shifts or classes. You'd better sharpen your
billhook and get yourself fit. The forestry station made
me the boss here. The three conditions the political director told you about weren't just hot air."

Wang Mutong was an intimidating sight as he stood
there, his arms akimbo and his eyes flaming with anger.
The One-hander gazed wide-eyed with horror, his
mouth hanging open and his face pale from shock.
Azure could not bear to see it, but she dared not pro-
voke her husband's savage and violent fury by showing
her own anger or speaking out of turn, so she could only
try to ease the tension by saying to the One-hander, "Li,
he's not very educated. He talks a bit rough. . . ." But
when she saw that her husband was on the point of exploding she shut up. "Rough I may be," Wang Mu-

tong said with a mocking laugh, "I suppose you're very smooth. The roughs control the smoothies these days. The roughs are in charge, Li Xingfu. Don't you forget that the leadership sent you here to be educated and re-moulded." With that he turned his massive body away and stormed off, putting his feet down so hard that they left deep footprints.

The One-hander's four suggestions had run up against the rock of Wang Mutong and disappeared without trace. He felt deflated. Yes, he had been sent to Green Hollow to be educated and reformed, but he could not help feeling afraid of Wang Mutong. He knew that there was very little he could do to improve his present state, but he was full of energy and could not let himself stay idle, because idleness made him de-pressed, lonely, fed up with life, and thinking he would do better to jump off a precipice and be done with it. He had two books that he had kept from before the "cultural revolution": *Trees* and *A Forest Fire Prevention Manual*. He took *Trees* with him on his daily patrols of the mountains and taught himself to recognize the hundreds of different kinds of broadleafed ever-greens that grew there with the help of the illustrations in the book. To prevent his time here from being completely wasted he decided to do a survey of the for-estry resources of Green Hollow that would be of use when felling began in the future. Thinking that Azure would understand him he told her of his plan, and she was as warm and friendly with him as if he'd been her own brother. "Silly thing. Go ahead and do it, but don't talk about it to anyone else." "Won't Wang mind?" "You won't be doing anything wrong. You...." When she said "You...." she drew the word out. Her dark eyes shone so bright he could see himself reflected in them; they shone straight into his heart. He was afraid to look into them, though he did not know why. Azure's "You. . . ." echoed over and over again in his heart.

It was autumn. The One-hander collected the seeds of some rare and valuable trees, including a rare fir, golden-leaf magnolias and south China camphor trees that he intended to raise in a little nursery. He planned to carry them into the forestry station later as seedlings for the technicians to raise. Some land had to be burnt and cleared for his nursery, and as he knew that Wang Mutong would not be at all interested he had to ask Azure to help him.

That day Wang Mutong was in the mountains setting traps. The One-hander and Azure had chosen the slope where wild aubergines grew next to the vegetable patch, a piece of land that Wang Mutong was intending to clear for cotton. They set it alight and soon thick smoke was billowing out above the roaring wind and flames. The two of them were relaxed and happy, laughing and shouting like brother and sister. They never expected Wang Mutong to come rushing down the mountainside in a high temper. He glared coldly at them, took the billhook from his belt and cut down a little pine tree that he wielded with both hands to put the fire out. The One-hander tried to explain, but Wang Mutong gave him a terrible glare and roared, "Cut out this new-fangled nonsense! I've got other plans for this land. Li Xingfu, write a self-criticism tonight for burning land without my permission." "Who am I to hand it to?" "Who to? Do you think that just because I don't read I can't be your leader? I'm telling you, you'd better behave yourself when you're under me." Hearing these awful things said Azure gave her husband a tearful look. "Go back and feed the pigs — the swill must be cooked by now," he said as harshly as if he were some malevolent deity.

The One-hander stole a lingering look filled with pity at Azure and watched her turn and go back without saying a word, wiping her tears away with the back of her hand.

Everyone needs to feel self-confidence and self-respect. Fail to mend a little crack and a yawning gap will open up: even the earth itself will split open. Wang Mutong felt that the One-hander had flung down a challenge. His own wife was getting out of hand: she wasn't as docile and tender as she used to be.

One day Wang Mutong had to go to the forestry station to fetch the family's grain. Normally he would spend the night there, but this time for some peculiar reason he had felt very uneasy as soon as he set out that morning. There was a worry nagging at him that he could not get out of his mind. He was a powerfully-built man and his blood was up, so he did the journey of some ninety kilometres there and back the same day, with a load of sixty kilogrammes of rice on the return leg. When he got back that night he stank of sweat. The door of his cabin was half open and the lamp was still on. His wife must still be up. That was odd. He went inside to find nobody there. Then he heard laughter and singing coming from the One-hander's hut. He felt the stove: It was cold. He was now ablaze with an anger that nothing was going to calm down. He rushed out and stood outside the One-hander's

window. He could see it all clearly: his own wife sitting
with her chin in her hands, Little Tong leaning against
her knees, and both of them listening with rapt attention to a woman singing devilish songs in that accursed
box.   And the One-hander had Little Qing on his knee
with his face touching hers.   He could hear that the
song coming from the black box was a Yao love song.

"It's lovely. My mum loved singing it when she was
alive. . . ." Wang Mutong could see his wife's eyes shining devilishly as she gazed at the One-hander so sweet-
ly.   "You Yaos have always been wonderful singers
and dancers. . . ." The One-hander was looking at her
in that shameless way too. Wang Mutong could bear
to see no more.   He had to control the flames of his
anger to stop himself from shouting obscenities when he
said, "Little Tong, Little Qing, like going to the music
hall, do you? Is this your way of shortening the wait
till daybreak?"   Only then did Azure realize that her
husband was back.   Pulling Little Tong with one hand
and Little Qing with the other she rushed to the door.
"Just look at you, you're so worn out you're soaked in
sweat," she said.   "Why didn't you spend the night at
the station?" He ignored her, and by keeping his teeth
clenched he prevented himself from saying something
that he did not want to say: "If I'd stayed the night at
the station I dare say you'd have spent it at his place."

Back in their own cabin Azure quickly lit the stove
and heated his water while cooking him a meal.   She
did not warm him up any wine because she was afraid
he might beat her up if he got drunk.   That night Wang
Mutong showed exceptional restraint.   His silence was
terrifying, freezing the atmosphere in the hut. He gave
himself a rub down and washed his feet with the warm

water then went to bed and to sleep without a word, paying no attention to the food his wife had set on the table. She seemed to understand what was upsetting him: several times she tried to make up with him by pushing hard at his naked back with both her hands, but he lay there as heavy and immobile as a gunpowder barrel. It was terrifying.

Wang Mutong was not only physically strong: he could work things out and think for himself. He felt that his position in Green Hollow was under threat, and the spark of mutiny was spreading from Azure to Little Tong and Little Qing. Was he going to sit there calmly watching the One-hander gradually luring away his wife and his children? Was an upright, tough and hard-working model forest warden going to be beaten by a weedy little one-armed city boy sent to the countryside? He decided to start by consolidating his position in his own cabin. The next morning his face was set and his eyes glaring as he announced in a voice like thunder, "Little Tong, Little Qing, kneel to your father! Kneel! Now, listen. From today onwards if either of you or your mum sets one foot inside the little cabin I'll gouge your eyes out and break your legs." Azure's face went pale as she heard this ban being proclaimed. Little Tong's and Little Qing's teeth were chattering as they knelt behind her. They were trembling like a pair of saplings in a cold wind.

Before the One-hander set out to work Wang Mutong went to his cabin to ask for the self-criticism he had demanded several days before. When the One-hander said he had not yet written it he said, "Do you think that what I say is just hot air that counts for nothing? I tell you frankly, Li Xingfu, that the leadership at the station put you completely in my power. From now onwards you won't be allowed to talk or act out of turn. All you'll be allowed to do is behave yourself. I'm giving you another day's grace. I want your written self-criticism first thing tomorrow morning."

Wang Mutong glared at him with his leopard eyes and shook two fists that were like sledge-hammers as he went on to lay down three new rules. "Listen! As from today you will report to me every evening here in your cabin on what you've done each day. If you're busy you can ask me for leave, and when you're not busy don't come into my cabin whenever you feel like it. And, thirdly, if you try to lead anyone in my family astray with that devilish box of yours you'll catch it from my fists. With just one finger I could pull out your fir pole with that wire on it and throw them over the hill."

He worked along two lines; internal pacification and resistance to outsiders. He also took some practical steps to enforce his prohibitions. Previously they had always gone past the One-hander's cabin whenever they left their own hut to take the dirt track that led east to the forestry station or to cross the stream westwards to sit in the fire watchtower on the mountain or to patrol. Wang Mutong now wielded his pick and shovel to cut a new path for his family. Of course, this meant making a detour of a good hundred paces when going to the mountain or the station.

This was the situation that the One-hander had no choice but to accept. Wang Mutong's status and position in Green Hollow was as strong and stable as that of a ruler of an ancient forest kingdom and it brooked no questioning. He had never gone to the One-hander's cabin very often before, but now that his wife and children dared not come any more he would go and sit there every evening to hear the One-hander's report on what he had done that day. He evidently enjoyed this taste of being a powerful leader and kept the One-hander as docile and well controlled as a so-called class enemy.

Thus it was that the One-hander withdrew into his little cabin like a snail pulling back into its shell. Even the songs from the little black box were quieter now. In the face of harsh reality, which had once again given him a black eye, the One-hander had to admit that he was beaten. Life in Green Hollow went back to its usual sleepy pace.

The weather was very odd that winter: it thundered constantly but there was no snow. Older people took it as an omen of a winter and spring drought. Every morning Green Hollow's vast ancient forest was hung with hoar frost shaped like dog's teeth, and the evergreens seemed to be wearing suits of jade sewn together with silver thread. It was a gleaming white world that did not disappear before noon. The two cabins at the bottom of the valley were crowned every morning with white jade, and the gurgling flow of the mountain stream behind them was now silenced by the hard shell that lay on it.

On these freezing frosty days Azure had no work to do outside apart from feeding the pigs twice and cooking a couple of meals, so she would turn out her basket of rags to sew soles for the children's shoes. When her husband took Little Tong and Little Qing out to play in the hills Azure would sit by the stove with a piece of cloth in her hands. Sometimes she would sit there lost in thought for half a morning. Every day Wang Mutong would bring back hares and badgers that he had caught on the mountains and take off their skins to be nailed up on the wall. The fat meat being stewed in the earthenware pot could be smelt for miles around. The strange thing was that the smell of the meat now made Azure feel sick, just as if she were expecting again. A great stone was crushing her heart, and underneath it there was still something alive. Her husband had been beating her a lot recently and she was covered in bruises. She could scarcely breathe in peace from morning till night as she watched his expression and his eyes. When he started hitting her she could only hope that his fists would land on her back or her legs or other places that did not matter. She wept till her tears ran dry and then till they flowed again; her fate was so bitter, and her husband so cruel. She felt that it was only the One-hander who respected her and treated her as a human being. That tyrant of a husband treated her like a criminal. She felt as sorry for the lad as she did for herself. But she was angry with him too. Of all the places he could have gone to why did it have to be Green Hollow? He'd ruined their lives.

The worst thing of all now for Azure was smelling her husband's acrid sweat in bed at night. Many nights of silent weeping gradually developed a spirit of resistance in her. Every evening when she went to bed she would obstinately turn her face to the wall. She might have been nailed there: she would not turn over however much he tugged and pushed. "I'll kill you," he muttered through teeth clenched in fury. "Go ahead!" "Whore! You just want your fancy man." "Are you going to beat me again? He'll hear, and the story will get out." "Bitch!" "Help! Mum! Hit me again, I'll scream." Azure now had the courage to stand up to her husband. She did not know why, but he was afraid of the One-hander hearing their secrets, and she was worried too about him knowing how she was mistreated and beaten every night.

Life can be very abnormal, and so too can emotions. Azure felt herself changing, though she did not know whether it was for the better or the worse. This freezing cold winter she wanted to dress herself up a little, which she had not before. She now liked wearing the silver grey woollen headscarf that she normally kept at the bottom of her trunk and her rose-red corduroy outer jacket. She kept herself as clean and tidy all day as if she were just about to go visiting, and even filled the copper basin her mother had left her with clear water from the stream to look at her own reflection. Some years ago she had asked her husband to buy her a looking-glass to hang on the wall from the forestry station, but every time he came back he said that he had forgotten. Now she realized that he had been doing it deliberately. He had been afraid that she'd see how pretty she was: a face like the moon, bright eyes, a mouth like a petal of red magnolia wet with dew, and two dimples. She looked lovely when she smiled and lovely when she didn't. Anyone would fancy her. The One-hander? No! How shameful. Her heart started to beat wildly. Her mind was in a whirl. She covered her burning cheeks with her hands and would not look up. It was as if she had done something wicked. Recently she hadn't been able to stop herself stealing looks at the One-hander's little hut. The strange thing was that the more her husband refused to let her go there the more attractive it seemed to her. The One-hander's radio, soap, face-cream, and all those other amazing things from the four corners of the globe were as alluring as a new world. Li Xingfu's name Xingfu meant "happiness", but was that skinny, pale-faced lad happy? Every day he had to chop the firewood, wash his clothes and cook his meals, all single-handed, and he did not so much as glance at her. When he saw Wang Mutong the poor thing looked as if he'd seen a tiger. She felt sympathy, tenderness for him often with the bewitching shyness of a Yao girl.

Once the One-hander came back from the forestry station with some sweets wrapped in silver and gold paper that he slipped unobtrusively into the children's hands. Little Qing was clever enough to unwrap one of them and pop it into her mother's mouth. Azure at once hugged her daughter tight and kissed her over and over again on the lips. "Little Qing," she asked as if in a dream, "does your mum's mouth have a nasty taste?" "No, no." "Does it taste sweet?" "Yes, very sweet." Heavens! What a thing to be saying to her own daughter! She blushed deeply, and as the sweet in her mouth slowly dissolved the delicious juice seemed to flow straight down into her heart. She covered her heart. She covered her daughter's soft pink cheeks with her own sweet kisses. Her strict husband saw none of this, and it was none of his business. If he had seen her he might have killed her there and then.

One day when Wang Mutong had gone into the mountains to set tree traps Azure went to the stream to fetch a bucket of water. She saw the One-hander rinsing his clothes in the water so icy it cut to the marrow of the bone. His only hand was red with cold. Putting the bucket down she went over to him, took the clothes, and started rinsing them out for him. He stood up at once and took a couple of paces back. "You shouldn't, Azure," he said. "If Wang sees you he'll. . . ."

She carried on rinsing without looking up. "Why shouldn't I? I'm not doing anything wrong."

"I know. . . . But he'll hit you again."

She stopped for a moment, not moving.

"Look. Your arm's all purple."

"Shut up, you fool. One of the pigs charged me in the sty."

It took all her self-control to hold back the tears that welled up. She longed to run somewhere where she could howl aloud. She rubbed and shook out his clothes several more times, then picked them out of the water, wrung them till they were a huge twisted knot, and dropped them without a word in his galvanized pail. She did not look back at him as she picked up her bucket and went, forgetting all about the water she had come to fetch. Once back in her cabin she leant against the door, weak in the limbs and completely drained of strength. Her heart was pounding so hard it seemed to be about to leap out of her chest. She did not cry. Indeed, she wanted to laugh. This was the first time in her life she had done something for another man behind her husband's back. This terrifying first time comes sooner or later in everyone's life. After the pounding of her heart had subsided Azure felt happy for a very long time. Her husband noticed nothing when he came back from the hills that night. She had won a victory.

The winter drought and the freeze went on till the

end of the year. The branches of many of the broad-leaved evergreens around Green Hollow were stripped bare, and they stretched their withered bony arms out to heaven like so many starving and thirsty old men. The hillsides were thickly covered in fallen leaves of every shape and colour that rustled as they blew around in the frosty wind, making the mountains resplendent with their rich colours of gold and jade.

The long drought made it impossible for the One-hander to go on lying low in his little cabin. He was up before dawn every morning to patrol the mountains with his billhook at his belt and his fire prevention manual under his arm. Several times he plucked up his courage to suggest to Wang Mutong that they ought to clear all the firebreaks and sweep the dead leaves from the paths. Because of his hostility to the One-hander Wang Mutong paid no attention to him and ignored nearly all of his suggestions. Wang Mutong was in charge of Green Hollow, and other people had better keep their mouths shut and stop being so bloody keen. But this time the One-hander had some kind of pre-monition and he did not give in. He decided to take some precautions himself. He persuaded Azure to clear all the undergrowth, firewood, dead leaves and fallen branches away from the two log cabins. He also used every spare moment he had to read aloud from his fire prevention manual to the children, which really amount-ed to reading it to their parents too. One morning Wang Mutong heard a conversation between the One-hander and Little Tong.

"Uncle Li, what does 'running into the wind' mean?"

"If there's a forest fire you can get away by running towards where it's coming from."

"Uncle, what do we do if our cabin catches fire?"

"Go and crouch down in the stream. Stay on this side where there aren't any big trees."

"Rubbish!" Wang Mutong was going to hear no more. "You're trying to bring us bad luck, talking like that." Having scared the boy off with his angry words he turned to the One-hander and demanded, "Li Xingfu, are you planning on starting a forest fire in Green Hollow?"

The question left the One-hander dumbfounded.

"Why else do you spend all day thinking about how to escape from one?"

"Brother Wang, fires and floods are cruel things."

"In that case do you think that there's bound to be a bush fire in Green Hollow this winter?" Wang Mutong contemptuously snatched the fire prevention manual from Li Xingfu's hand, flicked through it a couple of times without being able to read a word and threw it back to him. "I suppose this teaches you how to tell fortunes. You know what's going to happen, do you?"

"Brother Wang, the drought's gone on for so long and the hills are covered with fallen leaves. Every night the radio says...." The One-hander always looked sordid, guilty, pale and weak in Wang Mutong's presence. The word "radio" made Wang Mutong laugh derisively. "Has that black box of yours been singing any of those disgusting love songs recently?"

The One-hander did not know whether he wanted to laugh or to cry. Keeping a straight face, he replied, "Wang, I've got a suggestion to make. Shouldn't we put in a request to the forestry station asking them to get the telephone line repaired? Otherwise if there were an emergency here by any remote chance we'd have no way of contacting the outside world."

"If you want to make your request, go to the station and make it. I'll give you two days' leave. Why don't you see if they'll send a firefighting team to Green Hollow while you're about it?" Wang Mutong gave the One-hander a mocking glance, yawned unconcernedly, and added, "I can tell you without boasting that in the twenty or thirty years I've lived here I've never seen a forest fire."

After the evening meal Wang Mutong went to the One-hander's little cabin as usual. What the One-hander found different this evening was that instead of his usual hectoring manner as if he were dealing with a public enemy, Wang Mutong spoke very pleasantly. "Young Li, you're planning to go to the station, aren't you? I wonder if you could do me a favour." He produced a sheet of paper that he had brought with him and asked the One-hander to write out his application to join the Party. This was surprising enough, but the next thing was that Wang Mutong put his finger in his mouth and bit it open with a loud crunch. He waved the bleeding finger in front of the One-hander's face as if it were a tiny flag. "Soak your brush in this and write it quick for me. 'Dear forestry station leadership, I'm writing this letter in blood to apply for Party membership. I'm not educated, I'm a rough person, but I have a red heart and I do what the Party tells me....'" The horrified One-hander quickly found a battered old writing brush, soaked it in the fresh blood from Wang Mutong's finger, and wrote the application in blood as quickly as he could. The very sight of the blood made him tremble. He was covered in cold sweat.

When the blood letter was written Wang Mutong folded it up carefully and put into an inner pocket next to his skin. When it came down to it he could not trust the One-hander and allow a political unreliable to hand his sacred application in to the station.

The next morning Wang Mutong was out burning the undergrowth by his vegetable garden, which he was planning to extend. He had not even bandaged up the wound on his finger. He was a good worker and already had about a quarter of a hectare of land cleared for vegetables. The station required him and his wife to raise three pigs a year. These had to be smoked and handed over as cured meat at the end of the year; the rest they could slaughter and eat themselves. He cared nothing about ideology and isms, but he trusted the Party just as he trusted himself. He liked the Party and the Party liked him, and he reckoned that the Party ought to consist of people like himself. He collected huge piles of fallen branches and leaves, rotten stalks and dead plants from the hillside that he carried to his plot to burn. He collected ashes for fertilizer like this every year, and winter drought or no winter drought this year was going to be no different. The One-hander was very worried about him doing it in so dry a winter, but he did not dare say anything to Wang Mutong's face. He slept badly at night, troubled by nightmares of monstrous and terrible fires as beautiful as sunsets, fires flowing like great rivers. On two nights he got up quietly, went to cut himself a fir sapling from the hillside, and stood on guard by the bonfire that Wang Mutong had burned the previous day. He stayed there for most of the night, the icy wind cutting into his hands, feet and face as painfully as a knife. Why was he watching over the bonfire? He hadn't written a letter in his own blood, and even if he had nobody would have believed him. The flames were shooting up from the fire and the sparks were flying. It only needed a few of them to set the dry twigs and grass on the hillside alight for a forest fire to spread with the speed of the wind. He wondered whether he should go to the station and put in two requests, one for them to get the telephone line repaired straight away, and the other for someone to be sent to inspect the fire precautions in Green Hollow and persuade Wang Mutong to see sense. He secretly told Azure of what he wanted to do. The last few days her eyes had been swollen like peach stones and she wept as she nodded in reply. Her expression showed that there was much that she wanted to say to him, for whom she felt pity, love, resentment and anger.

That afternoon the One-hander was crouched over his stove cooking some rice to eat on his journey when Azure suddenly rushed into his cabin, openly defying the strict ban her husband had imposed on her. The One-hander stood up in confusion, not knowing what to do. She looked as if she had just come back from working on the vegetable patch. She was wearing only a thin shirt on her top half. It was rather tight and the top button had come open, showing the most alluring glimpses of her full breasts.

"Azure, you. . . ." The One-hander had not even the courage to finish asking his question. He was so flustered that he did not even look up.

"Idiot. Sometimes you're ever so clever, but sometimes you're such a fool. I'm not an evil spirit come to bewitch you." The sight of the One-hander's embarrassment and confusion made her feel more tender towards him than ever. It was a maternal tenderness.

"Azure . . . you. . . ."

"I've come to ask if you'll do something for me when you go to the station."

Only then did the One-hander calm himself enough to look her in the face.

"Here's a hundred yuan. I want you to buy us a radio like yours, and a round mirror, and some soap, and some of that cream with a nice smell you put on your face on frosty days, and a brush each for me and Little Tong and Little Qing to brush our teeth with every morning, and we want to put up a pine pole with a wire on it. . . ."

He stared at her with wide-eyed and utter astonishment. This woman from the forests was a goddess of beauty. Her breasts were full, her limbs were exquisitely proportioned and she was brimming with health. She was also tender and gentle, and her body was full of youth and life.

"What are you staring at me like that for? I'm a victim too, just like you." She turned aside with a touch of winning anger as her cheeks flushed and tears began to roll down them.

"All right, all right. Azure, you are good. I, I. . . ." The One-hander was as if spellbound by something about Azure that glistened and shone. A moment later he came to and blushed. "Azure, if you spend all that money at once won't you be afraid of what Wang. . . ?"

Azure had been gazing at him with happiness and

pleasure until "... won't you be afraid of what Wang...?" ruined everything. It was a handful of salt thrown into a heart full of sugar.

"Afraid? I've been afraid of him for ten years and more.... He's been catching animals every winter and selling their skins every spring. Besides, we both earn wages and don't spend much of them. There are piles of ten yuan notes at the bottom of our trunk.... He's too mean to spend them.... I'm not afraid.... Living with him here.... The worst he can do is kill me."

As she spoke the tears welled up in her eyes, as they did in his too. "Azure, I'll take the money and buy the things for you. Don't cry, don't cry. You're a victim too. I'm very sorry for you. I hate myself, hate myself.... Stop crying, Azure. There, there. If Wang sees you when he comes down the mountain he'll beat you again and swear at me...."

"You're no man," said Azure. "You're even less than one of the creepers on our cabin." She shot him a glare filled with all the anger in her heart, turned and went out of his cabin.

"Azure! Azure!" The One-hander followed her to the door and made an involuntary gesture, stretching out both his hands as if to embrace something beautiful. But all there was instead of his left arm was an empty sleeve.

The One-hander went to the forestry station. Big new slogans were being painted all over the place, such as "Down with the Rightist Reversal of Verdicts", "Criticize the Bourgeoisie Within the Party".* Cadres

---

* These were slogans raised in the political movement started by the "gang of four" to attack Comrade Deng Xiaoping in 1975.

and workers were arguing vociferously and going in and out of the spacious office of the station's political department. The One-hander felt that the right person to report to was the director of the political department, as he had sent him to Green Hollow in the first place. He had waited outside the office nearly all morning and only managed to squeeze in just before the lunch break.

"Oh, it's you, Li Xingfu," said the political director. "Why are you back here?" He was standing in front of his desk and just about to go out; Li Xingfu's arrival made him stay. He patted his aching head, then put his hands on his hips and shuffled his feet. But his manner was reasonably friendly.

The One-hander grabbed the chance to tell the director as briefly as he could about the need to restore the telephone line to Green Hollow.

"Restore a line that's been out of action for ten years or more?" The political director put on an expression of amazement. "Is that Wang Mutong's idea? Oh, it's yours. You'd better understand, Li Xingfu, that Wang Mutong's our man in Green Hollow. He may not have much education but he's politically reliable. He's been a model forester for a dozen years or more. . . . A telephone would need investment capital and materials. It couldn't be repaired just by shouting an order. Besides, a big movement's just beginning. The whole county from top to bottom is going to be attacking the Rightist tendency to overturn verdicts. That will be the main thing and much more important than everything else. Do you understand?"

The One-hander then made his request for the station to send people to inspect the forest protection and fire prevention in Green Hollow and reported how Wang Mutong was making bonfires in the dry season. He was terrified that the political director would be too impatient to knock off work to hear him through to the end.

"Oh dear, and it looked as though you'd been making a lot of progress recently, Li Xingfu." The political director put on another show of great astonishment, then looked very solemn as he continued, "Let me tell you once again. The station leadership has complete confidence in Wang Mutong. You should follow his leadership in Green Hollow and let him educate and reform you. Don't try to run your own show. And they say. . . . Well, his wife's young and very good-looking. Don't start getting any funny ideas. What would you do if someone cut off the arm you've got left? Eh? You're an educated youngster. You've got a future. . . ."

Thus it was that so far from being able to report the state of affairs to the station the One-hander was given a very cold dressing-down. It was perfectly obvious that the leadership did not trust him at all. He felt that there was no point in going on living like this as if he were a mangy, scabies-ridden dog who got kicked and driven away wherever he went. He spent a couple of days hanging around the co-op and the tree nursery on the little street at the forestry station. He wished his parents had never sent him to school and longed to be an illiterate, stupid boor like Wang Mutong. The way the world was now ignorance was something to be proud of. It had been decided that the more you knew, the more reactionary you were, and that only the likes of Wang Mutong could make revolution. Finally he started to miss Green Hollow, Azure, Little Tong and

Little Qing. At least there were three people in that remote and isolated corner who didn't look down on him and regard him as evil. The thought made the One-hander feel a little easier in his mind. He went to the station's grain store to buy two months' supplies of oil, salt and rice and then to the co-op to buy a transistor radio, soap, face-cream, toothpaste, toothbrushes, and a mirror the size of a small basin for Azure. Finally he went to the food store for steamed buns equivalent to a kilogram of flour. Early the next morning he set out back to Green Hollow with his purchases suspended from a carrying-pole.

He carried on till the sun was starting to set, by when he had reached Black Cwm. There was only one more ridge to cross before Green Hollow, and he would be back before dark in the little log cabin where he was to settle down and find his destiny. He had already noticed the black smoke rising above Green Hollow. Was Wang Mutong still making bonfires for ash? But why was there so much smoke? It didn't look like the smoke from bonfires.

Although he was exhausted he did not stop to rest but hurried up towards the pass. He could smell the fire on the other side of the mountain and hear the crackling of the flames. Had a forest fire really started in Green Hollow? Where else could the smell and the noise be coming from? As dusk gradually fell the sky reddened on the other side of the ridge. Was it the glow of sunset or the glare of a blazing forest?

He rushed up the path, his body soaked in sweat, and beads of it the size of fingertips on his forehead. Some kind of supernatural power seemed to be driving him towards the pass. All of a sudden the valley was filled with a sheet of red, flowing fire that shimmered beneath his eyes. Green Hollow! He almost passed out. Green Hollow was a sea of flame. The mountain wind whipped up tongues of fire, line after line of them, thousands of giant red centipedes writhing all over the hillsides around the hollow. Thick smoke poured up from the galloping flames in the valley. Ancient trees that had stood for a thousand years were now pillars of fire lighting up the heavens. Rocks were exploding in the heat like landmines. Rolling fireballs, red arrows and dancing crimson snakes merged into a burning torrent, the strange and terrifying beauty of a forest fire.

"Azure! Little Tong! Little Qing!"

Leaving his carrying-pole at the top of the pass the One-hander ran shouting down towards the blazing valley. In this crisis he could not abandon Azure, Little Tong and Little Qing. They were the only three people who meant anything to him in this valley. He ran flat out and only luck save him from tripping over. He did not know how far he had run through clouds of choking smoke when he saw a woman crawling towards him, her hair matted, her face covered in soot, and her clothes in tatters.

"Azure, dear Azure! What's happened? What's happened to you all?"

The One-hander shouted aloud for joy when he realized that this was Azure. But when she saw him she could only stretch her arms towards him imploringly and collapse on the ground. He rushed over to her and half squatted as he put his arm round her. "Dear, dear Azure. It's me, Li Xingfu, Li Xingfu. Dear Azure...."

The One-hander's throat went dry and his voice hoarse as he called to her and wept for ten full minutes until she came round. She opened her eyes and could only murmur, "It's you, it's you, I've found you. . . ." before lying back in his arms, sobbing.

"Don't cry, dear, don't cry. Tell me how the fire started. Where are Little Tong, Little Qing and Wang?" The One-hander shook Azure's shoulder as he asked.

"Let's go. Help me up." As she spoke she struggled to her feet and staggered up the mountainside. The One-hander helped her as he listened to her story. "That evil man . . . the cruel bastard. . . . At about noon on the day you went to the station he found out that there was a hundred yuan missing from the wooden box. He kept saying I'd stolen it to give my fancy man. He wouldn't believe a word I said. He just beat me up, and went on till every inch of me was bruised and aching. . . . May Hell take him. Then he locked me into your little cabin and left me there for three days and nights. He didn't even give me a drop of water. It was only very late last night that I finally scratched and pulled a plank loose and crawled to the stream for a drink. Then I saw that the mountain was on fire. It started from his bonfires. Let it burn. Let it kill all the animals in the mountains."

"What about Little Tong and Little Qing?"

"The hellhound! Once the fire started he put the box with the money in it on his back and took Little Qing and Little Tong down the stream . . . the way you'd taught them." Her body went weak and she leaned against the One-hander's shoulder. She was not weeping any more. There was even a kind of exultation in the way she ran her fingers through her own hair then stretched her hand out to run them through the hair plastered to the One-hander's forehead by his sweat.

The catastrophe numbed him with horror. They climbed till they reached the top of the pass and found the carrying-pole he had left there. Only then did he remember his steamed buns and his bottle of cold water. He got them out at once for her to eat. She was so hungry that she downed a steamed bun in three or four mouthfuls. After she had eaten four he would not give her any more, he only let her drink. She went on leaning against his chest, resting with her eyes shut.

He hugged her tight as he gazed in fascinated horror at the galloping flames twisting wildly in the wind. Suddenly he remembered that behind the mountain opposite was Love Hollow, where there was a stand full of rare firs and golden-leaf magnolias that the specialists in the station said were precious survivals from the last minor glaciation, living fossils on the verge of global extinction. At the thought of this he said to her, "Azure dearest, let's make our way round to the back of the mountain opposite while the fire's still only halfway up the mountainsides. We can go by the firebreak that runs along the top of the ridge. If we can save the trees in Love Hollow we'll at least have something to say for ourselves should we ever go back to the station."

As he spoke the One-hander looked back at the narrow track that led to the forestry station. His expression showed that it was a last farewell.

"Whatever you like. Wherever you go I'll go with

you." Food and the short rest had restored the life force in the Yao woman. She was strong.

The forest fire in Green Hollow was spotted by a military radar post over fifty kilometres away, and the forestry station of the Wujie Hills was immediately informed by telephone. Only then did the station's bosses begin to panic and mobilize large forces to go into the mountains to fight the fire. But by then a third of the thousands of hectares of primeval mixed broadleaf forest had been destroyed. All that was left in the valley were bare, charred trunks and branches looking like devil prisoners just released from hell.

A week later Wang Mutong turned up with the two children at the forestry station, his wooden box on his back. Nobody knew where he had gone to escape the disaster. Azure and Li Xingfu had disappeared. Wang Mutong swore with tears streaming down his face that the fire had been started by Azure and her lover, the One-hander. It had been nothing to do with his own bonfires. The station had made him a model forester for a dozen or more years now. To show where his heart lay he respectfully presented his application to join the Party written in his blood to the station Party committee. Naturally the station leadership believed his tearful story and sent militia to search for the culprits. But after combing the blackened mountains for several days all the militia found were the charred bones of wild animals. Nobody knew whether the One-hander and Azure were dead or alive.

As it happened the forestry station, like every other corner of China, was then preoccupied with a great class struggle that was supposedly going to settle the destiny of the country and the Party. Rather than disturb or deflect the main direction of the movement to "counter-attack the Rightist tendency to reverse correct political verdicts" they explained it by their usual class struggle theory and reported to their superiors that "the forest fire started by class enemies has been put out in good time by the revolutionary cadres and masses". There the matter ended.

Wang Mutong refused on his life to go back to Green Hollow. Fortunately the station was then also responsible for a stretch of ancient forest at Heaven's Gate Cave, next to the borders of Guangdong and Guangxi, where the old forest warden had died. So the leadership sent Wang Mutong with his two children to succeed the old warden in that rough, hard, self-sufficient way of life. It was said that Wang Mutong married a widow from Guangxi the same year. As before, he set out each day at dawn and went to bed at nightfall, and he was as full of energy and strength as ever. It happened that the widow had a son and a daughter too. It would only be natural if when they all grew up they married Wang Mutong's children and lived in the ancient log cabin at Heaven's Gate Cave for generations.

But after the fall of the "gang of four" there was a great deal of talk in the forestry station. Some people said that if the One-hander and Azure were still alive somewhere far away they would be living quite differently. Even more reckoned that with so many wrong and unjust verdicts being put right across the country Azure and Li Xingfu might turn up any day at the station demanding that justice be done to them too. Why not? In the last couple of years the mighty trees in Green Hollow that had survived the fire gaunt and blackened had been putting forth fresh green branches and new leaves.

Translated by W. J. F. Jenner

Gu Hua was born in Jiahe County, Hunan Province in 1942. In 1961 he studied at an agricultural college in Chenzhou and from 1962 to 1974 worked as a farm labourer in a local agricultural research institute. Since 1979 he has been a member of the Federation of Literary and Art Circles in Chenzhou.

Gu Hua's first short story, "Sister Apricot", was published in 1962. This was followed by collections of short stories and novelettes. "The Log Cabin Overgrown with Creepers" won an award in 1981 and "A Small Town Called Hibiscus" won him a Mao Dun Prize in 1982.

Gu Hua is a member of the Chinese Writers' Association and a council member of its Hunan branch.

A Tale of Big Nur

Wang Zengqi

IT is a queer name for a place, Big Nur. Mongolian they say, perhaps from the Yuan Dynasty (1271-1368). However, there is no way now to ascertain what people called it before that time.

A *nur* is a large expanse of water, not as big as a lake but much bigger than a pond. When the water level is high in spring and summer, Big Nur looks vast. At the source of two rivers, it has a narrow sandbank in the centre covered with cogongrass and reeds. In spring when the water is warm, the purplish red reed shoots and the greyish green southernwood on the sandbank turn emerald. In summer, the snow-white ears of the cogongrass and the reeds sway in the breeze. When they turn yellow in autumn, they are cut for thatching the roofs of houses. The sandbank is the first to turn white when it snows in winter and the last to thaw. The snow remains there glittering, while the ice melts in the river and the land grows green.

In the old days on the north-western side of the sandbank were several heated buildings. Through the clumps of green willows could be distinguished on a whitewashed wall, four conspicuous characters in black paint: "Chicken and Duckling Breeders". In front was a small clearing, where some people sat on tree stumps chatting in the shade. Now and then someone came out carrying two bamboo baskets full of cheeping yellow fluffy chicks and ducklings. East of the sandbank was a size shop. People starched their clothes and the underneaths of their quilts, for they liked to hear them rustle. Outside the shop dazzling white lumps of size were being sunned. Close to the shop were several stores selling fresh river produce such as water chestnuts, arrowheads, water caltrops and lotus roots. A fish market was collecting and distributing fish and crabs, and there was also a grass purchasing station. Beyond these were fields, cattle sheds and waterwheels. Big pats of cow dung were neatly pasted on cottage walls to dry. It was a truly rural scene. To the north were the villages in Beixiang, to the east the neighbouring prefecture of Xinghua.

On the southern shore of Big Nur stood a green wooden house, formerly the office of a boat company with a waiting-room at one side. At the waterside was a quay. A small steamer had plied between this spot and Xinghua, leaving on odd-numbered days and returning on even-numbered ones. Brightly painted and hung with colourful bunting, the boat had been a thrilling sight with its chugging engine and black smoke pouring from its funnel. While porters loaded and unloaded goods, passengers embarking or disembarking mingled with the pedlars selling beef, sorghum liquor, fried peanuts, melon seeds and candy covered with sesame seeds. After some heavy losses, the shareholders sold the boat and closed down the company, but the wooden building remained intact and empty. Only some mischievous boys living in the vicinity played in the waiting-room, fighting with rods and sticks or peeing from the quay. Standing seven or eight in a row, they pissed into the water to see who could aim the farthest.

Big Nur was also the name of the land around the water where the town and the countryside met. There was a long alley south of the boat company leading to a street outside the north gate of the town. There the hubbub of the town was faintly audible. Without a single shop, the place had its own colours, noises and odours. Even the residents were different. Their lives, customs and morals were quite unlike those of the town dwellers, who wore long gowns and studied Confucian philosophy.

2

To the east and west of the boat company were two small settlements, both dissimilar.

The one to the west was formed by some scattered low houses with tiled roofs. Most of the inhabitants were from places along the Lixia River. They were pedlars selling radishes, water chestnuts, Chinese hawthorns and lotus roots boiled with glutinous rice to fill in the holes. One man selling spectacles was from Baoying, while another from Hangzhou sold bamboo chopsticks. Like migrating birds, they would rent a room from an acquaintance and stay for a period of time, some longer, some shorter, leaving after they had sold their goods. They began work at sunrise and rested at sunset. After breakfast they went out carrying their wares, hawking and crying out for customers in various accents and tones. At dusk, they returned like birds to their nests. Before long smoke from damp fuel, a sweet yet pungent odour, wafted out through the low eaves. Because these men were from different places and made little money, they were polite and amiable. Their settlement was always peaceful, as bickering or scuffles were rare.

Among the residents were also about twenty tinsmiths from Xinghua. Tin articles were in demand, and every household had tin incense burners, candlesticks, spittoons, canisters, kettles, teapots and wine pots. Even chamber pots were made of tin. When marrying off a daughter, the parents would give her tin utensils for her dowry; at least two big tin containers which could hold four to five kilos of rice to put on top of a chest. When a woman gave birth to a baby, her parents traditionally sent, apart from two hens and one hundred eggs, two pots of glutinous rice porridge in the tin containers from her mother's chest. So even twenty tinsmiths did good business.

The tinsmiths were not highly skilled, and their tools were simple: a shoulder pole with a bellows and some tin plates on one end, a charcoal stove and two bricks two foot square with several layers of paper pasted on one side on the other. A tinsmith usually set his load on the porch of a customer's house or on the open ground by the roadside. There he worked the bellows, put the old tin to melt in the pot, poured the liquid in between the two bricks to press it into a plate, which he cut with a pair of metal shears and then beat with a wooden mallet on his anvil. In about the time it takes to eat a meal, the article began to take shape. To give it a finish, he scraped it, polished it with sandpaper and finally rubbed it till it shone with a kind of grass.

These tinsmiths were very loyal and helpful to each

other, looking after their sick companions and never competing for customers. If they went into partnership, they shared the profits. Their leader was an old man whom they all obeyed. An upright fellow, he was very strict with his juniors and apprentices, not letting them gamble, drink or flirt with women. He advised them to be honest, not cheat and avoid trouble. Except for business, they could not loiter on the streets.

The old tinsmith was good at Chinese boxing and taught the others. When they were not at work, he would take them out to practise in pairs, claiming this was a good way of passing time as well as useful for self-defence. For amusement, they also sang local operas. Whenever it rained and they could not go out, they sang. Girls and married women nearby crowded round to watch and listen.

One of the apprentices was the old tinsmith's nephew, whose pet name was Eleventh Boy, as he was the eleventh child in his family. Very intelligent and handsome, he was a worry to his uncle. Tall, broadshouldered, with a slender waist, he was well proportioned. Beneath his bushy brows shone a pair of large eyes. He wore a straw hat, neat, well-fitting clothes and black shoes. In hot weather, he unbuttoned his shirt, revealing his chest and spotless white cummerbund, five inches wide, wound tightly round his waist. He walked with a spring in his step. The old tinsmith was well aware that when the girls and women gathered to hear them sing, they really came to admire his nephew.

He constantly warned Eleventh Boy to steer clear of the local girls and women, especially those living at the east end. "They're different from us," the old man told him.

3

To the east of the boat company were houses with adobe walls and thatched roofs. The residents there had been porters for generations. Men and women, old and young, lived by their shoulders.

They mostly carried rice from the boats which landed at Big Nur. The rice was taken away by these porters to rice shops or the granaries of rich families, or to other big boats, moored at Loquat Sluice outside the south gate of the town, to be transported along the canal to other places. Sometimes they had to carry their loads to wharfs as far away as Cheluo or Mapeng Bay, one to three miles away. Without stopping for a rest, they walked with quick, even steps, chanting all the way. In a line of ten or twenty, each carried a load weighing two hundred catties. They shifted their loads from shoulder to shoulder in unison when the man at the front put his hand on his shoulder pole. For each load they were given a bamboo tag with one end painted red, the other white. At dusk they were paid according to the number of tags they had accumulated.

Apart from rice they also carried bricks, tiles, lime, bamboo poles, tung oil. . . . All year round they worked and never went hungry.

When their children reached their teens, they began work carrying half a load in two willow baskets. After one or two years, they were strong enough to bear the whole load and earned as much as the adults.

The porters led a very simple life: daily exerting all their strength, and eating three meals cooked on a small stove. No money was spent on fuel. Villagers carrying reeds to sell at the market always dropped some on the road. Children, too young to be porters, collected these with a bamboo rake and were nicknamed "Raking Devils". Sometimes, to save trouble, they simply snatched a bundle of reeds from a villager and took to their heels. By the time he had laid down his load and shouted curses, they were nowhere to be seen. Because there were no chimneys, smoke poured out from the windows or doors, drifting to the surface of the water and lingering there. These households never stored grain. They bought enough food only for each day. At meal times the men squatted outside their homes, holding big bowls of brown rice with vegetables, small fish, preserved beancurd or pickled hot peppers. They wolfed down their food with such relish that nothing in the world seemed more appetizing.

They celebrated New Year's Day and other festivals by changing into clean clothes, feasting and gambling. Each gambler took a stack of ten or twenty coins, then threw in turn another coin at the pile, keeping the coins that fell down. Another game was rolling the coins. Piles of coins were placed on the ground and a brick was propped up at one end to form a slope. The gambler rolled a coin down the brick. If it stopped at a spot five inches from a pile, he could take the money; if seven inches, he had to forfeit the same amount as the stack. The porters enjoyed themselves, while onlookers cheered loudly, adding to the fun.

The girls and women were as strong as the men. They concentrated on carrying fresh water products, perhaps because the men disdained to carry dripping loads. They had slender figures and put pomade on their thick black hair. The buns at the back of their heads were large and tied with red wool visible from far away. At

one side of their buns they liked to wear a decoration —
a tender willow twig twisted like a ball at the tip at the
Qingming Festival; some mugwort leaves at the
Dragon Boat Festival; a gardenia or an oleander in
season; or a big red velvet flower when they could not
get a fresh one. Because they carried their loads with
a shoulder pole all year round, nearly all the shoulders
of their blouses were patched. An old blouse, with new
and different coloured patches, was the distinctive dress
of the women at Big Nur. Twenty women with loads
of purple red water chestnuts, green water caltrops and
snow-white lotus roots walking in single file, like willows swaying in the wind, were a wonderful sight!

They earned the same money as the men and adopted
their fast way of walking like a gust of wind or sitting
with legs wide apart. They also wore straw sandals
and dyed their toenails red with garden balsam. They
did not avoid raw or cold food. They talked and cursed
like men. They even chanted the same rude songs. . . .

Unmarried women were more reticent, but once
married they behaved as boorishly as they liked. There
was an old bachelor called Huang Hailong, who had
been a porter when young. Later he hurt his leg and
was assigned to the wharf to look after the rice boats
and collect the bamboo tags. Old as he was, he loved
to fondle this woman's breast or pinch that one's bottom.
According to his age, the women ought to have addressed him politely as grand-uncle, but all of them
called him "Old Bawdy Beard". One day as he was
up to his old tricks again, several women made a plan.
Following a signal, they took immediate action. In the
twinkling of an eye, the old man's trousers were thrown
on to a tree-top. When the old fellow heard the bamboo

clappers for selling noodles with dumplings, he regained his high spirits.

"Who dares take a bath in the *nur*?" he challenged. "I bet each one of you two bowls of noodles with dumplings you won't!"

"Really?"

"Sure!"

"OK!"

The women stripped and splashed in the water. A moment later, climbing ashore they cried, "Boil the noodles!"

People here seldom married in a regular way, so sedan carriers and trumpeters were of no use. Women came to men of their own accord. Girls generally chose their spouses themselves. They were rather casual in their sexual relations. There was nothing strange about a girl giving birth to an illegitimate child at her mother's home. A married woman could have a lover. The only criterion for a woman to take delight in a man was her consent. Most girls or women asked their lovers for money to buy flowers, but some gave money to their lovers instead.

The townsfolk looked down on their morals and manners but were theirs any better? It was difficult to say.

4

To the east of Big Nur, there was a household of only two members — a father and his daughter. Huang Haijiao, the father, was Huang Hailong's cousin. He had been a fine porter, capable of going up steep gangplanks with his load. The grain bins of the big grain shops here were thirty to forty feet high with the planks sloping very steeply. One had to ascend them at one go. Whenever an older man or a woman hesitated at the foot, Huang would take their two hundred catty load and shoot to the top like an arrow. Raising his hands, he would pour the two baskets of rice into the bin and then stride down with only a few steps to the ground. Honest and faithful, he had not married until he was twenty-five. That year, when he carried grain to Cheluo, he met a girl asking the way. With a long fringe and a bun on the back of her head, she wore a little rouge on her face. Flurried and anxious she could not give the exact name of any place. Huang saw at a glance that she was a maidservant running away from some rich and influential family. He talked with her for a while, and finally she agreed to live with him. She called herself Lianzi, a common name for maidservants in the region.

A year later she gave birth to a girl. It was July when rosy clouds filled the sky, so they named her July Cloud.

Lianzi was deft and hard-working, but she liked to wear tight silk trousers, eat melon seeds and nibble between meals. She sang ballads such as "The cold moon rises and sheds light on my chamber. Giving a yawn, I stretch myself and feel sleepy. *Aiyo, aiyo,* I'm feeling sleepy...." All this was quite different from the local customs.

When July Cloud was three years old, Lianzi eloped with an actor of young gentlemen's parts in a theatrical troupe passing through the village. That day Huang had gone to Mapeng Bay. Lianzi washed and starched all her husband's clothes, gathered together her daughter's, cooked a pot of rice and purchased half a catty of wine. Entrusting the little girl to her neighbour, she said she had something to do. She locked the door and was never seen again.

Huang did not feel too sad, for things like that were not unusual. A caged bird sometimes flew away. But he adored the little creature she had left behind. Unwilling to see the child suffer at the hands of a cruel stepmother, he determined not to marry again. Shouldering the responsibilities of both father and mother, he brought her up by himself. He taught her how to make fishing nets and weave reed mats at the age of fourteen, because he was loath to see her be a porter.

At fifteen she was as beautiful as a flower, her figure and face like her mother's. With a dimple in one cheek, her face had an oval shape with long dark eyebrows. The corners of her eyes slightly tilted upwards and their long lashes made them look narrow. But when she suddenly looked round, they opened wide in a somewhat surprised and absorbed expression, as if someone was calling her from a distance. When she made a net or wove a mat by the waterside, some youths walked past her, pretending to be on business. If she went to the market to buy meat, vegetables, oil, wine, cloth or cosmetics, she got more and better quality than others for the same price. The women caught on to this and asked her to purchase things for them. Whenever she went to the market, she had to carry several bamboo baskets, returning home with aching arms. If there was a theatrical performance in the Taishan Temple, people had to carry a bench or a stool to sit on, but not July Cloud. She went there empty-handed and was always offered a good seat. Few people applauded the wonderful performance, because most feasted their eyes on her.

Soon she reached sixteen, the age she should consider marriage. But who would win such a beauty? First Boy at the breeders? Second Boy at the size shop? Or Third Boy at the fresh water food shop? Both Huang and his daughter knew they desired it, otherwise what was the point of hanging around July Cloud all the time? But the girl did not take them seriously.

At the age of seventeen, fate stepped in. Her father fell from a plank and injured his spine. At first he thought it was not serious. But the large quantities of medicinal wine and plasters did not produce the desired result. Eventually his legs were paralysed. Sometimes he got up from his bed and, taking hold of a high stool, shuffled a few steps forward. Most of the time, he lay propped up against a pile of quilts in bed. He could no longer earn money to buy his daughter new clothes or velvet flowers. Instead he had to depend on her to support him. Though still less than fifty, he could only do some old women's work, such as preparing bundles of string for his daughter to make nets. The girl did not neglect her poor invalid father. If anybody was willing to marry her, he must live with her and provide for the sick man. Who was prepared to do that? The only property they had was their thatched three-roomed house. The girl and her father each occupied a side room. The one in the middle was a small hall. First Boy, Second Boy and Third Boy came from time to time, glancing at the slender figure behind the fishing net or sitting on the snow-white mat. In their eyes admiration still shone, but their enthusiasm was dampened.

In spite of the old tinsmith's warning, Eleventh Boy still went to the east side of the *nur* frequently. Middle-aged women, young married women and girls liked to entice him there to mend old kettles. On the way from Big Nur to the town, there was a shady spot under the willows in front of July Cloud's house, a nice place to seek customers. One wove mats, while the other melted tin. Eleventh Boy and July Cloud were an ideal pair to keep each other company. Sometimes July Cloud stopped to help the young tinsmith work his bellows. When she went indoors to check on her father, she would ask Eleventh Boy if he wanted to have a smoke or a drink of water. He would cover the stove and take her place weaving. Once when her finger was cut by the sharp bamboo, he sucked the wound for her. Through their exchanges she knew that he had no sisters and that his mother had remained a widow for years, doing needlework for others, straining her eyes. Eleventh Boy feared she would become blind some day. . . .

People expected the two to fall in love, but how could they marry? One family needed a son-in-law, while the other a daughter-in-law. As for the two, they loved to sit side by side talking. They were old enough to love, but nothing was settled; they were like clouds floating back and forth in the sky, unable to form rain.

One moonlit night July Cloud went to wash some clothes on a boat. As she crouched down on the bow to rinse a jacket, a naughty boy crept stealthily up and tickled her from behind. Caught off her guard, she fell into the water. She could swim a little, but since she was scared and the current swift, she struggled, then shouted for help. After swallowing a lot of water, she was washed away by the current. It happened that Eleventh Boy was practising Chinese boxing on the level ground outside the breeders. He saw someone being carried along, her hair floating on the surface of the water. Quickly throwing off his shoes, he jumped into the *nur* and rescued her.

July Cloud was still unconscious. He had no choice but to lift her in his arms like a child and carry her home. Dripping wet, she was soft and warm. His heart throbbed as he sensed her nestling closer to him.

In her room she came to. As a matter of fact she had been conscious long before. He lay her on the bed. As she changed her wet clothes the moonlight shone on her beautiful body. He snatched up a bundle of grass and boiled her half a pot of sugary ginger soup. After she had eaten it, he left.

She got up, bolted the door and lay down again. She seemed to sense how she had looked, lying in bed. The moon was exceptionally fine.

"You're an idiot!" she thought to herself.

Then she repeated it aloud.

Before long she was sound asleep.

That same night a man prized open her door.

5

West of a street near an alley opposite the boat company was situated a Taoist temple named Lianyang Temple, in which was stationed a local armed force under the jurisdiction of the prefectural government in name, but paid by the local trade association. Bandits were rampant in the region. They kidnapped people by hiding their boats amid the reeds in the *nur,* from which they could easily escape when chased. The merchants felt they needed the protection of a special armed force. Well equipped, the troop had a boat with armour on three sides and bullet-proof iron plates chest high. Before setting out on a mission, the soldiers could be seen shouldering two machine-guns and carrying more than half a crate of bullets aboard the boat.

A week or a fortnight later they would return triumphantly with few casualties. Once ashore, in a column four abreast, they marched through the long alley led by a dozen trumpeters, heading for the big street leading to the prefectural government. When they reached the main street, the trumpeters began to blow. Behind them were the soldiers with loaded rifles. Their captives were sandwiched in the middle, sometimes three, five, or only one, with their hands bound behind their backs. What was amazing was that the captives also marched boldly and spiritedly in step with the music. They even followed the officer of the day, shouting loudly, "One, two, three, four!" All the shops and stores were informed beforehand to withdraw their birdcages of mynas or grey thrushes, because it might make the bandits unhappy to see them. As the captives would be thrown into prison after they arrived at the prefectural government, if they saw the caged birds, they would feel depressed. The glittering brass trumpets and bayonets and the militant column, with some legendary bandit heroes, made a fascinating spectacle for the residents living along this street. It was as wonderful as watching lion dances, dragon lanterns, stilt performances, children in fancy dress on high frames or a big funeral procession with all the required Taoists and monks.

Suppressing bandits in the countryside was the soldiers' sole duty. They seldom drilled, except for taking the two machine-guns to the waterside and firing several rounds of ammunition. What made others aware of their existence were the twelve trumpeters practising at the edge of the *nur* from eight to nine in the morning and four to five in the afternoon, first blowing a long note, then some sections separately and finally playing marches together. After that they were free to do whatever they liked. Some slipped away to the doors of certain households and with a cough, stepped inside, closing the doors behind them.

Most of the trumpeters liked to dress well. They had plenty of free time and earned their money. Their pay did not amount to much, but each time they returned from the countryside they got a reward. Sometimes they held secret talks with the bandits and did a deal with them. That was why they could spend lavishly. Because they protected the local gentry and merchants, they had strong backers, so even when they caused trouble, nobody made a fuss.

Their leader, Liu, was familiar with the women of several households. He was the man who had prized open July Cloud's door!

He left ten dollars when he took himself off.

It was not the first time something like that had happened. July Cloud's father learned about it that very night. Holding the money in his hand, he heaved a long sigh. When their neighbours heard, they did not say much. "That dirty beast!" the girls and women cursed.

July Cloud did not shed tears or try to drown herself in the *nur*. That kind of thing happened to a girl sooner or later, she thought philosophically. But why him? It should not have been him! What was to be done? Get a kitchen knife and kill him? Burn down Lianyang Temple? No! She had to consider her invalid father. Upset, she sat on the bed utterly confused. Then it dawned on her that it was time to get up and prepare breakfast. She had to make nets, weave mats and go to the market. She thought of her childhood when she had watched a bride wearing a pair of pink silk embroidered shoes. She missed her mother, who was now somewhere far away. She did not remember what her mother looked like, but recalled that she dipped a chopstick in some rouge to make a red dot between her brows. She picked up the mirror and stared at her reflection. It seemed that she saw herself for the first time. She reflected how Eleventh Boy had sucked her wound. She felt unworthy of him. Overcome with regret, she sighed, "Why didn't I give myself to him?"

This idea grew in her mind after each visit of the trumpet squad leader.

Then the troop went off on a mission again.

One day she went to see Eleventh Boy and said, "Come to the east bank this evening. I've something to tell you."

When Eleventh Boy arrived at the appointed spot, she stepped aboard a sampan for tending the ducks. It was too small for more than one person. Local people also used it to cut reeds or grass or gather wild duck eggs on the sandbank. She punted the sampan towards the sandbank, shouting over her shoulder, "Follow me!"

In no time Eleventh Boy swam to where she was waiting.

There they stayed in the grass until the moon was high in the sky.

6

The older apprentices knew about the affair but kept it secret from the old tinsmith. They left the door unlatched for Eleventh Boy and oiled its hinges to muffle the squeaks. Eleventh Boy often did not come back before dawn. One day he pushed the door open as usual and was about to slip into bed, when the old tinsmith boomed, "Are you courting death?"

Affairs of that kind could not be concealed. The news finally reached the ears of the trumpet squad leader. In fact, nobody had to tell him. He knew it himself, for July Cloud was cold and detested the sight of him. They were not married, so it was nothing to him if they broke up. But it was a loss of face to let a young tinsmith steal her away from him. That was unprecedented! He could not swallow such an insult, nor could his colleagues, who liked to bully others. If they ignored this, what would happen next?

One day before dawn, Liu with several men kicked open July Cloud's door, dragged the young tinsmith out from under her quilt and bound him up. They also tied up the girl and her father in case they summoned people to the rescue.

They dragged Eleventh Boy to the graveyard at the back of Taishan Temple and beat him up, wanting him to pack up and go back to his home in Xinghua.

The young tinsmith remained silent.

They ordered him not to enter Huang's house or lay a finger on July Cloud again.

He still refused to say a word.

They tried to make him beg for mercy and apologize. He gritted his teeth.

His toughness enraged them all the more. "See how stubborn he is!" one of them said. "Beat him to death!" Seven or eight sticks rained down on him again.

He was beaten almost to a pulp.

Hearing that Eleventh Boy had been kidnapped by the trumpeters, the other tinsmiths searched high and low for him until they finally came to the back of the temple.

Feeling there was still some life in him, his uncle hurriedly sent a man to fetch an old chamber pot. He knew that only the scales inside the pot could save the life of a dying man in such a condition.

Eleventh Boy clenched his teeth so tightly that the liquid could not be poured down his throat.

July Cloud took over and whispered in his ear, "Eleventh Boy, drink it!"

Seeming to hear a faint voice, he opened his eyes. The girl poured it down.

There was no knowing why, but she herself also tasted it.

Then the tinsmiths took off a door, lay Eleventh Boy on it and carried him away.

They reached the east end of the *nur* and were about to move westward, when July Cloud stopped them and said, "Carry him to my home."

The old tinsmith nodded.

July Cloud took all her fishing nets and reed mats to

sell in the market and bought medicine for Eleventh Boy's injuries.

Women killed their laying hens for him.

The tinsmiths pooled money to buy ginseng.

Porters, tinsmiths, women and girls came constantly to see him, expressing an affection and kindness they seldom showed in their hard, dull lives. They believed that what Eleventh Boy and July Cloud had done was correct and were proud that Big Nur had bred such a young fine pair. They felt as pleased as if they were celebrating the New Year.

Liu dared not show his face. His gang also barricaded themselves in their quarters with double sentries posted at the gate. Those "heroes" turned out to be cowards!

The tinsmiths held a meeting and submitted to the prefectural government a petition demanding that the trumpet squad leader be handed over to them.

The local government gave no reply.

Then tinsmiths took to the streets and demonstrated. It was a rare sight for there were no banners or slogans, just twenty men with their loads, parading slowly through the town. Silent and grave, they were dignified and determined.

The demonstration lasted for three days.

On the third day they sat in front of the screen wall facing the gate of the prefectural government. On each head was a wooden tray with incense burning in a burner. That was an ancient custom. When people had suffered grievous wrongs, and the officials concerned refused them redress, they could burn down the court with incense and go unpunished.

The tinsmiths never wavered. If they took action, the result would be serious. The prefectural magistrate invited the local gentry and merchants to talk the matter over and reached a consensus that the case could not be ignored any longer. So the head of the trade association invited an assistant as the representative of the prefectural magistrate, the adjutant of the troop, Eleventh Boy's uncle and two of the older tinsmiths, Huang Hailong for the porters, the spectacle seller from Baoying and the chopsticks pedlar from Hangzhou to meet in a big teahouse to settle the matter.

Agreement was reached. All medical expenses should be borne by the troop (actually the trade association gave the money), and Trumpet Squad Leader Liu was to leave the area and sign his consent to this. The old tinsmith accepted the terms but insisted that Liu add one more point. If he set foot in their prefecture again, the old tinsmith would settle accounts with him.

Two days later Liu left, quietly escorted by two of his men holding a gun. He had been transferred to Sanduo Prefecture to work as a customs officer.

When Eleventh Boy was able to take some food and speak, July Cloud asked him, "They said they'd stop beating you if only you promised not to come to my home again. Why didn't you agree?"

"You would have liked me to?"

"No."

"I knew you wouldn't."

"Was it worth it?"

"Yes, it was!"

"Oh, how wonderful you are! I love you! You must get well quickly."

"Kiss me and I'll recover soon."

"Yes, I will!"

There were three mouths to feed now and only one

wage-earner. They had no savings, and nothing to sell or pawn. Making fishing nets or weaving mats did not bring in money right away. Eleventh Boy's injuries would not heal quickly. July Cloud took the two baskets her father had used, knocked away the dust and went to earn money immediately. The local girls and women admired her. At first they were worried, but later they relaxed when they saw her carrying her loads with quick, steady steps. From then on, July Cloud worked as a woman porter, wearing a big red flower on one side of her hair. Her eyes were as bright as ever, but their expression was more profound. She had become a capable young wife.

Would Eleventh Boy recover?

Certainly!

Translated by Kuang Wendong

Wang Zengqi was born in 1920 in Gaoyao County, Jiangsu Province. After graduating from the Chinese language department of Southwest Union University in 1942, he became an editor and teacher. During the early 1960s he worked as a playwright in a Beijing opera troupe and in 1980 joined the Chinese Dramatists' Association.

A student of the celebrated writer Shen Congwen, Wang began publishing his work in the 1940s. "A Tale of Big Nur" won an award in 1981.

Our Corner

Jin Shui

OUR corner used to be different with its blotched walls under the low cobwebbed ceiling. We liked that corner, because it was on the lee side, as Tiezi put it, and Kejian said it was cosy. And me? I just wanted to keep away from the window, from which you could see a college, the gate of a song and dance troupe and the chimneys of some regular factories. We liked this corner. It was the technicians' corner to which our whole neighbourhood production team attached the greatest importance. There Tiezi designed graceful ladies of old which the women workers in the team copied painstakingly on furniture modelled after antiques. But only Kejian and I could give the finishing touches — give the ladies features expressing tenderness and love. The women were loud in their praise: "You're young fellows after all!" "Our team couldn't do without you."

Pleased with himself, Kejian began to whistle while Tiezi contentedly lit a cigarette.

"But what about free medical care?" I grumbled. "And our pay is still only eighty cents a day!"

"How you do grouse!" remarked one of the women. "There'd be no problem if we had any say. We all have children. . . ." She choked with tears.

We started humming *The Bodhi Tree* without looking at each other.

Before the gate a bodhi tree
Is standing by the well,
And in its green shade I have had
More dreams than I can tell.

We found the plaintive melody comforting. Tiezi and Kejian must be like me, I thought, recalling my dream-like childhood and our life in the countryside of Shaan-xi, the northeast and Inner Mongolia....

But what had become of us?

In the morning, at noon or in the evening you could see us walking together along the quiet alley. What we dreaded most was running into innocent, artless children.

"Look, mama!"

We all hung our heads.

"Those guys have been hurt, there's something wrong with their legs, so...."

Tiezi would speed up his wheel chair while Kejian and I tried to go a little faster.

"Are they cripples?" the child asked.

The mother's slap seemed a blow on our hearts.

What could we do about an innocent child and a kind-hearted mother? If it had been anyone else, we would have stopped to fight. What had we to lose? The cadres in the school vocational office tried to console us; factory recruiters eyed us superciliously — we didn't pass muster. And we were a worry to our parents, a burden to our brothers and sisters....

An elderly woman, wiping her eyes, had urged me, "Don't take things too hard. Your little sister will take care of you. She won't neglect you...." I can't imagine what I looked like then when she took me in her trembling arms and kept calling my name. So, that was all my life was worth. God! But our paintings were neither fewer nor less skilled than those done by regular workers. Enduring the pain, we worked extra hard to be independent, like normal people, to change our status as cripples.

"Forget it," Tiezi said. "Do you think we'll be so thick-skinned as to live on after our parents kick the bucket?"

"Get a pack of dynamite and we'll blow ourselves up with the next swine who sneers at us!" Kejian pounded his crutches so hard that he nearly fell down.

It is lucky that people can die. We seemed to have nothing to fear and in the quiet alley we sang:

> Today, as in the past,
> I roam till late at night,
> Wandering in the dark,
> My eyes closed tight.
>   . . . . . .

She came in the season when the spring wind began to turn the willows green.

"I'm Wang Xue. Can I sit here?" She came into our corner.

"Sure."

"If you like."

"Why not?"

Each of us gave a cold reply. Then Kejian whispered to me, "Disgusting, nauseous." Tiezi's frosty eyes glinted behind his spectacles, then he lowered his head with a grunt. Taking the offensive was a defensive tactic. But what were we on our guard against?

She was quite a pretty girl.

"Have you come back too because of illness?" I asked.

She shook her head. "No, my parents need my help. Are you waiting for jobs too?"

None of us uttered a word. Waiting for jobs? Heaven knows how many more years we would have to wait!

"I'll sit here and watch how you work first." She smiled at me, probably finding me less difficult to get on with.

The radio music for exercises from the college broke the silence of our corner.

Her head was close to Tiezi's and her eyebrows almost touched Kejian's shoulder. They were like schoolchildren holding their breath in fear, the fools! Where was their haughtiness of a moment ago? It was all I could do not to laugh. Neither of them had ever intruded into the heart of a girl. Only I . . . but that was all past.

Kejian made several faulty strokes in succession and the hair of the lady Tiezi was painting looked like old wool unravelled from a sweater. Many past events flashed through my mind. What were they? It was that letter again. . . .

Suddenly she burst out laughing.

We all raised our heads in bewilderment.

She kept on laughing.

An angry look appeared on Tiezi's face.

"I can see my own nose!" she exclaimed. "I was watching you painting and suddenly saw my own nose. I didn't realize it was possible!" She tilted her head slightly to squint down at her nose, chuckling.

We couldn't help laughing too. A gentle breeze blew a touch of warmth into our corner.

A flash of lightning through the fine spring drizzle aroused three atrophied hearts.

From morning till night our corner echoed with songs: *The Bodhi Tree, The Marmot, Fate, The Boundless Grasslands....* We started with a soft humming, then sang in low voices. Tiezi tried hard not to open his mouth too wide while Kejian, in order to sing the bass, pressed his chin as low as he could. I stole a glance at Wang Xue, and noticed that they were peeping at her too. Her head was swaying gently in time with the music, her plaits dangling over her shoulders. Our singing gained in volume.

> Ol' man river, dat ol' man river!
> He must know somethin'
> But don't say nothin'
>
> ......

"Why sing all these dismal songs?" she suddenly asked.

"What would you like to hear then?" Kejian flushed.

"*Making Hay.* I love to hear Hu Songhua* sing that." She cleared her throat and sang:

> With pitch and prong the whole day long,
> We both were making hay,
> And there she was and there I was,
> And we were worlds away.
>
> ......

I thought of that letter again. It had been written by a well-meaning fellow to my sweetheart. Forget it! That's over and done with.

---

* A famous folk-song singer.

Wang Xue was still singing softly, her plaits swinging with the lively rhythm.

The three of us just stopped work and stared blankly at her. The defences in our hearts had been dismantled. In our mind's eye a vast expanse of spring water glimmering with patches of sunlight as gems, gently lapping at the solitary embankment appeared. How beautiful she was! But unlike certain actresses, she didn't make eyes at the audience or put on airs to please them. No, she was her natural self. And her thoughts were written on her face: she didn't look down on us.

All of a sudden Tiezi's voice rang out:

> I wish I were a little lamb,
> To follow by her side.
> I wish she'd take a little whip
> To flick my woolly hide.

Wang Xue doubled up with laughter, nearly choking. "What sort of rubbishy song is that! Who wants to be whipped? You must have made it up yourself." She casually took hold of Tiezi's arm and shook it.

She seemed more like a little girl than someone in her twenties.

Just like in the song, we worked together all day long. We would paint while singing *Making Hay, Auld Lang Syne, Aiyo Mama* and other lively songs. Our output increased with each passing day, surprising the rest of the team. Wang Xue was eager to learn, and we vied to teach her all our special skills. Soon we were all talking to her in an avuncular way:

"Wang Xue, you ought to take more exercise."

"Wang Xue, you should learn a foreign language. It's not too difficult. Where there's a will there's a way."

"Or learn to play the violin. There's nothing you can't do, if you put your mind to it."

"You must make something of your life, Wang Xue. You're not like us...."

And Wang Xue? Such advice delighted her. She would fish some sweets from her pocket and quietly put them in front of us, or pour us each a cup of fragrant tea.

"Is this a reward, little girl?"

"No!" She was delightfully naive. "It's a punishment."

"A punishment?"

"Yes. Why should you expect so much from me, but not from yourselves?"

We fell silent again. Sweets taste sweet but we felt bitter.

"I ... I haven't offended you, have I?" She glanced at us, then lowering her eyes, added, "What I mean is, you should live like that too. Am I right?"

Quite right, Wang Xue, but wait, we have to think things over carefully....

After that, she came half an hour earlier than usual to tidy up the workshop and our corner. She was always cheerful, conscientious about everything, and thoroughly enjoyed life. Amidst her singing, the dust in our corner vanished. A beautiful calendar was hung on the shabby wall. Gradually we three, who had formerly limped into our corner only when the bell sounded, also came earlier and earlier, each trying to arrive before the others. I was not at first aware of what was happening. Only when I sensed a certain constraint among the three of us did I realize that it was due to unconscious jealousy. Every one of us hoped to stay a little longer with Wang Xue. Eight hours a day was too little. What was the meaning of this jealousy?

After that I gave up going to work too early. I was by no means the kind of noble lover you read about in novels who makes way for his rival. It was precisely because I loved Wang Xue so deeply that I quite naturally rebuilt the defence in my heart. It was a trench, a deep scar inscribed with the glaring warning: "Impossible!" Besides, there was that letter! That letter.... Ah, just as my heart was seeking a little happiness in life, it underwent bitter pain. All I could do was stifle that pain in my heart, turning it into an apathetic smile to conceal what my heart sought.

Later, Tiezi and Kejian stopped coming earlier too. I daresay it was for the same reason!

Wang Xue really was like a little girl. She failed to see these subtle changes. One summer evening she begged us to accompany her to a film to be shown in a nearby park. Holding up four tickets she declared, *"To Make Life Sweeter*, a good film. Come along!"

Tiezi shook his head and Kejian said, "I won't go either. What sweeter life?"

"Won't you go with me?" She turned to me. "It's very dark on the way back after the film...."

"Are you afraid?" we all asked together.

"Mm." She knitted her eyebrows, nodding sheepishly.

Then we all agreed to go with her. I felt rather proud because we could protect her. No doubt so did Tiezi and Kejian.

In the park the gentle evening breeze carried the **faint**

scent of flowers. How many years now? Five! Ever since I'd had to use crutches, I'd never come here. Why should I? It would only remind me of the past. This was my childhood playground. I seemed to have sung and laughed here only yesterday. Here I felt the hopes of my boyhood. However, I could not recognize the poplars I had planted. On that lawn there had gathered many youngsters ready to settle down in the countryside, who used their simple, heartfelt verses to express their magnificent ideals. But what had happened later?

It was not yet dark. There were only a few children sitting there quietly, looking up at the blank screen. Tiezi and Kejian were also silent.

Suddenly Wang Xue laughed.

In the grove young lovers were strolling arm in arm, kissing.

"What's so funny? You'll do that yourself some day." I blurted out.

"What nonsense! I won't!" she stammered, red in the face.

Well, better not think of such things.

However, Tiezi burst out, "Doesn't it give you the creeps being with us, Wang Xue?"

"Why should it?" She jumped up to pick two leaves and mischievously stuffed them into Kejian's collar.

"Aren't you afraid?" I asked.

"Of what?"

I was tongue-tied. That letter! It read, "Don't be too friendly with him. Better keep your distance. Otherwise he will probably fall in love with you and you can only make him suffer. . . ."

"What's there to be afraid of, eh?" She gave me a

punch, holding a ladybird in her other hand. Oh, if only she could stay like a little girl for ever!

"Well, I mean, are you scared of the dark?"

"Don't be silly!" She blushed. "Are we going to see the film or not?"

Humming a song, we turned back along the small path. Still holding the ladybird she chattered away, keeping Tiezi and Kejian in fits of laughter. All at once I felt that the world was beautiful and sweet, and that we had become three happy elder brothers keeping their lovable sister company.

She was really like a little sister. As soon as the film started she began to giggle, clutching at my crutches. Her laughter made it hard to hear what the actors were saying. I wished time would stand still so that she would remain a little sister and we her happy brothers, forgetting the past, the present and the future, and everything on earth. . . . In fact, I so far forgot myself that I bent down, without the support of my crutches, to pick up a ball of knitting wool she had dropped. I fell flat on my face and cut my arm. . . . But I would gladly have fallen ten more times, because when she was on the verge of tears the casual way I passed it off made her laugh again.

One day Wang Xue was suddenly depressed, staring blankly and sighing without a word. When asked what was wrong, she hummed and hawed, glancing at us with embarrassment.

"Tell us what's up," said Tiezi anxiously. "Who's bullied you?"

"Who's tired of living? Tell me who?" Kejian clenched his fists.

"No, nobody's bullied me," she stuttered. "It's my mother. She wants me to meet that man. . . ."

There was dead silence in our corner.

"A university student. Introduced by my second aunt. . . ."

We heard the whistling of the wind along the electric wires.

That was something to be expected and I had already built up my defences, yet I seemed to feel my heart rolling down a dry well. I was not clear what went through my mind at that instant. It seemed that I was only thinking about how to get through the coming day. I longed for a cigarette. Tiezi and Kejian had already lit theirs and handed the lighter to me. My heart hit the bottom of the pitch-dark well. I wished I could stay there for ever, forgetting the world and forgotten by the world.

However, fixing expectant eyes on us, Wang Xue asked timidly, "Should I go to meet him?"

A girl like Wang Xue really deserved more happiness than other people. Just because she was too simple-minded to shun us, how could we undermine her happiness? Must she sacrifice it to prove her fine qualities?

"I don't want to meet him. What's the point? . . ."

She was expecting our help; she needed our help. A moment ago I had really been too selfish!

"You should go." Tiezi was the first to return to his senses.

"Love is something that can make you happy," I said. "Then you'll work and study harder. Even the world will become more beautiful. . . ."

"That's right!" chimed in Kejian.

We held forth on love, and Wang Xue listened trustingly and raptly. We could see from her shining eyes that she admired us and thought highly of us. We were prompted by a sense of pride to give our "little sister" good advice without any thought of ourselves. . . .

Still, when we left by the small alley that evening, we once again sang the song that had been banished from our minds all through the summer.

> Today, as in the past,
> I roam till late at night,
> Wandering in the dark,
> My eyes closed tight.
> It seems the leaves are calling without cease:
> Come back to me, friend, to find peace.

The following day in our corner there were indications that Wang Xue wanted to talk with the three of us alone. But better not, Wang Xue. I felt somewhat anxious. She smiled at us, looking so relaxed that my heart felt as if gripped by an icy hand. I kept reminding myself: You are glad of your sister's happiness, right?

"Sing a song, Tiezi," I suggested.

"Yes, let's sing, Kejian," Tiezi responded.

But we were in no mood to sing.

At the break Wang Xue finally found a chance and told us hastily, "Hey, I met that man last night and broke off with him."

We made neither head nor tail of this at first, looking at each other tensely. The next moment Tiezi started to splutter with laughter. You silly girl! You talk of breaking off, as if you'd known him for ages.

"It's true, I'm not kidding you." She sounded anxious.

"That means she didn't agree to see any more of him. Is that right?" Kejian turned to ask me cheerfully.

The icy hand on my heart had loosened its grip. It

was no good, really, gloating over someone else's misfortune.

"Why didn't you agree?" I asked her.

"He kept a straight face like a big cadre, and lectured me all the time as if he didn't even know how to smile. He said I was naive. Not just rather naive but *extremely* naive. Dear me! My head started buzzing. Oh, spare me, I'm not short of tutors." She rattled this off, her nose twitching, then dashed out, calling over her shoulder, "I'm going to find a newspaper and see if there's a film show in the park tonight!"

I found I had started humming a tune already. Why? Because I was happy? What if she were my real sister? Even so I'd never agree to her marrying such a man.

We went to the small park again. That summer we spent many a sweet evening together in that small park. Wang Xue told me many things about herself. I can't remember now what film we saw. What remains in my memory is the setting sun, the evening wind, the moon, the stars and little Wang Xue who loved us as if we were her own brothers. And we began to love everything around us just as she did.

As I recall them now, those memories are as precious as gold. . . .

University? Oh, yes. Wang Xue was admitted to a university later. It was in the autumn of that year when she and her mother were at loggerheads over that university student that the news spread apace: Students must be enrolled through an entrance examination.*

---

* During the "cultural revolution", students were admitted through recommendation.

The day we heard that Tiezi sat there lost in thought, I knew what he was thinking about. He had been one of the best students in a well-known middle school.

"Forget it, Tiezi," I said. "Just ignore the whole business."

"You can only deceive yourself," he countered with a wry smile.

The street lamps swayed in the wind. Tiezi and I sat face to face at the door of his house without a word. The autumn cicadas would go on chirping till midnight.

"Wang Xue!" Teizi exclaimed as if he were dreaming.

"Where?" I looked round.

"I mean Wang Xue can go to university now."

"Sure! But can she pass the exam?"

"She told me she did quite well in it the year Zhang Tiesheng** was enrolled."

"Right!" My eyes sparkled. "You can help her with maths and physics."

"And you with Chinese, mainly composition."

"Exactly!"

From then on every evening the light in our corner was on while crickets chirped away outside.

Bending over the table Teizi and Wang Xue were engrossed in points, lines, logarithms, sines, drawing and ciphering. As for me, I taught her grammar and classical prose, and wrote classical essays for her to imitate. Only Kejian sat silently outside the door boiling water for us, occasionally poking his head in with an envious grin when he heard us laughing. The kettle sang merrily

---

** The student who handed in a blank paper, caiming to have been too busy working to revise for the examinations. In 1973 the "gang of four" instructed universities to recruit students according to their political attitude, not their examination results.

over the blue-tongued flames. There was a look of depression in his bright eyes, for he could not understand what we were talking about. In fact, he had not even finished primary school.

Using my crutches, I walked over to him and patted him on the shoulder. "Perhaps you have some useful books at home?"

He didn't answer. He was feeling upset because he could not give Wang Xue a hand. Poor Kejian!

The next day he limped over with a book entitled *The Absolute Discrimination of Sound*, which he gave to Wang Xue, not knowing what it was about. It turned out to be a foreign novel. Pretending to be overjoyed, the kind-hearted girl said she loved to read such books.

The lamplight was serene and soft. I'd seen that kind of lamplight when I was a boy and my mother came home from work and kissed me on the neck. Why can't we spread such a light over all darkness around?

The light was still on when the crickets stopped chirping.

The light was still on when the leaves fell.

The light was still on when the north wind grew colder and colder.

One evening we sang *Lamplight*:

> A young girl
> Sees a soldier off to the war.
> They bid farewell in the dark.
> Those steps before. . . .

Wang Xue's voice suddenly broke, tears filled her eyes. "If I'm admitted to a university far away from here, we won't be able to be together again."

A shooting star swiftly disappeared on the horizon.

None of us spoke, as if aware of this problem. To be frank, we were worried about her, prayed for her every day and felt comforted when we imagined her sitting in a lecture room. . . .

"You'll write to me, won't you?"

There was only the rustling of fallen leaves on the pavement in the small, dark alley.

"Anyway, I'll write to you whenever I have time."

The wheelchair creaked, crutches thumped.

"Promise me just one thing, please. . . ." She sounded choked.

"What?"

She halted and all of a sudden burst out sobbing.

"Yes, we will, Wang Xue," we chorused. "We will write to you!" We were only too pleased to say this.

"Just one thing." She stopped crying with a great effort. "'Never talk about death again; never talk about dynamite packs. . . .'"

She knew everything.   She had never brought that up before but she knew everything! She probably hadn't mentioned it because she hated to talk like that "big cadre with a straight face". However, she told us all that was in her heart.   She liked to hear us singing cheerful songs.   She liked us to go to films with her and to tell us amusing "news". All this had converged into a warm stream that thawed out our frozen hearts. Thank you, little girl! No, you weren't a little girl and we shouldn't thank you.   We shouldn't let your painstaking efforts come to nothing.

"Do you promise me? OK?"

That reminded me of a fairy tale: A mother sheep told her three lambs before she went out, "Wolves have long snouts and pointed ears. Don't open the door for them. Promise me?" So we were like three little lambs Wang Xue worried about.

"OK, Wang Xue, we do!" we promised her.

A street lamp flashed past, lighting up her anxious face. We had not set her mind at ease. We passed another light. Putting on an air of cheerfulness she said, "I may not pass the exam!"

Well, well, she was the first to comfort us again.

I felt something rending my heart as I said, "Don't worry, Wang Xue! We'll bite that wolf to death!"

"Wolf?" She faced me, her eyes glistening with tears. Oh, little girl, you still didn't understand!

I began to talk excitedly about Jack London's novel *Love of Life* and Lenin's comments on it. How the hero fought with a wolf; how he overcame hunger, piercing cold and weakness; how steadfast he was and how strong his will to live. As I went on Wang Xue's eyes shone, so did Tiezi's and Kejian's. The three of us struck up a tune and then Wang Xue joined in. Our spirited, stirring singing made the quiet alley ring....

That winter, just as she had predicted, Wang Xue was admitted to a medical college in another province. She had always wondered why our legs could not be cured now that there were so many hospitals in our country. Clinging to the window of the southward bound train, she said earnestly, "Just wait and be patient. I'm taking your medical records with me." We waved goodbye to her as we had as boys when we saw our brothers and sisters off to school. She didn't seem to be leaving us for a remote city in the south but for somewhere so close that she could come back at any time.

Look, here is our corner. The beautiful calendar is the one Wang Xue hung there. There's not a speck of dust on it, I can assure you! We no longer sing those melancholy songs. Whenever dusk falls in that little alley, we seem to hear Wang Xue's voice and call to mind the story about the wolf. Here in this world, at this moment, a kind and beautiful girl is concerned about us. She has kindled the light in our hearts. We should be her brave fighters. As to the future ... friends, no need to remind us. We've thought of everything. We wish Wang Xue a happy life. And the warm stream in our hearts will never run dry nor grow cold. What if I could pour a warm stream into all other icy hearts as Wang Xue has done? Then, wouldn't the world in which we live turn into a better place?

Translated by Kuang Wendong

Jin Shui is the nom-de-plume of Shi Tiesheng, born in Beijing in 1951. He graduated from middle school in 1967. Paralysed while working in the countryside, he joined a neighbourhood factory in 1974. His first short story "The Professor of Law and His Wife" appeared in the magazine **Contemporary Era**, No. 2, 1979. This was followed by the "Half Hour Lunch Break" and "Brothers".

Outside the Marriage Bureau

He Xiaohu

PEOPLE all say that I've made a good match and should be grateful to the marriage bureau. In reality, our marriage was not arranged inside, but outside the bureau. You don't believe me? Then listen to this.

Marriage between men and women is necessary. But although I had met half a dozen possible partners and was approaching the age of twenty-nine, I was still single. Unmarried youths are especially sensitive about their ages. The greater the number, the heavier the pressure on their hearts.

Was it because I was ugly? No, last year, when I was named as an advanced teacher, a newspaper reporter described my appearance thus: "Although he cannot be considered handsome, his pair of black, shining eyes, under long eyelashes, radiate the vitality of youth, and his strong athletic physique makes him an attractive young man."

The principal reason for my failure in love was my profession. I am a primary-school sports teacher. My reversals in the affairs of the heart provided me with a mirror, in which I could clearly see my position in the eyes of some people.

My first love was an old schoolmate, a worker in a textile factory. I often walked with her hand in hand by the banks of the river, looking at the orange yellow setting sun, the magnificent evening clouds, feeling that our two hearts were beating in time together. Songs of joy reverberated round us. Ah, those were really golden days, the days of youthful dreams. Once, she put her head on my shoulder and said in a tender, soft voice, "Weiyang . . . can't you get another job? My friends at work are all making fun of me."

My heart felt as if it had been pierced.

She urged, "Please change your job. My father can help you . . ." and she pressed more closely against me.

A wave of coolness rose in my heart. I looked at her eyes; I saw her pleading. But I saw more distinctly her pity for me, and it was just this which I could not bear. It was really a contempt for my work, destroying my self-respect. Many scornful words rose in my throat, but I managed to choke them back. We parted without an angry word.

My last discussion like this occurred last year. A neighbour had introduced me to a fashionable young girl. When we met, her two large, alluring eyes blinked and looked at me as if I was some rare animal. When she learned of my profession, her eyes suddenly became dim, like fading electric light bulbs. She moved away without any explanation. I followed her. Outside my neighbour's window, I heard her giving vent to her anger, "Auntie, you treat me like dirt! You said you were introducing me to an athlete. Some athlete! He's a primary-school sports teacher. What sort of a job is that? Primary-school teachers are looked down on as second-class citizens. Useless!"

The setting up of a marriage bureau was announced in a match-box-sized advertisement on the lower right-hand corner of the fourth page of the local newspaper. The reaction this aroused far surpassed any front-page news! The office was located in Huasheng Lane, a quiet, small back street known to very few people. It suddenly became full of beautiful colours as many young girls in flowery dresses and many young men appeared. The lane was filled with the tinkling of bicycle bells, laughter, smiles, soft guitar music, taped electronic music and songs of famous singers. Some poets romantically called this ordinary small lane the "road of love and beauty".

Urged repeatedly by my mother, I found my residence card, work permit and a photograph of myself. Dressed in a brand-new woollen suit, I proceeded to the "road of love and beauty".

My thoughts were cut short by a burst of electronic music. Three or four long-haired, fashionable young men, with tape recorders in their hands, rushed in ostentatiously. One of them I knew was a well-known young hooligan in the northern city district. My high spirits were at once dampened. Should I try to find love in the company of such bad characters? The love I required was evidently of a different kind from theirs.

As I was hesitating, I heard a melodious, charming voice asking, "Teacher Wang, where are you going?" A tall, slim, graceful girl was standing before me.

She was the elder sister of a pupil of mine. I only knew that her surname was Bai. "Ah, Xiao Bai, I'm going to. . . ." Damn! How could I tell a strange girl that I was going to the marriage bureau to look for a mate? "I . . . I'm going to visit the parents of one of my pupils. And you . . . where are you going?"

Xiao Bai smiled, "I'm going to a hardware shop in the east city."

"I see," I nodded, and hurriedly took my leave.

I walked a little distance, and, supposing that Xiao Bai had gone, turned back. I espied that she had also turned back. She shook her pigtails, turned and stepped briskly through the vermilion door of the bureau. I was overjoyed. "With girls like Xiao Bai there, I'll find true love," I thought to myself. The unpleasant impression made by the young men a moment earlier was at once dispelled. I stepped quickly through the door and entered the reception room for men.

I stood at the window and looked into the reception room opposite for women. Among the crowd of girls in pretty clothes was one who looked like Xiao Bai. She was filling in a form, her head down. I watched until she had completed it and left.

I smiled.

One of the staff of the bureau, a man of about forty years of age, came over and patted my shoulder, "Don't look so dazed. Fill in the forms first. You can depend on me. My name's Chen. I'll find you happiness." I nodded my head gratefully and took the two forms he handed me. Newly printed, they still smelled of ink. The first form was easy to fill in, like filling in a curriculum vitae. The second one, however, gave me quite a headache. It was headed "Requirements for a Partner". Underneath were ten columns, including the girl's possible occupation, age, character, appearance, financial situation, height, native place, nationality, hobbies and general family circumstances. Through these abstract entries I saw a concrete, lively human being, a warm-hearted girl, from whose rosy, oval face shone a pair of bright, black eyes, expressing the purity of her mind. Moreover, she had an easy manner, a graceful figure and a bewitching black mole under her left ear.

How could I forget her, although I hardly knew her name and had only met her three times?

The first time I had met her had been in the winter of last year. I had taken my pupils skating in the park. One boy went outside the boundary and suddenly fell through a hole in the ice. Alarmed, I jumped into the water and got him out. Fortunately, I saved him in time; after his clothes were changed, he quickly recovered. Another teacher warned me, "Wait till his parents come to complain! Last time when I was giving a P. T. lesson, a pupil sprained his ankle vaulting over a horse. His parents raised hell. You've done worse, nearly drowning a boy!"

Accompanying the boy back home, I was nervous, anticipating a confrontation with an irate parent. On entering the boy's home, the only person who received me was his elder sister, Xiao Bai. Instead of blaming me when she heard my story, she looked at me with grateful eyes, thanked me again and again and brought tea and cigarettes for me. I had become a hero. Feeling very uneasy, I criticized myself. When I left and reached the entrance to their lane, I turned back and could still see, under the dim street light, her graceful figure as she repeatedly waved her hand to me.

The second time I saw her was in the early spring of this year. I took some students to see a gymnastics display in the stadium. After the show, it began to rain so hard that it was impossible for us to go back. This was a difficult problem for a teacher to solve. It would soon be lunch time. As I was wondering what to do, the door of the ticket-office opened. Xiao Bai beckoned to me with her hand. "Teacher Wang, since you can't go back to school yet, come in here and get warm." I refused. "I don't want to interrupt your work." I had only met her once before. How could I give her so much trouble? She had invited me out of politeness. I could not accept.

Xiao Bai, however, came over and insisted, "You're a teacher, but what about your pupils? It's very cold outside and the rain won't stop soon. Come inside and have some hot water to drink. It's almost noon. You can buy some bread for the children. I've money and food coupons here. You can use them."

How carefully she had thought of everything! Seeing that she was sincere, I no longer refused. I let the children cram into her room, while she brought two large kettles and searched for and found some bowls and lunch-boxes for us. Then she suggested, "Teacher Wang, have some water first. I'll go to buy the bread."

Psychologists, when describing the mental state of unmarried youths, have written: "With approaching maturity, the image of an 'ideal person' is gradually formed in the mind, a mixture of one's own character, preferences, behaviour and habits. In chance contacts or conversations with a person of the opposite sex, one is always gauging and guessing about the opposite party in terms of the imagined 'ideal person'." I was then just in such a state. To the sound of the rain, I chatted and ate with Xiao Bai. Our warm glances expressed a tender, fluctuating affection. In our conversation, we were assessing each other, trying to find some common ground.

The rain stopped and the sun came out again. I cursed. Why should the sun be so unaccommodating as to end our interesting conversation?

For several days my mind was in a turmoil. Certain vague longings and anxieties possessed me. My equilibrium was disturbed. I knew what was required to restore it. At last, the holidays came. I went by bike to return the money and food coupons to Xiao Bai, hoping we could continue our conversation.

She was playing volley-ball with two young men on the sports ground in front of the stadium. I knew that one of the men was a well-known centre in the provincial basket-ball team; the other was a top-notch volley-ball player. On seeing me Xiao Bai exclaimed joyfully, "Here's another athlete." She introduced me to the two players. When they heard I was only a primary-school sports teacher, the basket-ball centre did not conceal his contempt and reluctantly shook hands with me.

I realized the distance between such sportsmen and myself, hearing again the words, "Second-class citizens. Useless!" How could a pretty young girl surrounded by such heroes fall in love with a "second-class citizen" like me? She had acted purely out of kindness, but I, love-sick, had imbued it with a deeper significance. I must control myself. Six girls before her had rejected me. Need there be a seventh?

I therefore returned the money and food coupons to Xiao Bai, gave her a faint smile and immediately went away.

Now, I had spotted her in the marriage bureau. This meant she had not yet found a sweetheart. Wonderful news! Through the marriage bureau, I could continue my conversations with Xiao Bai and discuss things with her more openly and sincerely. Even if it didn't work out, I would not feel humiliated or embarrassed.

"The marriage bureau is really good!" I exclaimed from my heart.

According to what I knew of Xiao Bai, I filled in the second form as follows:

Age: About twenty-five.

Occupation: Connected with sports.

Character: Warm-hearted, kind and tolerant.

Speciality: Eager to help other people.

Appearance: Regular features, graceful and pretty, with a black mole under the left ear.

As for financial conditions and general family circumstances, I just wrote "Doesn't matter", or "No particular demands".

I handed the forms to Old Chen. He asked some questions while looking them over.

"*Ai*? Connected with sports? What does that mean?"

I replied, "I'm a sports teacher. I hope my future wife will appreciate such work."

"Of course," said Old Chen, tapping his head. "You mean occupations like being a salesgirl in a sports shop or a sports advertiser?"

I nodded and added, "Or a ticket-seller in a stadium."

"What's this?" Old Chen queried again. "You put down 'having regular features, graceful and pretty, with a black mole under the left ear'. What does that mean?"

"That is. . . ." I quickly made up a wild answer. "My mother said our native place had such a custom. A black mole under the left ear symbolizes good luck. A girl with such a mark is thought to be dutiful."

"Good, you're a filial son. Not many young men like you around these days." With these words he put the two forms I handed to him into the files. Then he said, "Please leave your telephone number and wait for a happy meeting." He accompanied me out of the door and tightly pressed my hand, adding, "Now don't worry. I was thirty-five years old when I got married. I understand your fears. Although your requirements are rather unusual, we'll do our utmost to find a suitable partner for you."

The days that followed were full of hope and longing. The telephone, to which I normally paid no attention, suddenly dominated my thoughts. Whenever it rang, I was always the first to snatch up the receiver. When I wasn't teaching, I used to sit beside it, stroking the receiver with my hand. It was the first time that I realized the beauty of the telephone: It was of a rosy colour with a chromium-plated dial, which glittered brightly, and a green cord, like a streamer decorating the streets on festive days. This was the coloured thread that would bring me a happy marriage.

Ten days later, the beautiful telephone brought me a message from the marriage bureau: "We've found a possible partner for you. Your first meeting will take place in the pavilion near the eastern gate of the municipal park at three o'clock tomorrow afternoon. The girl will hold a newspaper in her right hand. In order to avoid a mistake, you should carry a magazine."

I lost no time in shaving myself and going to the barber's. Then, in my best suit, I set out for the park as if I were a diplomat going abroad on an important mission.

The result was most disappointing. The girl was not Xiao Bai. She also looked quite graceful and had a black mole under her left ear, but to me, her eyes lacked lustre. Her voice also lacked charm. She spoke in a monotone, swallowing the ends of her words. In short, it was just like listening to funeral music. I simply couldn't stand it.

According to the rules of the bureau, a report had to be made after the first meeting. I went directly there.

"She won't do!" I told Old Chen. "Please find another one for me."

"Why not?" Old Chen took out my forms, looked over them slowly and asked, "She doesn't meet your requirements?"

"Her eyes don't sparkle!" I answered.

"Don't sparkle?" Old Chen smiled generously. Pointing at one of the forms, he went on, "You didn't write that down here! You youngsters are really choosy. You want a girl not only with a black mole under her ear, but also with eyes that sparkle! How odd! Ha! Ha!..."

"Anyway, we're not suited to each other."

"All right, all right! You left one column blank, so I'll help you to fill it in right now: 'Her eyes must sparkle.'" Standing up, Old Chen kindly patted my shoulder and saw me off as usual to the door. Shaking hands with me, he added, "Now don't worry. I was thirty-five years old when I got married. I understand your fears. Although your requirements are rather unusual, we'll do our utmost to find a suitable partner for you."

My second date was a champion markswoman. She was good-looking, perhaps even prettier than Xiao Bai.

Though she also had a black mole under her left ear, I hadn't the same joyful, comfortable feeling as when I met Xiao Bai. Her eyes were very big, like the muzzles of rifles, and they gleamed with a black light as if she were taking aim at me. I got goose-pimples all over.

Once again I rushed back to the bureau to report to Old Chen. As usual, he smiled at me warmly, saying, "How about it this time? You can't say that her eyes weren't sparkling...."

"Sparkling? They were like laser beams. I couldn't bear them."

As usual, Old Chen saw me off to the door. Shaking hands with me he added, "Now don't worry! I was thirty-five years old...."

The third time I ran away before Old Chen could begin, "Now don't worry!..."

At the entrance to the lane, I sat down miserably on a stone step with my head in my hands. I'd been disappointed three times. It was clear that the "ideal person" in Xiao Bai's mind was not a man like me.

Raising my head, I suddenly saw Xiao Bai. She was smiling at me. Refreshed, I stood up.

"Teacher Wang, where are you going?" Xiao Bai asked in her musical voice.

"I ... I'm going to visit the parents of one of my pupils," I answered hastily.

"So why are you sitting here?"

"Oh, I got tired walking ... I was just taking a rest." I felt very uneasy: It was obvious I was telling a lie. I tried to conceal my embarrassment, saying lamely, "See you again. I've something to do. Goodbye...." With that, I beat a retreat.

After a few steps, I stood still and cursed myself.

"Why should I, a grown-up man, be so timid?" When I had gone to the bureau, I had hoped they would introduce me to Xiao Bai, but now she had been standing before me and I had been too scared to speak to her. Would she eat me?

I turned my head and saw she was still standing there motionless, like a statue of a Greek goddess, staring at me.

I plucked up my courage and walked back to her. After heaving a deep sigh, I fixed my eyes on the ground, saying in a very low voice, "I went to the marriage bureau, but the dates they arranged for me were all useless. This was the third one. I'm feeling very depressed."

"So am I," confessed Xiao Bai. "I also went there and they made three dates for me too. None of them worked out."

"So, you. . . ." An unexpected hope rose in my breast, and my heart beat fast.

Xiao Bai said nothing. We began to walk side by side along the road. I couldn't stop myself from asking, "In your job, you have many opportunities to meet the stars of the sports world. It should be easy for you to find your ideal man. Why do you need to resort to a marriage bureau?"

"A man's position and character are two different things," she argued.

I relaxed like a soldier hearing the command, "At ease!" I felt bold enough to joke, "The marriage bureau gave both of us disappointments. So we're fellow-sufferers!"

"Not necessarily so," she replied. "Arithmetically speaking, one disappointment plus another equals two disappointments. But, in life, the result is sometimes just the opposite. One disappointment plus another may equal a hope."

What she said was amusing, yet it had some philosophical truth. My heart beat rapidly, but I didn't know the right thing to say. I began to taste the exquisite, deep sensation of love, more interesting and magnificent than those dull, matter-of-fact appointments made by the bureau. The words slipped out of my mouth, "The work of the bureau is rather like that of my elder brother. He's studying biogenetics. Every day he writes down on his cards lots of data such as the species, weight, hair colour and so on. . . ."

Xiao Bai giggled, "What a sharp tongue you have!"

"Of course the staff of the bureau work hard. Take Old Chen for instance. Every time I went there, he was always friendly. But I wasn't introduced to a girl I liked. They were all a great disappointment."

"Since you've already got your ideal girl in mind, why didn't you contact her directly. Why give so much trouble to the marriage bureau?"

"Easier said than done. I'd been snubbed too many times. Though I'm keen on a certain girl, how can I be sure she's interested in me? I'm only a primary-school sports teacher." I darted her a meaningful glance.

Her face suddenly turned red.

We were both silent, walking slowly together, staring at the ground. More conjectures. . . .

After a short while, Xiao Bai asked in a low voice, "What do you want then?"

I looked at her. Her head was still down, and she was holding a red handkerchief in her hand. I summoned up my courage and answered, "She must have a black mole under her left ear."

"And?"

"Her job must be connected with sports."

"Anything more?"

"She must be kind-hearted, eager to help others, and her eyes must sparkle...." I poured out all my requirements.

"Anything else?"

"Nothing more. That's all!" I gesticulated vigorously.

"But," Xiao Bai raised her head and cast a sidelong glance at me, "how did you know the girl you fancied had also gone to the marriage bureau?"

I had no answer to that.

Frowning, she went on, "Put yourself in the girl's place. How can she fall in love with a man, who follows her stealthily like a secret agent?"

Greatly alarmed, I hastened to protest loudly, "I didn't follow her. I only spotted her in the reception room for women when I was in the one for men."

Xiao Bai smiled and pointed at me with her red handkerchief, "You beast! I never imagined you could play such a trick...."

......

One month later, I went to the marriage bureau together with Xiao Bai.

Old Chen received me as warmly as ever. He began as soon as he saw me, "I'm very much concerned about your problem. I've found out that there are eleven girls, who fit your requirements. Do you want me to arrange a meeting with one of them?"

Pointing at Xiao Bai, who was standing behind me, I replied, "No, thank you. No need now. I came here specially to tell you I've already found a girlfriend. I won't bother you any more."

"A girlfriend?" In surprise, Old Chen gazed at me and then looked at Xiao Bai, asking, "You didn't register with us, did you?"

"Yes," she answered with a smile. "I did register here, but nothing worked out."

Old Chen was silent. Turning round, he took out a bundle of forms and began to flick rapidly through them.

"Don't look at them any more. It's not easy to classify people according to the ten entries on your forms. Rather create a better life for single people. Let them have more opportunities to meet each other. You should organize tours, dances, get-togethers, many activities. In my opinion, that's the best way."

So my story had a happy ending.

Translated by Hu Zhihui

He Xiaohu was born in Taiyuan, Shanxi in 1950. After graduating from middle school, he worked as a welder at a power plant. Since 1972 he has published several short stories including "Structural Beauty" and "Outside the Marriage Bureau" which won awards in 1980 and 1981 respectively.

He Xiaohu is now a member of the Shanxi branch of the Chinese Writers' Association.

Deaf-Mute and His "Suona"

Han Shaogong

ONE day, while I was lodging at the team leader's, I heard someone playing a *suona* trumpet, sporadically, as if the player was being throttled. A little while later, it sounded just like a goose honking. Looking out, I saw a man of about thirty with a *suona* in his belt and an armful of fresh branches, scowling at the children in front of him. The children were holding sickles. Judging by his guttural noises, gestures and excited facial expressions, the man was a deaf-mute.

Unafraid, the children pointed at him, cursing and swearing, "You're a fake, Deaf-mute! You're a phoney!"

He laughed and then turned to leave, but the hem of his jacket was caught by one of the boys. The man's face clouded and he made as if to strike him. At this, the children ran away swearing, "Hey, Deaf-mute! Deaf-mute, you're just a phoney!" He made no response but carried the branches away towards the piggery. Who was he, I wondered. Perhaps he was a forest warden who watched over the trees. But was a deaf-mute capable of doing that kind of job? And was it he who had played the *suona*?

When he saw me, he broke into a broad grin, revealing his simple nature. His head was covered with hemp-like black and white hairs, a symbol of youth and old age at one and the same time. He had a protruding jaw and retroussé nose and his clothes were badly worn. Like many other peasants, his body had been deformed by too much hard labour. Had it not been for his clothes and his plimsolls, he would have looked like a gorilla.

He uttered something which sounded like "*ao, ao*" at me and made a number of baffling signs: He pointed first to himself and then to me, then put his hands out as though grasping a steering-wheel. He pointed at my wrist watch, made a circle in the air and held up his thumb, laughing. What did he mean?

Seeing I couldn't understand him, he was annoyed and immediately repeated his gestures, then seemed to ask: Don't you understand yet?

At this point, the team leader came in with an armful of thatch and smiled at me. "Of course, you can't understand his signs yet. He meant he knows you're a cadre and a good one from the county and that you came here by bus. Your name is Yuan."

Pointing at my watch had meant I was a cadre. The circle he described meant my name Yuan.* His peculiar language made me laugh.

Seeing my laughter, he appeared relieved and much happier. The team leader told me, "His name is Deqi. After a childhood illness he became a deaf-mute. Worse still, his mother is dead. Though he's ugly, he's very clever and knows a lot about nature." With this, he held up his little finger and asked him, "Who are the most wicked and treacherous people?"

Deaf-mute frowned before snorting contemptuously and holding up four fingers — the "gang of four"!

---

* The word for "circle" is a homophone of the surname "Yuan" in Chinese.

I laughed.

Proud of his successful demonstration, he was cheered, and his face acquired an almost rosy glow. He became more "talkative". Hands behind his back, he swaggered into my room and looked around, then signed to the team leader, pointing at the window to indicate that he should help me to paper it well. He held his right palm like a cleaver slicing meat and rubbed his hands, meaning that he was inviting me to his home to have meat dumplings with him when next a festival occurred. Still pointing to the upper terrace, he held up three fingers and pinched his nose, meaning that Lao San, the old cowherd who lived there, was too cruel to his animals. Again he shook his little finger — he's no good.

After the team leader interpreted his sign language, I nodded to Deqi to indicate that I set much store by his information. He happily patted me on the shoulder and walked away.

That was how I made his acquaintance.

Long years have elapsed and his image is still fresh in my mind, although I am far away from that mountain village. My pad of writing paper under the bright table lamp in front of me, I look out of the window. Beneath neon lights, sedans and limousines are swishing along the street. The crowds eddy along with the noisy traffic. There are so many people in this world. . . .

2

Now let me tell you the story from the beginning.

Deaf-mute of Wu Village was a good fellow —

everybody there said so. Even though he couldn't hear the broadcast summoning people to work, he got up early every morning. Sometimes he even went to knock at the team leader's window to wake him up and ask him for work. He was the only man excused from attending meetings. However, he eagerly attended every one, whether it was a mass meeting or a cadres' meeting, although some quite normal people contrived to evade them on the grounds of having a "stomach-ache" or "going to find a lost chicken". During meetings, he would look this way and that. No one knew what he came to the meetings for, whether it was only for amusement or whether he sat there envying other people who could communicate with each other with their mouths and ears. When the kettle boiled, he would blow the dust off the lid and make tea for the others.

During the "cultural revolution", duty and obligation were ignored, and callousness was the consequence of poverty. Those bullied tried to bully others. Taking advantage of Deaf-mute's simplicity and docility, some people used to make him do all the hard jobs. When building houses, carrying coffins or unloading for the supply and marketing co-operative, they would always think of him. He didn't mind whether or not he stood to gain anything from his labour. But once free, he left as soon as he could. If, after the job, the host had prepared a meal for him, he would eat several bowls. If there was no meal, he simply dusted himself off and went home. When called upon next time, he would do the same. He was a lover of certificates of merit. So, before getting him to do some work, the employer always offered him one, "Come on, you'll get a certificate for this."

He would nod and follow along smiling. When the work was done, he would be happy with any kind of certificate, even one without an official seal. People often gave him schoolchildren's certificates and changed the names on them.

He collected numerous certificates, ranging from those issued by the county government to those from the old cowherd living on the upper terrace. One had originally not been his, but had belonged to a county level cadre, and had been awarded when the advanced agricultural producers' co-op was set up. A favourite of Deaf-mute's friends, the cadre had slept in the same bed with him and had helped him with money when his mother had been ill. He had also given him a pair of cotton-padded shoes. In winter he helped the peasants to protect their paddy shoots against the cold. The following year they had a bumper harvest. Deaf-mute had plenty of glutinous rice buns to eat, and could even afford to go by bus to the county town with the cadre. When staying at the cadre's, he was very taken by the certificate of merit on the wall and so it was given to him. From that day on, he felt highly honoured. Now he had a pile of them, ones which included genuine praise as well as genuine deceit. The moment he made a new acquaintance, such as a cadre just come from the county town, he would smugly display them. When the villagers around him laughed, so did he, although he didn't know why they laughed. As far as he was concerned, he was proud of them, and particularly proud of his favourite friend, the cadre who had given him the special certificate.

In a word, he was a man who belonged to the public and to society. People needed him, his sweat and his smiles more than they respected him. In his silent world, he was like an ox, a stone, or a limpid brook flowing peacefully day in and day out.

3

Deaf-mute lived with his brother Decheng.

Once when he was helping someone work, Decheng came and dragged him away, swearing at the other man, "You wicked devil, how can you have the heart to take advantage of a deaf-mute?" When some carried a joke with him too far, Decheng would also curse vehemently, "Damn you! You barren, rotten pig!"

Wu Decheng had a round face and a trunk-like body and was a resourceful man, able to turn his hand to anything and nicknamed "weirdo" in the village. In his youth, he had helped his uncle to set up a butcher's shop, and had then earned his living by selling buffalos and firing bricks. Well-to-do, he had cigarettes to smoke, meat to eat and tea to drink every day. His newly built large house with its bright window-panes occupied a long stretch of the street, one symbol of his considerable wealth which attracted much attention. After all he was only a peasant. When the unprecedented "cultural revolution" broke out, he was robbed of his pigs and a brick kiln, and two of his rooms were pulled down. He was prohibited from doing any private business, and could only work in the paddy fields. The only way he could vent his anger was to use violent language at home. Luckily for him, his burden was not such a heavy one, because the workpoints Deaf-mute earned were put to his credit, so he didn't need to tighten his belt that much.

Deaf-mute's sister-in-law was a lovely young woman from a distant village. Her first name was Fragrance and nobody bothered about her surname. On the wedding day, villagers thronged to see her and jabbered admiringly about her fine features, her pretty feet, the exquisite lace edging of her jacket and the delicacy of her skin. She looked as though she had just walked out of a painting. If she went to the river to wash, she would but enhance its natural beauty, they said. And if she went up the mountain to pick tea leaves, she was sure to augment the perfume of the flowers.

Happier even than his brother, Deaf-mute smiled, bustled about and played his *suona* all day long. No one knew who had taught him to play. Some said it was his best friend, the cadre.

In the village there was an old-fashioned, slightly barbaric custom: On the wedding day guests could behave in a familiar way with the bride and the bridegroom could not stop them. Just as some mischievous lads winked at each other to start, Deaf-mute elbowed through the crowd and positioned himself in front of them, brandishing his *suona* like an axe.

"What? Has Deaf-mute gone mad?"

"So you came here to join us, eh?"

"*Ao ao.* . . ." He stood his ground glowering, like a fighting bull or a Vajra spirit guarding heavenly flowers.

Disappointed, the young men could do nothing but glance at the wine cups, peanuts and sweet-potatoes. Some yawned, others began looking for their companions and for lanterns to make their way home.

"Just our luck. Deaf-mute put a spanner in the works," one of them grumbled.

"Perhaps he thinks his sister-in-law's made of sugar, and would crumble easily."

Other sneered. "Ha, if he had a wife, I bet he wouldn't even let others look at her."

"You mean he might get married one day? I'm afraid the woman who'd marry him hasn't been born yet."

People thought Deaf-mute would never marry. Did it ever worry him? No one knew, but they always found him glowing with happiness and playing his *suona* when he saw others get married. On such occasions, he always had a few firecrackers in his pocket.

After the guests left, the exhausted Fragrance gave a deep sigh of relief. Bashfully she threw a grateful glance at Deaf-mute before saying to her husband Decheng, "Your brother has a heart of gold."

"Hum. . . ." He was paying her little attention since he was calculating whether the presents and his expenditure balanced.

4

Soon after the wedding day, the young bride started to join the commune work. One day, after washing the dishes, she went off with the other women to a place beyond the mountain to cut grass for the pigs. As soon as she was out of the door, a woman nudged her. "What?" Fragrance asked.

"Look! What's he up to?"

Following the direction of her finger, Fragrance saw Deaf-mute gazing at a jacket of hers drying on a pole in front of the door. Staring a while, he turned away, then turned back again. The jacket was made of bright pink cloth with an apricot flower design. What was he looking at? Was it the brilliant colour, or the exquisite lace edging? Or did he associate it with her slim figure? Gracious! He had the nerve to stretch out his calloused hand to feel the shoulder and cuff.

The other women burst out laughing.

Unaware of their presence, Deaf-mute remained lost in his reverie.

Fragrance flushed, scolding, "Deaf-mute!" She decided to forget it, but on second thoughts, went towards him. "Go off and get the cow!" She slapped his hand away from her jacket. "Don't you understand? Go on, quick! You're grown-up now. You should know better."

Taken aback at seeing Fragrance and the others standing there, he blushed slightly, rubbed his hands in an embarrassed manner and tried to smile, but couldn't.

"Quick!" She chivvied him, her lips pursed, then took in her washing.

When she came out again, she saw Deaf-mute going off with two baskets hanging at either end of his shoulder-pole. Two women teased, "How is it that you're so pretty, Fragrance? Because you have such good looks even your clothes are attractive."

"Your clothes attract attention when you put them on. Even when drying outside, people fondle them. Soon they will be worn out." With this they laughed.

"Don't be silly!"

Brushing away a lock of hair, Fragrance lowered her head. She knew she was attractive from the looks in the eyes around her and from her reflection in the water, but that made her worried and cautious. She wished she wasn't a delicate flower but simply a leaf on a tree, not a beautiful cloud, but a transparent raindrop sinking into the parched soil. That silly deaf-mute! What was wrong with him at the moment, staring at her jacket and stroking it with his rough hand?

Fragrance would not go into Deaf-mute's room to sweep his floor as before. Instead, from that day on, she was more sober with him. Previously, she used to laugh when she saw his certificates and when she puzzled out his gestures. Her happy giggles were like the twitters of birds or like pearls dropping on a plate.

His conscience guilty, Deaf-mute didn't see her for a long time, and busied himself chopping sweet-potato vines, carrying water from the well, making straw sandals, repairing baskets and piling up firewood.

Shrewd as his brother Decheng was, he still didn't know what had happened at home. He gave Deaf-mute a cigarette and praised him, "Eh, you've been very diligent lately."

Fragrance didn't utter a sound while finishing the last stitch in a pair of shoes for Deaf-mute.

5

Paralleled by Decheng's increasing invective, the ultra-Left became more virulent than before. After the harvest, cart after cart of rice was sent to the state grain depot. The certificate awarded to the team tempted only children to look at it. But the peasants in the village, who owed too much to their team, could only heave deep sighs every day. And those who had earned sufficient workpoints could not be paid in cash. Consequently, quarrels about rations and living allowances took place. The new cadre from the county decided that the debtors must settle their accounts and, if necessary, their houses would have to be pulled down to pay their debts. This made the debtors furious but their creditors applauded the decision. Though most of the peasants and some of the team bosses shook their heads, the cadre insisted on his decision, so they could do nothing but puff away at their pipes.

Only when the day to demolish houses arrived did Deaf-mute learn of the decision. Usually he poked his nose into everything. When he saw the old cowherd beating his animals, he would complain to the team leader about it. Because of this, the cowherd's wife had unleashed a torrent of abuse. But today the tears the cowherd shed for his tile-roofed house moved him greatly. He strode boldly forward with a shoulder-pole in his hands to stop the team leader. Pointing to the house, he vehemently shook his fist at him. "*Ah, yi....*"

The man brushed him away and told his men to climb up on to the roof to begin the demolition.

His eyes wide, Deaf-mute ran after them.

The team leader gave him a bitter smile.

"*Ao, ao....*" The veins on his forehead standing out, he made signs to stop them, while his face flushed crimson with indignation. Some roared with laughter and others, seeing Deaf-mute take the lead, suggested, "As far as I'm concerned, we should stop. Don't pull it down."

"Spring is not the right time to sell grain; winter is not the right time to demolish houses. Don't be so merciless!" seconded another.

"Doing a good deed is worth more than praying ten years to God."

Only Decheng, representing the creditors, opposed them. He fidgeted with his tobacco pouch. "Not demolishing the house is all right," he smiled. "If only I could get payment from the team cashier. I can't work a whole year for nothing."

"I agree with him," another creditor chimed in. "I'm waiting for payment so I can treat my friends."

A heated dispute broke out.

A long time passed. Decheng had to bring the new cadre over and gave him a cigarette. The cadre pulled a long face saying that his decision must be carried out. The team leader patted Deaf-mute on the shoulder and pointed at the loud-speaker in the tree-top, meaning that it was an order from above, and that the house had to be pulled down. "Do you understand now? Go on, quickly!"

Amazed, Deaf-mute reacted as though cold water had been thrown over him. He indignantly stamped his foot and went home.

"Swine!" Decheng's face was livid with rage. "Where're you going? Well, you wait and see!"

Deaf-mute had never stayed away from work in his life, but this time was an exception, as he lay on his bed in broad daylight. Everyone knew that he was a partially disabled man and could sleep or take a rest any time he liked. There was no one who could complain, even the team leader had to let him alone. But Decheng hated him, for he had lost workpoints.

When lunchtime came, Decheng went to Deaf-mute's room and, yanking back the mosquito-net around his bed, snarled, "How have you got the nerve to at home. Come with me this afternoon to carry bricks."

Deaf-mute sat fidgeting with his *suona*.

"Aren't you listening to me?" Decheng snatched away the *suona* before going on, "Carry bricks, carry bricks...." He made a sign to him.

Deaf-mute blinked and lay on the bed with the floral quilt pulled over his head.

"Humph! Are you rolling in money? Or are you a cadre too? I won't let you eat for nothing."

Decheng managed his household strictly and had, particularly over the last two years, become more and more irritable.

6

At supper time, Deaf-mute got nothing to eat. I can't remember how many times he went hungry. On previous occasions, when he came back after helping others to do some work, he would be given little to eat. Then he would go to the mountain and bake chestnuts or gather melons to stave off his hunger. But now nothing was left there. Wandering in the fields, carrying his *suona*, he thought he would go to the team leader's home, since the man used to smile at him whenever they met. A long way in the distance, he saw his wife scrubbing out a pan — he knew that their family did not have enough food to eat either. Deaf-mute had no choice but to think again. Suddenly it struck him that the woman in charge of the pig farm must have gone home to eat and that there ought to be some of the pigs' sweet potatoes left over.

The gate was locked, but he still managed to get in. In the kitchen he found two little potatoes. Wiping them on his sleeve, he took a mouthful out of one. Pugh! Rotten.

"Deaf-mute's a thief! Stealing potatoes! A thief. . . ."

He didn't know where the children sprang from. At long last they had seized the opportunity to pay him back.

Flustered, he finished off the potatoes.

"Let's catch him and turn him in to the team," one of them suggested.

"Humph, he wants to get certificates, does he? This time he'll be paraded through the streets so others can see the phoney."

"Yes, we caught him in the act."

Deaf-mute put on a smiling face to play down the matter.

"No, no, nothing doing!" They had the upper hand now. "Go on, quickly!"

"Don't play any tricks on us!"

Several little hands dragged him out of the pig farm. Deaf-mute knew that he had got himself into trouble and kept signing to them, telling them they should not deal with him in this way. He would make each of them a bird cage.

"No, we don't want one."

Then he promised to make a fish trap for them.

"No!"

At last he gestured that he would play the *suona*.

The children gave in, saying, "That's a bit more like it. Go on then."

As he was blowing his *suona*, his belly shook, his cheeks blew up like balloons and saliva dribbled from the corners of his mouth. Perhaps he could still distinguish some sounds, or still retained some ability to sense rhythm. The sounds he made were like roosters crowing, ducks honking, dogs playing, or buffalos romping, or like the beating of gongs and drums when the villagers brought in the harvest.

"Wonderful, wonderful!" some of the children cheered.

"Nothing doing," one mischievous boy said, raising his little finger. "Blow your *suona* with your nose, your nose!"

Deaf-mute angrily shook his head.

"You must, you must...." With this, the children started kicking up a fuss. Some of them climbed on to his head, some held on to his jacket, another snatched away his instrument....

"*Aiya*...." Fragrance suddenly turned up, frowning at them. "You...." Pale with anger, she took him by the wrist and pulled him away like a child.

"Deaf-mute's a thief, a thief...." the children continued.

"Down with him. Admit your crime...." They mimicked what their fathers and brothers had shouted at struggle meetings.

"That's enough shouting, you boys." She turned and patted their heads. "The sun's setting. Be good boys. Go off home, all right?" She fished some fried beans out of her pocket to get rid of them.

Luckily, his brother was not in. Fragrance sat Deaf-mute in a chair in the kitchen, then brought him a basin of warm water so he could wash before eating. The food, pickled cabbage and a fried egg, were all brought to him by her delicate hands....

"*Ao, ao. . . .*" Deaf-mute tried to express his gratitude.

Fragrance didn't see him and crouched next to the stove poking the fire. After a long time had gone by, she heaved a deep sigh.

7

Deaf-mute saw his brother quarrelling with his sister-in-law. Angrily kicking over a chair, he held out his trembling fist and cursed, "You wasteful creature! You curry favour with him behind my back. . . ."

"So what? Do you want to beat me? Just you dare!" Fragrance wasn't cowed. She was given a blow on the ear. His brother had a reputation in the village for fighting with people. Several burly young men beaten up by him had had to receive medical treatment. Fragrance, weeping, dropped the vegetables, went inside, bundled up some clothes and walked out. What were they quarrelling about? Deaf-mute had a vague idea — it probably concerned him!

Full of remorse, Deaf-mute hid in a corner as if he had stolen silver at home, or gold that belonged to the team, or had done something very wrong. He regretted his action at the pig farm. Now great trouble had befallen his sister-in-law, and he repeatedly thumped his head with his fist.

The team leader and neighbours came to calm Decheng down. Slightly tipsy, the team leader went up to Deaf-mute, and made a series of signs, meaning, "Your brother has a bad temper. Don't work tomorrow. Take a bus to your sister-in-law's and fetch her back. Do you understand?"

Deaf-mute nodded.

He didn't get to sleep that night. Before daybreak he had put on his best outfit, brand-new blue suit and plimsolls, and set out with an umbrella under his arm. But on the way, he tripped over a stone and fell, the blood from his nose staining his cuff.

His sister-in-law was brought back with the help of the team leader.

However, his brother still had a long face. Deaf-mute tried to draw him out and make him smile at his wife. But all he could do was work. In winter, he wore only a lined jacket. He carried compost to spread on the vegetables in the garden, climbed up mountains to cut firewood, cleaned out the pigsty, and the chicken and duck coops. Finding droppings in a corner he would kneel down to clean the area carefully with a broken tile.

But troubles arrived one after another. He was about to carry compost to the vegetable garden when the new cadre brought some people to collect it. Their hens began to lay eggs when the cadre came to "collect" chickens and ducks.... Decheng could do nothing but force a smile. After they left, he flung curses behind their backs. To vent his anger, he often went out drinking. At home, he would kick over chairs and stools. Sometimes he blew his top over the smallest thing.

Now Deaf-mute hated not only himself, but also the new cadre. Whenever he saw him passing by in the fields, he would point at him with his little finger to express his indignation.

"You're pretty daring!" a fellow villager teased. "You pointed at the official with your little finger."

"Don't forget he's an activist — often been awarded certificates of merit just like you. Ha, ha. . . ."

Deaf-mute pouted and snorted.

He was determined to make the new cadre lose face. Soon people found the names of the cadre and the team scratched off of the red honour roll pasted on the wall. Of course, everyone knew who had done it, but nobody could prevent his arriving at such a "verdict". Even the cadre himself could only smile bitterly.

He hadn't attended mass meetings for a long time. In the past, he would go whenever there was something lively, and mingle with the children, tooting his *suona*. Although there were lots of deafening firecrackers, gaily-coloured bunting and streamers and slogans everywhere, and a new gadget for broadcasting opera arias, the villagers missed his smiling face and the clear strains of his *suona*.

8

The cold brook flowing in front of their gate grew warm again, and its turbid waters became clear. The crops in the fields were harvested season by season. The peasants in the mountain village experienced dramatic changes. After the fall of the "gang of four", the chalk slogans on the walls became blurred. People began to visit one another to talk about the new policy of fixing farm output quotas for each production group, which had already been put into effect in the village beyond the mountain. Traditional operas were staged again in the county town and some families made a good profit on their private businesses. Though there were fewer peasants in the fields, the vegetable trellises were better and the rows of seedlings longer than ever. And there were no weeds to be found on the ridges and slopes. Decheng was naturally very busy too. It was said that at first he felt slightly nervous when he took his capsicums to the free market to sell, but gradually he became ambitious and aggressive. With his friends he went to Hubei to sell tea and to Guangdong to sell fish fry. Coming back, he was all smiles and talked about this and that happening in other provinces. After a meal and tea, he was often surrounded by admirers. Instead of the title "Brother Decheng", he was now addressed as "Uncle Decheng", though he hadn't changed at all.

Both poverty and wealth can help an evil seed to grow. As he rapidly became richer, Decheng would often pace up and down the room with his chest held out and his hands behind his back. When meeting old friends on the road, he would cut them dead or put on airs. "Hey, your next litter of piglets will be mine. Don't sell them to anyone else." "Huh, you old cowherd, you've got a cheek borrowing money from me! Do you still remember what bank-notes look like? Are they round or square?"

Some people dared not offend him, because this former butcher was resourceful. Several bottles of fine wine were offered to an organization and he was able to get a lot of sought-after goods. Furthermore, he was planning to open a shop and also pool money with his friends to buy a truck and start a transportation service.

The wealth Decheng attained didn't bring the family any comfort and happiness. Deaf-mute found his brother always scowling at his sister-in-law. She grew thinner and seldom smiled. It seemed to Deaf-mute that she had tried her best to please her husband. Under her care, every pig in the sty was fat. Vegetables in the garden behind the house were thriving and there was not a weed in sight. A clever woman, she could do any kind of work in the field. She was warm-hearted and hospitable to her neighbours too. She bustled in and out all day long, and never stopped for a moment. Everything she did was admired by the villagers. But Decheng still looked surly.

One evening when Decheng was having his rice, he suddenly slammed his bowl down on the table, complaining, "What is this? Taste it!"

Pale with fright, she quickly did so. "I'm sorry, I put a little too much water in the pot."

"God dammit! You can't even cook well. What can you do? I told you to collect debts, but you say you're soft-hearted. I told you to go and work in the fields, but you can't fight for a good job. You're a real sow, damn you!"

"I'll go and make some more," she said timidly.

"Make some more? What, so I have to wait until tomorrow morning? Don't you know I'm going to the brigade headquarters to see the opera?"

Decheng, tired of waiting, took up the rice again. He ate half of it and tossed his chopsticks on the table. Throwing the bowl on the floor, he swore and went out, carrying an electric torch. A few chickens ran in and pecked at the scattered rice.

Fragrance was frightened into silence for a long while before she stooped to pick up the broken bowl. Deaf-mute saw that when she picked up the last fragment, tears dropped on to the back of her hand.

The mountain village hadn't seen traditional operas

for ages.   This time the biggest troupe in the county had come to perform in the brigade, thanks to the brigade cadres who had sent people to help them transport their costumes and props. Their drums and gongs made an ear-splitting din. Beneath the makeshift stage of planks and door slats, vendors sold melon seeds and sweetmeats. For them it was a treat just to squeeze through the crowds, let alone sit and watch the opera. Deafmute, however, didn't show up that day. He unobtrusively slipped into the kitchen to find Fragrance sitting staring blankly by the stove.   The flames danced on her face.   He wrung his hands wondering what he could do to comfort her.   He poured her a cup of tea and placed two sweets next to it. They had been given him by the team leader the previous day, and he hated to eat them himself.

Fragrance didn't want to drink. Taking the cup, her trembling hand spilt most of it.

What a pity! Deaf-mute wished he could scoop up the spilt tea. Why didn't she drink it? Tears were coursing down her cheeks.

"*Ao, ao....*" He thought that he must have done something wrong. The only remedy was to take out his *suona* and blow it. His tempo was first brisk, then slow. Through it, he expressed his love for sunlight, a happy life, their forefathers, their children, the old mountains and the fields they had ploughed for generations. The notes he made could be likened to scarlet strawberries on the mountains — sweet and sour.

Why was she so pale, so excited, trying to keep away from him? "Don't play any more," she begged. "Go to see the opera, will you? Don't play any more, I want to boil some water...."

But Deaf-mute kept on playing.

"Don't play any more!" Fragrance, irritated, stood up and glared at him. Deaf-mute was disappointed. He moved back. When he was nearing the door, Fragrance, saddened, unthinkingly threw her hand out and grasped his. "No, you can't leave me, you can't!"

The *suona* dropped to the floor.

Fragrance bit her lips, and finally burst into tears. "It's fate, fate!" she cried, heartbroken. "You don't know how much your brother hates me, dislikes me and beats me. Look here, and here. . . ." She showed him her hands, then unbuttoned her collar to display bruises on her shoulders. "He closes the door first, so nobody will hear. He says that I can't manage the household well and calls me a wild beast. . . ."

Deaf-mute was astonished at the bruises.

"I thought he would treat me better if I gave him a child. But unfortunately I didn't. I must have done something evil in a previous existence, otherwise, why have I been so severely punished by Heaven? Some women are a lot uglier or poorer than me, but they have children. I haven't, though I've taken a lot of medicine and burned bundles of incense praying to Heaven. What should I do? When will things get better? . . ."

"*Wu . . . wu . . .*" Deaf-mute tried to comfort her.

"I know I'm fated to suffer. During my childhood, my parents were disgusted with me because I was a girl. I followed behind my sister begging for porridge from door to door. But the porridge we got was rotten. I didn't like it. All I could do was cry. Then I came here. Although I've worn myself out, I still can't please your brother. In the bitter cold winter, I had a back-ache, but I still had to carry water and wash clothes. The water was freezing cold, and my hands felt as if they had been cut by a knife. I squatted down by the pond washing and washing, and fainted several times. You never knew about that, did you?"

She buried her face in her hands, forgetting that the listener was a deaf-mute. To whom could she complain about her fate? To whom could she cry over her misfortune? Where would her hot tears flow? All of a sudden, a drop of cold water fell on her hand. She lifted her head to see tears welling up in his eyes. He really could understand, she thought. "*Wu....*" the rasping sounds coming from his throat were like the moaning of a mountain.

They stopped crying, and sitting by the fire stared at each other, like two separate mountains whose feelings had been joined.

Suddenly Fragrance fainted.

9

Deaf-mute anxiously helped her to the bed and took off her shoes and apron. He felt her forehead, which was burning hot. Then he hurried off and banged at the neighbour's door. An old woman emerged grumbling. When she was taken in and felt Fragrance's forehead, she was alarmed. "Goodness! She's extremely ill, why don't you send for the doctor?"

Carrying a lantern, someone went to fetch the doctor, while Deaf-mute was sent to find Decheng. A kettle of water was boiled. The footsteps from the direction of the performance were first continuous, then sporadic. But Decheng had still not shown up. Where was he? Deaf-mute knocked at the team leader's door, and after they had exchanged a series of signs, they made their way to the edge of the village.

Outside a young widow's house, they overheard laughter and smelt liquor. Peeping through a crack in the door, Deaf-mute saw his brother's large head. Beside him was a man and on the table were winecups. Someone was dealing cards and the hostess was laughing.

Walking in, he patted Decheng on his shoulder, pointed outside and signalled to him that his wife had fallen ill.

Decheng flung a card on the table and spat out a cigarette end, "What did you come here for, fool," he barked.

"*Ao, ao....*" Deaf-mute pointed outside once more.

"Dammit! You must have gone off your head!"

At this the team leader went up to him, "Don't play any more, Decheng. Your wife's fallen seriously ill. I'm afraid she had to be rushed to hospital."

Decheng's heart missed a beat. "Goddam! What lousy luck! Well, you go on back first. I'll be on my way soon." With this he flung down another card and, giving the table a hard thump, barked again, "Trumps! This time you definitely have to drink as a penalty."

"Decheng...." The hostess saw the team leader's expression.

"Go on...." He took no notice of her warning. "It's just her old trouble. She won't snuff it yet." He watched his cards.

Suddenly, Deaf-mute, who had been standing next to his brother all this time, gave the chair a violent pull and Decheng slumped to the ground. Before he knew what had happened, Deaf-mute had yanked the table and the cards and winecups were all dashed to the floor. The hostess screamed in fear.

"You!" At last Decheng recovered from his stupefaction. "You bastard! You're asking for a beating, aren't you?"

Deaf-mute stood firmly, glaring at him.

"I. . . ." A hand on his backside, Decheng staggered to his feet, looking 'ound. He grabbed a shoulder-pole and struck at his brother, but was stopped by the team leader, who snatched it away. Decheng shook off the team leader and flung out his fist to punch Deaf-mute.

Suddenly Decheng yelled. His hand had been bitten by his brother.

"Damn!" With difficulty, he got away. Before he could stand steady, however, Deaf-mute threw a teacup at his brother which hit him on the forehead. Blood immediately ran down his face.

People in the room began trying to calm Deaf-mute down.

As though becoming hysterical, Deaf-mute moved to pick up the barrow near the wall, his eyes blazing. But he didn't throw it after all. He just stood there holding it, his lips trembling. How badly he wanted to speak, to explain his anger. But he couldn't, though reason judgements, truth, principles and laws welled up in his heart.

"You hit me! You wait, you animal!" His brother's voice followed him as he went out.

Outside the door a dog was barking.

10

After the fierce fight, both of them were criticized by the security section of the brigade. As a result, the family broke up and lived apart. Deaf-mute was allowed to take two boxes and a bed. The villagers said that Decheng was too mean. He reiterated that it was he who had brought Deaf-mute up since their parents died. And he had refused to give a hand when the new cadre gave instructions to pull down the old cowherd's house, from which he could have been paid for his workpoints. To crown it all, he had spent a lot to heal the wound on his forehead.... "What? You say I've taken advantage of him? Well, he and I live apart now. I hope he makes a fortune, makes a fortune...."

The team felt it was impossible to mediate between them.

As he had nowhere to live, Deaf-mute had to lodge at one of the team's rooms. The team leader and some kind-hearted villagers gave him a table, some chairs and household utensils. And they lent him two piles of bricks to help him build a house after autumn. Now that the free markets were brisk, he would be able to get some money from the cashier if he needed to. But he still didn't manage too well. Without Fragrance, his clothes became tattered and dirty.

Decheng's home was not far from the house where Deaf-mute lived. Fragrance went to see him several times. Each time she sent him some glutinous rice and a pair of new shoes, she was ruthlessly beaten by her husband afterwards. Then Decheng would pour forth a stream of coarse invective, implying that she was unfaithful. He knew his doubts were groundless, but it helped him to take out his venom on her. Some of the women began to gossip about Fragrance, who wasn't afraid of cruelty but did fear rumours. She secretly made a new suit and another pair of shoes, but took them apart again.

Near the house where Deaf-mute lived was a lotus pond. Fragrance was often seen to go out of her way to wash clothes there. And on each occasion she would spend a lot of time on her laundry. Amid the raucous, mocking laughter of the women around her, she knelt on a stone slab with her head bent over her old pink jacket. The jacket with the apricot design was kneaded again and again on the stone until its colour faded. The fresh water squeezed out of it flowed back into the pond, in which the reflection of a woman staring woodenly scattered itself in various directions and then reformed again. What was she gazing at?

The following year, she didn't go there to wash her clothes. She had decided to divorce her husband. On the day she was leaving, the women villagers came to see her off. On such occasions, they sniffed and their eyes moistened with tears. Even the mischievous young boys behaved properly. Her hair had been carefully combed that day. She said not a word until she made a bow to the women and then asked the team leader, "Where's Deqi?"

Deaf-mute's real name was seldom used, but now she did so calmly, as if relieved of a heavy burden.

The team leader hesitated.

"Where's Deqi?" she asked again, in a louder voice, her eyes moist.

The team leader hurriedly looked around.

Smoothing her jacket, she walked towards the team house. The pink jacket she had on that day was worn out, but well-mended and clean, and had an aroma of fresh water and sunlight. Step by step she crossed the ditch, the hill and the threshing ground, until the small window of the house came into view. "Deqi, I'm coming to say goodbye to you. Why didn't you come out to meet me? Do you want to keep away from me? Or do you blame me for not looking after you?"

There wasn't a soul in the room.

The team leader hurried to the upper terrace to call, "Have you seen Deqi?"

The people about him chimed in, "Have you seen Deqi?"

"Have you seen Deqi?"

The question echoed in the mountains.

They called out for a long while but in vain. Fragrance's lips trembled with disappointment. After a pause, she went up to the team leader and asked him to look after Deqi. "His nose is apt to bleed. On hot days, don't let him be out in the sun too long. He loves to eat buns. After harvest, please give him more glutinous rice. And that padded coat of his is worn out. I would have made him a new one, but it's too late now. When autumn sets in, please ask a tailor to make one for him. . . ."

"Yes, I will, I will. . . ." The team leader nodded.

"He likes drinking cold water while he's working in the fields. Don't let him. And he likes sleeping on the threshing ground at night in summer. Don't let him do that either, will you."

"All right. . . ." The team leader's voice grew hoarse.

"He is meddlesome and often offends people. In fact, he's like that for the sake of the team, for the sake of the village. Please don't hold it against him, will you."

"You. . . ." The team leader's eyes filled with tears, while some of the women near him were openly sobbing.

Imperturbably calm, she passed her hand over her hair before going on, "As for Decheng, I hate him. He was kinder to me before. It's only recently that he's changed. Perhaps he'll change back again in future. I hope all of you advise him: If he takes a wife again, tell him to take back his brother. With a new sister-in-law managing the household, they'll get along alright."

The team leader was choked with sobs, and tears coursed down the children's faces. "Aunty!" They held on to her jacket, begging, "Don't go away, don't. . . ."

"If you leave us, we'll miss you," a boy said.

"Why do you want to go?" another protested. "Aren't our mountains green? Isn't our water sweet? Aren't the chirps of birds here cheerful? Is it because the flowers here aren't beautiful? . . ."

Fragrance squatted down to stroke the boy's head and set her cheek against his, her eyes moist with tears, "Oh yes, my little one! The mountains here are green, the water is sweet, the chirps of the birds here are cheerful and the flowers beautiful. I'm going to leave you, and I'll always remember you. It's because I have no choice but. . . ."

"Aunty, will you come back to see us?" the children asked, holding on to the hem of her jacket.

"Of course, of course." Fragrance turned up her skirt to wipe away her tears. "Do what your parents say and work hard, will you? And I beg you all not to bother Uncle Deqi again."

"No, never, never," they replied. "We'll give him good food to eat, and give him good toys to play with. . . ."

"Good . . . good!"

Finally, holding two boys in her arms, she cried out loud. She cried not because she felt grief, but because she was reluctant to part with those barefooted, dirty-nosed children. She was grateful to them for their promises. She would have given her own life to ensure they would never go hungry, nor suffer from cold. . . .

And so, Fragrance left.

Taking the cool, clean and winding flagstone road, she headed towards the entrance to the village. Her shadow grew smaller and smaller and then became a black dot. At the end of the road the black dot halted. No one knew whether she was going ahead or whether she had stopped to look back.

At length, the black dot vanished. Everything under the sky remained the same as before: Green and yellow mountains overlapped one another. The dim edges skirting the mountain terraces were like wrinkles on the forehead of a brooding old man.

Deaf-mute was nowhere to be found.

In the evening, he returned from the mountain with a bundle of firewood on his back, then took up his *suona* and blew in the direction of the window overlooking the lotus pond. He blew until his mouth was dry, his lips were swollen and the sound died away. His cheeks remained a little distended. Perhaps he thought his *suona* was still emitting a sound. His face was sallow and calm. Like a wild animal after a fierce battle, he returned to his den to rest. Like a crag after torrential rainfall, he recovered his serenity.

He fell ill and everyone in the village was worried about him. The brigade Party secretary, the team leader and all his neighbours came to see him. The children came too and stuffed chestnuts and sweet potatoes into his hands. Even Decheng put in an appearance, bringing him two catties of sugar, some liver and a reprimand. His table was cluttered with eggs, glutinous rice, dates and cured fish. Deaf-mute, tears in his eyes, touched none of them. Some said that he had been possessed.

II

As a matter of fact I had not been particularly close to Deaf-mute and wondered whether it was worthwhile including him in my story. I decided to go back and see him again.

When I got to Wu Village, I could hardly recognize it. Here and there new houses had been put up. A number of people had wrist watches. All of them looked healthy and cheerful. But when asked about Deqi, their faces immediately clouded over. He had never recovered from his illness; and had recklessly thrown himself into hard work. Perhaps he wanted to wash away his memories with sweat. One day while pushing a cartful of stones up a dike, he slipped and fell down the slope. Hundreds of catties of stone spilled over....

Even today people still mention Fragrance and Deaf-mute. Every time they plough paddy fields, extract oil, or build houses, they think of Deaf-mute's miserable life.

"*Ai!* He was a good boy," an old man said sighing.

"Good people don't always live long. What a pity!"

"His good deeds were known to everyone. Even the King of Hell has got to grant him that." This was the sort of chatter to be heard by the stove in winter while people were having their ginger tea.

People used to speak of Decheng too. After he took a new wife, he was constantly at loggerheads with her. Because of his smuggling, he was fined by the government, and he was often a target of criticism behind his back.

The day his new house was completed, the team should have pooled some money and invited an opera troupe to celebrate. But nobody in the village stirred that day. Afraid to lose face, Decheng preferred to pay the cost of the opera himself and provide the villagers with wine, meat and cigarettes. He would not bother people about erecting a stage. All this, however, had no effect. He could only celebrate without the opera. He set up a few tables and begged people to go to have dinner at his home. Finding me, he said humbly, "Please come and have a simple meal with me, will you?" With this he gave me a cigarette and lit it. "Because you are a distinguished guest. . . ."

I smoked his cigarette but didn't go to his home, and neither did the villagers. I saw him standing embarrassed before people's critical eyes. Was he worried? I hope eyes like that may be seen everywhere.

The *suona* sounded again. It was blown by a boy who could not play it in tune; it sounded just like a crying baby. Verdigris had formed on this *suona* deserted by its owner.

The *suona* trumpet! It made my mind wander again.

Had it happened yesterday? Or the day before yesterday? Like a guard, Deqi sat at my door to stop the children from entering, in case they should interrupt my study. Sitting there, it seemed as though he wanted to have a chat, but was afraid to disturb me. At length, he shook his head and nudged me, rubbing his hands to indicate that he wanted to treat me to meat dumplings, then slowly went away. He had intended to "talk" to me and make friends with me, a cadre from outside the village. I should have "talked" to him, even if it was about "nonsense". At least it would have warmed his lonely heart. But I didn't do that. Was it because I was busy, or had nothing to say to him? Or perhaps because I had been bored by his naive hospitality.

Today I would like to, but I can't. He has melted into the green mountains and no longer has anything to do with me. Fate, in fact, placed us in two different dimensions. However, I still remember those days and nights. For the rest of my life they will help me to understand poverty and wealth, to understand how to defy oppression. And they will remind me each dawn of the goodness and beauty which, like eternal starlight, shines over men and which, through the darkness, points to a splendid future.

Only after excitement has settled can a person's mind become clear and peaceful. The wind from the mountain moans again, and the fog creeps in. The chugging noise from the oil press is punctuated by the sporadic barking of dogs. And the water flowing over the ridge opposite my door gurgles as before. The bright moon in the sky reminds me of a place a long way away. Is it even on the same planet? Beneath the neon lights shiny sedans swish past and crowds of people jostle like whirlpools amidst the noise. There are people everywhere. . . .

I feel that I must lead a proper life.

Translated by Song Shouquan

Han Shaogong was born in Changsha, Hunan in 1953. After graduating from junior middle school, he worked as a farm labourer in Miluo County. In 1974 he was transferred to work at a local cultural centre where he began writing short stories and collaborated with a friend on a biography of the veteran Communist leader Ren Bishi. In 1978 he became a student in the Chinese language department of Hunan Teachers College. "Deaf-mute and His 'Suona'" has been adapted as a film.

In 1979 Han became a member of the Chinese Writers' Association. He is also a council member of its Hunan branch and a committee member of the provincial Federation of Literary and Art Circles and now works as an editor in the provincial Trade Union Federation.

A Summer Experience

Ge Wujue

I was thirty-two on my last birthday. This all happened during summer. Since then I have often felt as though I have been in a sort of trance, a strange sensation lingering in my mind — sweetness, bitterness, sourness? ...

There are two people in my family — Sha Sha, my four-year-old daughter and myself. Last spring I was able to get a three-room suite with a balcony front and rear. Then I began to understand that being a member of the Provincial Overseas Chinese Association was not merely an empty title.

But the spacious rooms brought inconvenience too. I have to spend a lot of time and energy looking after them. In the past I had only one room twelve square metres in size and could clean it easily just by standing in the middle and turning around. Also the new place is a long way from the kindergarten Sha Sha attends every day. When I go to fetch her, I have to change buses twice. But it's the best kindergarten in the city and thanks to my status as an overseas Chinese I can send Sha Sha there. The third inconvenience is having a female visitor by the name of Yang Na, whom I first met by chance at a friend's house. After I moved she came around to have a look and since then has been a frequent visitor. Perhaps this shouldn't be considered an inconvenience.

Yang Na is very beautiful.

My ex-wife was also very beautiful. I remember being in a park once and seeing a young couple hand in hand, shoulder to shoulder, posing for a picture. The young girl was rather ugly and the young man thin and short. But I was touched by the scene, and even thought that real love perhaps only existed between ugly couples. She Sha's mother always used to hum her favourite song, "Love is like a wanderer, or a bird flying free in the sky." She used to think that this song from an Indian film was from *Carmen*. A year ago, when we left the Civil Affairs Bureau after finalizing our divorce, she turned and asked me with a smile, "Will you buy me a pair of brown boots as a memento? They've just come in. We'll never go shopping together again." As the department store was opposite the bureau, I complied with her request.

I was only thirty-two, but in matters of love I had already proved myself something of a pessimist. Sports competitions are real games which can be judged by marks, and in seconds or millimetres. But love is the product of ignorance and impetuous emotion. Now you can add money, overseas connections and housing to that. I decided to remain unmarried, rejecting anyone who was recommended by others or who introduced herself. Of course I had dropped large hints about this to Yang Na.

Yang Na was an elegant young woman, who would tilt her head slightly backwards when she looked at me. Then she would smile and appealing lines would appear at the corners of her mouth. "You've been unlucky," she said.

No, I'd prefer to say that I managed to escape my bad luck. Yang Na's eyebrows had been carefully plucked into fine and delicate lines. I hoped she hadn't come to bring me more bad luck.

2

Since I was a basketball coach for the provincial team and my timetable was determined by the training schedule, I was often the last parent to fetch my daughter at the kindergarten.

One windy day, the sort that is quite common in north China in May, our training session ended early. When I got to the kindergarten, the children had just finished their dinner and were playing in the courtyard, their eyes glued to the front door. Once the parents arrived, the place exploded with joyful noises.

Sha Sha wasn't in the playground so I went to the third grade classroom where the children were gathered around in a circle singing and dancing.

> Little friends, clap your hands
> And follow one by one.
> Don't talk, don't turn
> Just circle round and round, like a rubber ball.

"Sha Sha, here comes your father." The young teacher playing with the children called out in a low voice. I hadn't seen her before. Perhaps she was new.

Turning her head Sha Sha walked straight through the circle and threw the dancing group into disorder.

Without saying a word, she gave me her hand and I led her out of the classroom.

"Mr Wang! Mr Wang! Please hold on a minute," the young teacher called out. "Sha Sha's dress should be mended. Would you ask her mother to do it?"

"All right, all right," I muttered.

"I don't have a mother. Daddy and Mummy are divorced," offered Sha Sha.

My daughter was only telling the truth. But she had put me in an awkward position.

"Oh, I'm sorry! I didn't know. I've only been with this class for a little while." The teacher blushed and looked even more uncomfortable than I did.

"That's all right. I'll mend it. I'm afraid I'm too careless," I tried to comfort her.

On the bus home I asked Sha Sha, "What's your new teacher's name?"

She shrugged her shoulders.

Sha Sha's teacher couldn't be called beautiful. Her eyes weren't large, her forehead was narrow, and she was a little heavy by current standards. Her mouth was somewhat large too, but she had a small exquisite nose and moved very gracefully when she ran. She would race in and out of the classroom and I couldn't help thinking that with her long legs she could, with some coaching, hit the 12.5-second record for the 100-metre dash.

Back home, after putting the rice on the stove, I started mending the clothes. Sha Sha sat on a small stool preparing shallots which made her eyes water. I heard footsteps on the stairs. I knew that it was Yang Na and immediately put the clothes away. I was afraid she would take a look at them and repeat in that affected manner (who knows whether she meant it or not), "Hey, you really are unlucky!"

Yang Na was standing at the door smiling. She wore a pair of white high-heeled shoes and a white sweater with a blue brooch. Her skirt was made of black velvet with a gold-coloured trim. Her dark, long hair hung loose, fastened together with a large white clip. She had bright eyes and ivory white skin. She was really a beauty and she knew it. Perhaps my expression told her. At any rate her face was glowing with health and she was brimming with confidence.

Waving her artificial crocodile handbag, Yang Na made a mock bow and said with a smile, "Here I am again."

"Come in."

She went into the frontroom ahead of me and took some attractively packaged chocolates from her handbag.

"This is a birthday present for Sha Sha. They're made in Switzerland."

"But Sha Sha's birthday's on the sixteenth of next month. It's still a whole month away," I said.

"Really?" she laughed. Her frequent laughter seemed slightly unnatural, designed only to create an effect. She could start and stop at will. "Then I'll have to come over again next month. Every time I come here I have to rack my brains to find an excuse. You really are impossible!"

She sat down gracefully.

"You really ought to buy a suite of furniture with your overseas remittance certificates. I'd like to advise you on what to get."

I headed her off with a vague reply, "Some other time."

"When? When you invite me to your wedding?" She started laughing again.

The joke annoyed me. Just then I heard the water boiling. "I'll go and cook. Do you mind if I leave you by yourself for a while?"

"Go ahead." She stood up and walked over to the balcony. I didn't like her standing there where she could be seen from outside.

"Would you like to listen to some new tape? One is by that famous Japanese singer, Yamaguchi Momoe."

She turned on the tape-recorder, but then suddenly said, "I'll do the cooking. I'll make something really nice. Have you got some slippers? I like to change out of these shoes."

Wearing my slippers, walking about the place as though she owned it, what did it all mean?

"I was just going to make some noodles and eggs. It's easy enough."

"Oh, you really are unlucky!" Heaving a sigh, she picked up a rattan chair, and walked over to the balcony.

3

Sha Sha was a slightly eccentric child who had been brought up in the shadow of family quarrels. When she was a year old, it was I who had looked after her, coaxing her to go to sleep. "That's a good girl. Don't cry, don't cry. Your mummy has gone out dancing." When she grew up, she often heard her mother say, "Go away! Go and see your 'darling' daddy!" or from me, "Go and get your mother!" Sha Sha had a fierce temper. Whenever she was in a bad mood she would shriek whether we had guests or not. When she was only two she already knew how to register her complaints by breaking things. Her mother and I were surprised when we saw her do it the first time, but what could we say — she was only imitating us.

We had been divorced a year. It frightened me that Sha Sha never once asked for her mother. Somewhere, there was a murky area in her mind, a very profound recess indeed. Sometimes when I woke up during the middle of the night, I would look at the plump child asleep beside me and feel guilty. It wasn't her fault — it was the two of us who were to blame.

Then one day, probably about half a month after I first talked with the new teacher, I once again arrived late to fetch Sha Sha. I'd bought a red balloon on the way.

"Sha Sha, look at the balloon. Isn't it wonderful?" I tried to interest her.

Sha Sha, pulling a long face, didn't pay much attention, but the teacher took the balloon and asked, "Can it fly all the way up to the sky?"

I thought the teacher seemed more childlike than the child.

"Yes," I said.

"Sha Sha here, hold it." The teacher wound the string around Sha Sha's finger. "Don't you like it?"

"Thank you, Daddy." Sha Sha looked up at me. She seemed more concerned about saying this than in watching the balloon.

I felt a slight tugging at my heart, moved by these very ordinary words. My daughter had now started to learn manners. In the past she had been unconcerned about courtesy. She had seemed to be indifferent to any toys I bought her too, and sometimes even threw them away.

I wanted to kiss her, but the teacher was one step ahead of me. She hugged Sha Sha, kissed her, and said, "Sha Sha, that's a good girl. You really are a clever girl."

From that moment on I began to like Sha Sha's teacher.

I am a rather careless father. Once I found a button on Sha Sha's clothing that had been replaced by some-one else and another time I found that the elastic band in her sleeve had been renewed. And so I knew that Sha Sha had a good, dedicated teacher. However, a special reflex activated by Yang Na's visits warned me to be on the alert.

That day the training was longer than usual and the water had stopped while I was taking a bath, so I was an hour late when I went to the kindergarten to fetch Sha Sha. Only Sha Sha and her teacher were in the classroom. They sat facing each other on stools, sing-ing children's songs and clapping hands:

Row, row, row the boat,
Row to Granny's bridge.
I don't cry, I'm not naughty,
Granny calls me her little darling.

Intrigued I stood by the window watching them.

Sha Sha sat upright, saying, "Teacher, do you know my granny?"

The young teacher answered, "No, I don't. Does she love you?"

Sha Sha said, "Yes, she does.   She lives in America.
See my shoes.   Granny bought them for me."

Sha Sha raised one foot and then the other.   As I
entered the classroom, she jumped up immediately, and
the teacher helped her to straighten out her clothes.

I apologized, "I am very sorry to have kept you waiting for so long."

The teacher just smiled and asked, "Where do you
live?"

"South Zhongshan Street."

"That's convenient.   My family live there too.   You
have to go out of your way to get here from the sports
association.   It'd be better for me to bring Sha Sha
home."

I politely refused, not so much from worrying about
inconveniencing her, as from worrying about bringing
myself more trouble — that special reflex had put me on
guard.

"The buses are too crowded to take a child on.   I'll
come earlier next time.   But thank you very much."

Sha Sha clapped her hands, shouting, "Daddy can say
'thank you' too." We all laughed and the tense atmosphere relaxed.

Although I had rejected her offer she still called on
me a little while later.

Sha Sha had tonsillitis and couldn't go to kindergarten.   The next day there was an unexpected knock at
the door.   It was the teacher.

My place was in a mess.   The bed wasn't made,
dishes were unwashed, there was a mop in the centre of
the room and clothes thrown on chairs.   I had never
been much good at doing housework.

Sha Sha's teacher seemed not to notice that I had

such a fine flat with modern facilities. She asked quickly, "How is Sha Sha?"

"She's still sick. She has a temperature of thirty-nine degrees."

"Teacher! Teacher!" hearing her voice Sha Sha shouted out.

She quickly made for Sha Sha's room. Sha Sha welcomed her warmly. She kissed the child's forehead and said, "You're quite hot, just like a little fireball."

Sha Sha asked, "What did you bring me?"

What a child — asking for things!

The teacher fished out a sopping wet plastic bag from her multi-coloured satchel.

Sha Sha asked, "What's that?"

"My swimsuit." She put it aside and took out a batch of white papers, saying, "These are for you. Do you know what they are?"

"White papers." Sha Sha took the papers, staring at them disappointedly.

"You're wrong. There's a little dog, that's a little boat. This is a frog and that's a camel. This one is an old hunchback.... You just hold them for me." She was skilled at folding the paper into different shapes and gradually she spread them out over the bed.

Having set my mind at rest I went to turn on the television. Tonight was a video relay of the basketball final between the U.S.S.R. and the U.S. from the World Student Games. Since basketball was my job I needed to watch it.

After a while the teacher came in and asked, "Mr Wang, do you have any mung beans?"

I had more than ten tins of green soya beans but no mung beans. "No, I haven't," I answered.

"Well, do you have a saucepan?"

"Yes, in the kitchen. What a great shot!" I didn't want to move from the TV. The American No. 11 had just made a beautiful backhand shot. It took a strong player with several years' hard training to do that! Now he made another block and then, dribbling behind his back, he moved to shoot again.

"Teacher!" Sha Sha shouted from her room.

"I'm coming," she answered cheerfully. She was standing right behind me, fascinated by the game. Hearing Sha Sha call she smiled. "I've brought some mung beans. Sha Sha likes mung bean puree. Where's your saucepan?" I ran to the kitchen and handed her the pan and hurried back to the TV. "It's not the best time for Sha Sha to get sick," she chortled.

While the puree was boiling, the teacher wandered about, comforting Sha Sha and occasionally watching the television. My flat was full of the sound of her busy footsteps and warm laughter.

The American team won. Sha Sha had finished the mung bean puree and had fallen asleep. I discovered that the teacher had also tidied up my rooms. Now she was about to leave. Suddenly I realized I didn't even know her name.

"What's your name?"

"Call me Meiqing," she answered with a smile.

Sometimes you feel perfectly relaxed, perhaps from drinking good wine, from listening to good music, or watching a good film. Tonight, I'd enjoyed the best-played basketball game I'd ever seen. I asked the teacher, "What do you think of this television?" By this question I was just showing off because I was in such a good mood.

"It's very nice. After watching a colour TV no one likes black-and-white. Was it expensive?"

I told her the price. She was astonished, "That's a lot! Unless I got a raise, it would take me five years of saving my whole salary to buy one." She laughed again and I thought how pleasant she was. "I'm on my way now. I'll come over tomorrow night."

"I'm sorry to have troubled you." Having said this I immediately regretted it. From then on I didn't really give it much more thought.

The next day I tidied up, then bought five ice-lollies to make ice cream the way Yang Na had taught me.

The red and green traffic lights were glittering one after another and the evening streets were bustling with noise and excitement. In the distance I saw Meiqing turning a corner at a good pace, her vigorous, lithe strides bathed in the bright lights.

4

In the end I decided that whenever my training finished late, I would ask her to bring Sha Sha home. I used to stand on the balcony waiting for them, waiting to see Meiqing holding Sha Sha's hand as they turned the corner. A little later on I changed my routine. In the past, I used to ring up the kindergarten if I had time to go and fetch Sha Sha. Now I hardly ever rang, and instead waited for them on the balcony every evening.

And now a new problem vexed me; that of whether I should give a key to Meiqing or not. It was a serious decision.

Yang Na still came to my place once or twice a week.

She hadn't met Meiqing yet because Meiqing only saw Sha Sha to the stairs and didn't come in. She was reserved and seemed only to be interested in her work.

One rainy day my department held a long meeting to discuss our training programme before going abroad. Afterwards I raced home to find Meiqing teaching Sha Sha to sing. "Come on, let's sing it again:

"Little alarm clock, ding-a-ling-a-ling,
Our little room, silent, silent and silent."

The two, their clothes drenched, sat by the front door. Meiqing cuddled Sha Sha and held her small hand to beat time. They only noticed me when I stood directly in front of them.

Meiqing rose to her feet quickly, smoothing out her wet dress. She had a nice figure, full and athletic, like a professional swimmer.

"Sha Sha, your daddy's here."

Sha Sha's eyes narrowed in annoyance.

"We've been waiting ages for you. We're both nearly frozen to death." The tense atmosphere was dispersed by the frank, light tone of Meiqing's complaint. She was someone who treated even hardships and difficulties as jokes. I saw that her lips had turned purple from the cold.

As I took Sha Sha in my arms, her small hands were like ice. I then let slip what I had previously been reluctant to say, "Meiqing, I think I'd better give you a key."

She laughed, "How can you do that? I can't pay for any losses. If something in your place got stolen, I couldn't possibly pay for it. My wages wouldn't cover anything like that."

She meant what she said. There was something both naive and charming in the way she spoke. She said goodbye and quickly ran downstairs, seeming almost afraid that she might have to make a decision which would affect the rest of her life. There was obviously something on her mind.

From the corridor came the sound of footsteps. It was Yang Na.

Her waterproof black silk mackintosh was dripping wet. She looked very elegant, her face white, eyes wide.

"Here I am again. Am I welcome?" she said with a smile.

I opened the door, "Come in. I've just come back myself."

"Was that girl on the stairs a nurse at the kindergarten?" Yang Na took off her hat, and her hair tumbled down loosely like a waterfall.

"She's a teacher there."

"Well, what's the difference between a nurse or a teacher in the kindergarten. They're the same thing," she said contemptuously. I wondered what she thought of her own job as a worker at the water-supply company. I was angry, but decided not to say anything.

I silently did my routine housework, helped Sha Sha change her dress, dried her hair with a towel and then put the water on to cook noodles and eggs. Sha Sha was watching TV and I imagined Yang Na would be watching too, although she was not usually that interested. She often liked to bring tapes of popular music to listen to, though she had never made much comment on my cassette recorder. "Not bad" was her pet phrase about all of these things, and I wondered what might actually elicit the word "fine" from her. While I'd been lost in thought, the water had come to a boil. Removing it from the stove, I turned round to see Yang Na leaning against the kitchen door. She held her head high and her large eyes were full of tears.

"You don't like me, do you?"

I couldn't really answer her question then. She was like a calendar photograph of a movie star. I could hang it on the wall to appreciate it, but there was no real connection between us. Whether she was happy or not, Yang Na always looked good. She had a kind of graceful bearing, but she was not a very substantial person.

Sha Sha's mother was also pretty, but she was always worried about this heaven-sent endowment being spoiled. To her it had actually been a burden. Her beauty was only in her appearance, in the large sentimental eyes, the refined nose and the soft lips ... but her innermost heart was empty, poor and barren, like an abandoned well. If you live with a woman like that you often feel deceived. Only the inner beauty, the beauty of personality, like a clean, murmuring spring, flows for ever and makes you aware of the sweetness and warmth of life.

"You're very pretty. You will be happy," I said comfortingly after thinking a bit.

"No. I'm not. You're the lucky one." She continued leaning against the door, staring at me without moving.

5

Every day I would see Meiqing twice — in the morning when she came to fetch Sha Sha and in the evening when she brought her home.

I consciously tried to test her several times, for I didn't completely trust her. In any case I was ten years older than she was. Of course these tests were usually related to Sha Sha. Meiqing would wash Sha Sha's dirty clothes, although I had a washing machine; she mended Sha Sha's worn out socks, although I could do that myself or even buy a new pair. She would also wash Sha Sha's hair, comb out her plaits and cut her fingernails, and once even made an apron for her. In the kindergarten, a movement to give children as much affection as their own mothers had been launched and Meiqing had already given Sha Sha the kind of affection she would have given her own children. She was like a good mother in every respect.

One day while we were chatting, she told me, "In my family there are only three of us, my mother, my brother and myself." What had she meant by this remark? Another time when we were talking about the children in the kindergarten she said, "Sha Sha has no mother. That really is a shame." Was this a hint?

One Sunday I met her on the street by chance. It was then that I found out that she didn't live near my place but in fact quite a distance away, more than one bus stop's walk. But she had never once mentioned it to me, pretending instead that she lived close by. Suddenly I felt that I could read her mind.

Once I asked, "Do you get tired of children?" She answered, "Of course. Sometimes I get so annoyed that I want to pinch them to shut them up. Every day when I get home, I like to sit quietly just to get rid of all the crying and shouting still ringing in my ears. But I'll get used to it." So why was she so kind and concerned with Sha Sha?

... Now her motives seemed crystal clear.

No fiancée could be absolutely perfect so I started looking for her faults. I decided not to indulge in any kind of lovesickness, since I had already tasted the sourness of love once. Certainly her job wasn't ideal. People say that doctors and nurses don't pay much attention to their spouses because they see too much suffering. But what about Meiqing? As a kindergarten teacher she saw too many children, so would she still be able to love Sha Sha? She was attractive and lively, but she lacked a certain elegance and dignity and these things were very important when one grew older. Would my mother like her when we went abroad? And her eyes were a little too small. People say that double-fold eyelids and wide eyes are accepted norms of beauty. It would be ideal if Meiqing had eyes like Yang Na.

Perhaps my attitude to falling in love was too sober.

In September our basketball team was to go abroad to play for two weeks. I was pleased at this opportunity to force myself to make a decision.

It was then the second of August. I waited on the balcony as usual. Meiqing was wearing a white round-necked blouse, green skirt and a pair of high-heeled shoes in pastel yellow. Holding Sha Sha's hand, she waited for the buses to pass and then they crossed the street. She liked to laugh and run, both of which made her even more attractive. I calculated that in three minutes she would be knocking on the door. I stood behind it and immediately opened it when she did.

Surprised, she said with a smile, "You gave me a scare. You saw us coming?"

"Intuition. Please come in."

She hesitated. Ordinarily she wouldn't have entered. After saying goodbye to Sha Sha, she always left in a hurry. But that day she came in, asking, "Was there something else?"

I asked casually, "Did you go swimming today?"

"Yes. I go every lunchtime. You see how tanned I am."

"What about in winter?"

"I go skating."

She was probably a good skater too I thought.

"Which do you like best? Figure skating or racing?"

"I like racing. It's much more exciting. I like to compete with people who can skate fast."

She had an amiable disposition, and talked about all sorts of things with genuine enthusiasm. I decided to come to the point.

"Three days from now I am going abroad with the basketball team. May I ask a favour of you? Can Sha Sha stay with you for a couple of weeks?" I watched her reaction.

"Sha Sha, would you like to stay with me?" She took Sha Sha in her arms. She didn't seem to take the whole business that seriously and I felt a little disappointed.

Sha Sha said, "Daddy has already told me and I said all right. Daddy, didn't you mention it yet?"

It had been three nights ago. Since then I had repeatedly told her, "Daddy is going abroad. You will stay with Meiqing for a couple of weeks. I hope the two of you will get along."

"All right, Sha Sha. I'm sure we'll get along very well." Meiqing was still pretending to talk to Sha Sha. She really was clever.

I then took out a key from the drawer and handed it to her, "Please take this."

Slightly irritated she said, "Do you want me to stay here?"

"I'd like you to take care of my home too."   I stared at her, smiling.

"May I watch the television then?"   It seemed an odd question, asked in innocence.

"Of course."   I wanted to say something more meaningful but I stopped myself.

6

I returned home from the trip at four in the afternoon.

I could sense the presence of Meiqing everywhere. The rooms were tidy and there was even a white gauze cover on the pillow. A bottle of orange juice and three freshly cleaned radishes were in the refrigerator. On the balcony two small chairs leaned against the wall side by side.

Yang Na must have been here too. She would have been rather surprised to meet Meiqing since she knew that I was still abroad.   She would think herself unluckier still.   The opportunity to go abroad carries considerable weight on the scales of love.   But I didn't feel any responsibility for Yang Na.   In any case she would have had to experience sadness sooner or later.

I didn't know whether or not to go to the kindergarten or just wait at home.   To stay home would be more convenient, but I would have to put up with waiting about for more than three hours.

I decided to wait.   The truly wonderful moments in

one's life are few. When next we met and I said those most important words to her, then a new life would begin.

I just sat on the balcony for those three hours. I knew that she wouldn't be appearing around the corner, but I was content all the same just to stare at the street she walked along every day. It was a street I had often thought about while abroad.

At half past seven she and Sha Sha appeared beneath the traffic light. They were coming. She would be able to see the light from my flat. I turned on the lights in all three rooms, the hanging lamp, the table lamps and the wall and floor lamps. I saw Meiqing with Sha Sha waiting for the cars to pass by one after another. Perhaps she was too impatient to wait any longer, for she took Sha Sha in her arms and carried her across the street.

I felt my heart beating and the wrist watch in my pocket ticking. The watch was an expensive foreign kind which Meiqing had once admired in a television advertisement. I had bought one abroad to give to her.

I went downstairs but then I thought it better to wait for them in the flat and returned. I heard them walking up the stairs. When they came in, Sha Sha was hugging Meiqing, shouting at the top of her lungs, "Daddy! Daddy!"

Meiqing was also very excited, "I am glad to see you back. We saw the light on in the distance. I even made a bet with Sha Sha about it last night."

She was genuinely overjoyed. I was sure then that I liked her more than I ever had before. Her large mouth seemed quite in keeping with her open-minded character. Her eyes needn't have been any bigger, since they made her seem gentle, friendly and innocent. Her figure was well-developed, not overly lean. She seemed so graceful and unrestrained.

We finished exchanging greetings and she asked about my trip, the team and the condition of my health. She was interested in knowing everything. The watch kept ticking in my pocket. I decided not to bring up what was on my mind just then, but to wait for exactly the right moment.

Meiqing looked at the clock, "Oh, it's quite late. Are you working tomorrow?"

"No. I've got a couple of days off."

"That's good." She went into Sha Sha's room and sorted out some of the laundry before emerging. "Sha Sha, don't forget to wash your feet before you go to bed."

Now I felt ready to bring up the most important matter. I couldn't even guess at what her reaction would be. Perhaps she would throw herself into my arms with joyful tears in her eyes. Perhaps she would pretend to decline, or stall for the time being, saying, "Let me think it over. I'll tell you tomorrow."

"Are you going home?" I asked calmly.

She smiled, "Oh, I nearly forgot!"

Fishing a key out of her pocket, she handed it to me, saying, "Sha Sha won't be going to kindergarten tomorrow, and it so happens that I'm taking time off too. I'm getting married the day after tomorrow."

I was stunned. I couldn't even pretend to be calm and just stared at her dumbfounded.

"You must have seen him." She obviously realized there was something odd about my expression.

"Who ... who is he?" I asked abruptly.

"You've met him twice. Let me see ... no, three times. Once when we were going to a film, we met you on the street. He even gave Sha Sha a sweet. ..."

I couldn't remember that at all. I hadn't ever noticed her with any young men. Perhaps it was because I felt that there wouldn't be anyone who could match me ... my first-class living conditions, my job and all of the material possessions which ought to have impressed her. I couldn't help looking around the room.

"Where does he work?" I stammered out the question almost as though I hoped it would change things.

She chortled, "Where does he work? He can't even get a job in a factory. He works at a stall he set up with other young people. They've just got their licence for it. I've got to go now. Goodbye, Sha Sha!"

Sha Sha ran to the door, "Bye-bye, teacher!"

She was gone. The key was on the table and I suddenly found that I had the watch in my hand. I couldn't even remember taking it out of my pocket.

On the balcony I stood staring as she crossed the street and then was swallowed up by the crowd. I hadn't even said thank-you to her and had just taken everything for granted. Now I understood and was deeply ashamed. I felt my cheeks burning.

The sky was studded with a myriad twinkling lights and the fragrance of summer flowers filled the colourful, noisy streets.

Summer has ended now, and after autumn winter will come and then spring. ...

Meiqing still comes over twice a day. In the morning she knocks on the door, calling, "Sha Sha, hurry up!

It's late!" In the afternoon she always says "I'm leaving, Sha Sha. Goodbye!" after she brings Sha Sha home.

I've never really dared express the gratitude I feel, afraid as I am of profaning what is to me the most precious thing in the world. . . .

Translated by Shen Zhen

Ge Wujue, born in 1937 in Wenzhou, Zhejiang Province, is now deputy director of the literature and art department of the **Ningxia Daily**. He took an early interest in literature and in 1955 went to Beijing University to study journalism. After graduation he was assigned to the **Ningxia Daily.**

His first short story "The Wedding" was published in 1961. During the "cultural revolution" he was labelled a counter-revolutionary and he started writing again after his rehabilitation in 1977. Since then he has written a number of works including "The Visitor" which was awarded a prize by the literary magazine **October,** "The Visit of Malong" and other novelettes and short stories. In 1980 he joined the Chinese Writers' Association.

He also likes sports, painting, calligraphy and music. He has published "A Journalist and Her Story", a short story collection.

Han the Forger

Deng Youmei

HE hadn't walked down this road for more than thirty years. Now it was asphalted and lined with buildings and a school. In his youth Gan Ziqian used to come along here to Taoran Pavilion Park to sketch. Now, standing beside the historic lake, he felt lost. "Where on earth can Han be?" A man who would be useful for the country's modernization, Han had been ousted from the antiques trade decades ago. Like a sputtering candle, Gan knew his days were numbered. If he didn't find Han he wouldn't find peace even after death.

The misunderstanding between Gan and Han had started with a prank. Gan could paint well in the traditional style, and sometimes copied old works. Seeing a masterly copy of an early painting one day tempted him to do likewise. On an impulse he made a painting called *The Cold Food Festival* and attributed it to the celebrated 12th-century artist Zhang Zeduan, using a well-preserved sheet of Song paper and ink. Originally he did it just for fun, never expecting his copy would attract a newspaper correspondent, one Na Wu by name, who came from an impoverished Manchu noble family. Na Wu took it away and asked a famous craftsman to mount it, colour it with tea and then fake the seal of the Qing emperor Qianlong. When this was done he brought it back to Gan saying, "Look, it exceeds even Master Zhang's skill. And it's certainly as accomplished as Han's."

As a dealer, connoisseur of painting and well-known copyist, Han had been appointed assistant manager of the Gongmao Pawnshop.

"You flatter me. I don't think my skill is nearly as great as Han's," he protested.

"Flatter you? Never!" retorted Na Wu. "If you don't believe me, let's put it to the test."

"How?"

"I'll take it to Gongmao Pawnshop. If Han tells me it's a fake, then I'll say we were only joking. But if I can fool him, then it proves that you do have a remarkable skill. What's more we can share the money between us. Then you can treat me to a roast duck." With this, he carried the painting away wrapped in a blue cloth.

At first Na Wu had only wanted to pawn the painting in order to make the bet with Gan and it was only when he actually had it in his hands that he changed his mind. To fool people he needed to be dressed in his finest clothes, since the pawnshop looked first at the customer and then at the goods. So on the appointed day, he wore his silk gown, a fashionable waist coat, black satin slippers and white silk socks. Between his fingers he balanced an exquisite cigarette-holder with a fine cigarette, lit but unsmoked. Placing the painting on the counter, he asked a price of a thousand yuan and then turned away to look at the wall. From his appearance, Han assumed that he must be a ne'er-do-well from an impoverished Manchu family and that he had stolen the heirloom to pawn. Men of his ilk never sold things and usually never redeemed what they pawned.

Fooled perhaps by Na Wu's appearance, frightened by the high asking price or owing to sheer negligence, Han, after haggling for a long time, chanted in his Shanxi accent, "An antique painting. We can loan you six hundred yuan...." In those days, a bag of flour was only two yuan forty *fen* and six hundred was an enormous sum. When Na Wu returned and told him the story, Gan laughed heartily. But on second thoughts, he was scared stiff. If the story got about, it would discredit him with his friends and offend Han as well. Although the relationship between them was not particularly close, they were still friends. And both were fond of Beijing opera, especially of performances by Sheng Shiyuan. Whenever an opera was staged starring Sheng, they would both go to see him. And as a result of their frequent attendance and vocal support, Sheng became convinced that if they were not at the theatre and cheering, his performance would be below par.

Seeing Gan's misgivings, Na Wu coaxed, "Don't get so worried about it. Everybody already knows Han makes a living from fake paintings. It's time he got his comeuppance. If you're worried about your reputation, we won't do it again. Nobody will find out if neither of us let on. What we did this time wasn't to make money but to put your technique to the test. Now that he's offered us money though, we mustn't be so foolish as to turn it down. Are you really going to pay it back with interest and redeem the painting?"

"I can't afford to."

"You couldn't even if you had the money since the pawn ticket belongs to me now."

Gan had no choice but to give him three hundred yuan. Finishing his duck, Na Wu declared, "Now I'm going to take the ticket to the Japanese pawnshop. I should be able to bluff him out of two or three hundred yuan. So let me pay the bill."

"You're a little too clever at times," remarked Gan.

"Well, don't you agree that to cheat Japanese is patriotic?"

And soon Gan heard others gossiping, saying that Han was used to cheating people with his fakes, but that he had never expected to be swindled himself. Shortly thereafter Gan received an invitation from Han to celebrate his birthday on August 16.

When the day arrived, Han rented Listening to Lotus Hall overlooking a lake in a garden behind Beihai Park and set ten tables under a corrugated iron shade to treat his friends. Gan expected to find a dispirited Han but instead he looked more cheerful than ever. After three cups of wine, he stood up and bowed to the guests with his hands folded, saying, "It's not only because it's my birthday that I invited you here today. I also want to tell you that I've made a blunder.

"I'm sure you've already heard — I've been taken in by a fake. When I was poor, I lived on fake paintings. Now I've been caught myself. It is a sort of retribution, and I've no one to blame but myself. But I think all of us are basically honest men, so to save you from suffering a similar loss, I've brought it here for you to have a look at. Bear this lesson in mind and don't make mistakes yourselves." Then he ordered the painting to be brought out.

With this, his two apprentices approached, one holding the painting, the other carrying a pole with a double-pronged tip which he used to hang the painting on to a bronze hook. All the guests gathered round to examine the work. "Looks genuine all right. How amazing!"

"Don't you be taken in by it. Try to spot its weakness and then we will learn something from it." Turning to look at Gan, Han smiled, adding, "Ziqian has a good eye. You try first."

Gan's face had already turned crimson, but since he had been drinking, no one became suspicious. Moving forward, he first looked at the lower left-hand corner of the painting and spotted his thumb-print, positive proof that the work was his, but he was unable to detect any discrepancies. Had he known of any, of course, he would have corrected them in advance. Secretly he admitted that his brushwork was not up to that of the original painting. He commented, "The brush strokes are weak, and the style a little vulgar. Mr Han's really been deceived by the fact that the artist has used 12th-century paper and ink."

Han laughed saying, "I was duped this time not because the faker was so skilful but because I was too conceited and negligent. So today I'd like to advise you all, don't follow in my footsteps and always keep your eyes open. The painting looks genuine but if you're observant enough, its weakness can be easily detected. For instance, the subject is *The Cold Food Festival* and that takes place in spring.* The painter Zhang Zeduan lived in Kaifeng where at that time of year people

---

* The Cold Food Festival used to be celebrated on April 4.

would have been wearing spring clothes. But look, the boy in the painting is still wearing a cotton-padded hat with flaps. Do you think Zhang would have made such a mistake? For another thing, the young woman by the grave is weeping over her dead husband. The word 'husband' has a closed syllable at the end, but her mouth is open saying 'ah'. Judging from this, I would venture to suggest that this painting is not by Zhang Zeduan."

It was an explanation that won everyone's admiration, even Gan's.

At this, Han threw a cup of wine over the fake, struck a match and set fire to it. Then he laughed again, saying, "Getting rid of it saves anyone else from being swindled. Now let's have another drink before the opera begins."

With the destruction of the painting, Gan felt greatly relieved and calmly sat enjoying the entertainment. As a gesture of friendship, Sheng Shiyuan appeared and performed especially well. Han, on his part, cheered loudly and Gan couldn't refrain from following suit. When the performance was over, Han went backstage to express his appreciation. Sheng asked, "The man who often accompanies you to the theatre hasn't come to see me for a long time. Who is he? Won't you introduce us next time he comes?" Since he'd been cheated, Han had felt so miserable that he hadn't been to the theatre for several days and consequently wasn't aware that Gan had also been staying home. Sheng's words startled him. He knew that the faker must be someone from the same trade and had therefore invited a number of them in order to watch what would happen during dinner. However, he had never been even remotely suspicious of Gan. Immediately he looked around to search him out but was told by his apprentice that Mr Gan had just been called away unexpectedly.

Later, called to the side door of the garden by Na Wu, Gan was annoyed. "What the devil did you come here for?" he growled.

"I apologize but I must tell you. I went to pledge the pawn ticket with the Japanese but he asked me to let him inspect the painting first. Dare we run the risk? If it passes, then there's no problem. If the Japanese spots anything wrong with it though, he won't be as easy to deal with as Han — we'll be sent to prison."

"You're too greedy!" Gan scolded. "In any case, the painting has already been destroyed by Han."

At first Na Wu was stunned by the news. Then all of a sudden he slapped his thigh and exclaimed, "Wonderful! It's time Han got what was coming to him."

"What are you going to do? We've already made him lose six hundred yuan. Don't be so cruel! He and I are friends and see one another frequently."

"Friends? No. Business is business. It's foolish to let a good opportunity slip through your fingers. Come, stay awhile. I'll treat you to some crabs."

After Na Wu's departure, Gan was uneasy. Han was a better man than Na Wu and even if he himself had nothing further to do with this, he didn't have the heart to let Na Wu extort any more money from him. So he made up his mind to visit the pawnshop and inform him of Na Wu's intention in order to avoid any further trouble.

When he arrived at Gongmao Pawnshop, Han came out to meet him and graciously ushered him into a private room behind the accountant's office. Shortly an apprentice appeared bringing Gan a cup of tea. Han puffed at his hookah for a while before breaking the silence, "I haven't seen you lately. Where've you been?"

Before Gan could reply, the accountant, looking upset, scurried in and stuttered, "Something's wrong, sir!"

"What's wrong?" Han asked nonchalantly.

"There's a man here to redeem his pledge."

"Redeem his pledge? What's wrong with that? It's natural that people come here to redeem their pledges."

"But, he wants to redeem the. . . ." The accountant glanced at Gan, then approached Han and whispered.

"Speak up!" ordered Han. "Mr Gan is not a stranger."

The accountant couldn't help blurting out, " . . . that painting!"

"Which one?"

The Cold Food Festival that you burnt yesterday."

Gan, shocked, felt a shiver run down his spine, for he had never expected that Na Wu would carry his trick so far.

But Han said calmly, "Tell him the painting he pawned is a fake and that he should be content with the sum he got from me. If not, I'll take him to court."

"I'm sorry, sir. But you can't speak to a customer that way. He came here to redeem his pledge and even if the pledge was a bit of toilet paper, we are still supposed to return it to him. If we can't, then we should pay him twice the loan. Even if we do, I'm not sure he'll take it. How can I tell him we'll go to court?"

The accountant's argument reduced Han to silence. Just then they heard a commotion outside. Na Wu shouted, "What! You want to keep my heirloom, do you? If you're not going to return it to me, you'd better pay me a proper price for it!"

"Outrageous! I'd better go and see what's happening," said Han. "Excuse me, Ziqian."

Angry and embarrassed, Gan ignored form and followed Han out of the room.

The shop's counter was over a foot higher than the customer. Behind the counter stood Han, surrounded by his accountant and assistants, all looking down at Na Wu, who challenged, "If you have the painting here, then return it to me. If not, we'll have to settle the matter another way."

Gan peered out from behind Han and saw a swarthy, heavy-set fellow standing behind Na Wu. He was dressed in grey clothes, his sleeve cuffs covering his hands. Beneath his unbuttoned jacket Han could see a white calico vest edged with black trimming, and recognized him immediately as a police detective. It certainly looked as though Na Wu was determined to continue hounding Han. Winking at him, Gan began tentatively, "Oh, it's you, Mr Na. Well, we're all friends here. Why do you want. . . ."

"Mr Gan, what we're talking about is no laughing matter. Please don't get mixed up in this. I pawned a scroll painting inherited from my forefathers. Today I've come here to redeem it. First they tell me it's a fake. Then they promise I can get it back another day. Does it surprise you that my patience has run out?"

As Gan was about to try and coax him out of continuing, Han edged forward saying to Na Wu, "So you've run out of patience, have you? Well, I'm much more impatient than you are. I reckoned you'd be here as soon as the shop opened. Why did it take you so long? You want to redeem the painting, do you? Then first please show me the money!"

"So you're afraid I haven't brought it." With this, Na Wu threw a white packet on to the counter containing the principal and interest, amounting together to over eight hundred yuan. Having counted the sum and placed the interest to one side, Han handed six hundred yuan to the accountant, then removed a package from under the counter and handed it downwards.

"Here. Now take it away."

Hearing this, Gan and the assembled assistants were taken aback. Na Wu stood stunned before nervously reaching out for the package, his hands trembling so much that he could not even hold it. The detective reached out and steadied him, saying, "You'd better have a look. Is it the one you pawned?"

No sooner had he untied the bundle than the sweat stood out on his brow, and his lips trembled. Pretending to talk to himself, he said so that Gan could hear, "Wasn't this burnt yesterday?"

"If I hadn't burnt it yesterday, would you have come here today?" replied Han sarcastically.

"So there are two such paintings in existence!" uttered Na Wu.

"If you like, I'll produce another one for you tonight," added Han.

Incredulously Gan asked, "What on earth is it, Mr Na? Won't you let me have a look?"

Holding the painting, Gan blushed scarlet with shame. First of all, he examined the lower left-hand corner, and looked hard at the thumb-print, which though very pale could barely be distinguished from that in the destroyed painting and had they been placed together in front of him, he would have been unable even to identify his own work. It was said that some craftsmen were so skilful they could peel off the top layer of a painting to make two. "Can Han do that?" he wondered.

"It looks like there's nothing for me to do here." The detective was growing impatient. "Settle with me and I'll be off."

Paying him, Na Wu turned towards Han with a contrite smile and folded his hands in a gesture of respect, "I've learned a lesson from you and paid two hundred yuan for the privilege."

"Take the interest back!" Han handed it over to him and laughed. "It was you who brought the painting here and I imagine your slippers must be worn out, so you'd better use the money to buy a new pair. By the way, please tell the man who made the fake. . . ." With this he turned to the dumbfounded and embarrassed Gan before going on, "Does he think he's clever enough to fool me? Not until he can fool the painter himself with his fakes, will he be properly qualified. So I suggest he study for another couple of years."

Ashamed, Gan slunk out of Gongmao Pawnshop, head bowed, and from then on never appeared when Han was around. Although Han was a man of good reputation, his master dared not run the risk of losing any more money and in the first month of the following year he was dismissed. Later he was reduced to working as a junk dealer for two years, but since business was bad, he finally supported himself by collecting and selling scrap. Gan, despite suffering a temporary loss of credibility, got a good job restoring damaged paintings.

As a result of his background, clear record, progressive ideology and loyalty to the Party, after Liberation Gan was elected to the leadership of the antiques trade and became vice-chairman of the trade association during the socialist transformation of capitalist enterprise.

To reinforce the leadership after the changeover, someone suggested that they should appoint Han to a job. But the authorities did not know much about his past and asked Gan for an opinion. Gan was evasive, saying he didn't know much about him and asked them to wait until he found out a little more. Returning home, he turned the affair over in his mind. Though he hadn't intended to cheat Han, he certainly wouldn't be able to explain it away. "If Han isn't hired, then no one will rake up the past," he thought. "If he is, however, he may raise it against me. What's more, I'm applying for Party membership. Why should I bother to recommend him?" But Gan also couldn't lie to the authorities. When asked for his opinion, he said, "Han lived on fakes and used to be an assistant manager in a pawnshop. He was quite well off before Liberation. On his birthday the famous Beijing opera actor Sheng Shiyuan even performed at his home. . . ."

"It's said that he's an able man. What do you think about our employing him?"

"The decision rests with you," Gan replied evasively. "My political standard is low, and I'm not sure."

In the end Han was rejected.

According to the conventions of the antiques trade,

people who had been vetted could do anything except assess or deal in antiques. From that day on Han sank into obscurity.

Many years passed. Gan didn't feel guilty and, as time went on, forgot about Han.

During the "cultural revolution", Gan was deeply wronged. After the fall of the "gang of four", he was rehabilitated and had his savings, which had been confiscated, returned. What pleased him most was that he was able to go and work at an antiques studio, where he could put his knowledge to full use. But time takes its toll. When he was elected a people's representative, he was given a medical certificate stating that if he didn't rest, his chances of recovery were nil. At length he recalled Han.

In the antique world some old craftsmen had died, others had fallen ill. During recent years few talented successors had turned up, and a shortage of able people became a big problem. The international antique market was brisk. Han was good at both assessing and copying ancient paintings and should have had a position which would have given full play to his unique skills. If Gan had said yes before, then he would have been employed, but instead, the man had been barred for many years.

Gan was so filled with remorse that he confessed everything to the Party committee. The secretary praised him and asked him to try and locate Han.

But Beijing was so big, where was Han? First Gan was told that he was a boilerman for a teahouse at Tianqiao, but when he got there he found the place had closed down. Then he was told that Han and another old bachelor had rented a house to breed goldfish near the Goldfish Pond. When he went to look for him, the house had been razed. Half a month passed but Han was nowhere to be found. All Gan knew was that he was still alive, and sometimes went to Taoran Pavilion Park to practise shadow-boxing at dawn.

He was determined to find him. Despite the doctor's warnings, he went with his cane first thing in the morning to the park. As the sun had not yet risen, only a few dim figures could be discerned running along the edge of the lake. Others were singing, walking or fishing. But whom should he approach?

Just then an old man with a beard and a cane, wearing traditional-style clothes, came towards him. He was so absorbed in humming a Beijing opera aria that he didn't notice the people around him. Out of habit, Gan spontaneously cheered, "Wonderful!"

The old man stopped to look up towards the shaded trees by the lake. "Why, that cheering sounds familiar to me, but I haven't heard it for more than thirty years."

"I haven't heard such a sweet voice for over thirty years either," Gan chimed in. "Aren't you Mr Sheng?"

"Oh my goodness!" The old man stepped forward, and grasped Gan by the hand. "It's you, the man who used to come with Han to see my performances."

"Yes. My name is Gan Ziqian."

"I've heard of you. Once after a performance, I wanted to meet you, but you had already left. Thirty years have passed since that day. How are you getting along? Where do you work now?"

Told that Gan was an adviser at an antiques studio, Sheng said, "I'm with a Beijing opera company now. I lost my voice in 1945 when the Japanese surrendered and was jobless. But after Liberation, the government showed a lot of concern for us and gave us the opportunity to use our talents, so I became a teacher at a Beijing opera school, but that was interrupted by the 'cultural revolution'. . . ."

"Mr Sheng," Gan cut him short, "you mentioned Mr Han to me just now. Do you know where he is?"

"Why yes. He lives with me."

"Eh?" Surprised, Gan stared at him for a long time before he asked cautiously, "Really?"

"Of course. Anybody who comes here to practise shadow-boxing knows he's lodging with me. During the 'cultural revolution' the teahouse where he worked closed down. Since he couldn't earn a living, I told him not to worry and to stay with me for the time being. My wife died and my son was transferred to another province, so I was alone. I told him he could come and keep house and that as long as I had an income, he wouldn't go hungry. So he's been living in my place for the past ten years."

"If he's there now," Gan said impatiently, "may I go with you to see him?"

"No."

"Why?"

"Because he's gone into hospital with a stroke."

Gan heaved a sigh.

"Don't worry," Sheng added. "He's out of danger, but the doctor won't let him have any visitors yet."

Relieved, Gan asked again, "What caused it?"

"Overwork. Last year the doctor insisted that he take it easy, but he was busier than ever with his work. He said that his ancestors were connoisseurs of painting and had the knack of being able to tell genuine works from fakes. While he was able he wanted to write it down so that the knowledge would not be lost."

Gan sighed. "If only he could have done it earlier!"

"Years ago he used to complain to me that the higher-ups in the antique world were a bunch of laymen who'd insulted him and that he would rather die with his skills than teach others. But in the last couple of years, since I've been cleared of the false accusations made against me in the 'cultural revolution' and we've had a bit more money, he's changed his mind. Now he says he won't withhold his knowledge any longer and has decided to write it all down. I was delighted and provided him with paper, ink, fine tea and tobacco, but I forgot to remind him to take care of his health."

Hearing this Gan was moved. "You really have been a loyal friend!"

"Oh, I owe a great deal to the way things have improved since those chaotic years, otherwise I couldn't have afforded to help him."

With a heavy heart Gan walked silently beside Sheng for a while before asking, "Is he able to talk?"

"Yes, but his tongue gets a little stiff sometimes."

"So he can still be cured." Gan was cheered, thinking he should suggest sending someone to Sheng's house to have Han's speech recorded. When the next National People's Congress opened, someone should propose helping old scholars and craftsmen to pass on their knowledge.

Saying goodbye to Gan, Sheng promised, "As soon as I have the doctor's permission, I'll take you to see him."

On his way home, Gan felt much more at ease; at long last he had found an opportunity to make amends for his error. Now he could die with a clear conscience.

Translated by Song Shouquan

Deng Youmei was born in Tianjin in 1931. In 1945 he served in the New Fourth Army as a messenger, a member of a cultural troupe and student correspondent. Entering the Central Research Institute of Literature in 1949, he was under the guidance of the celebrated woman writer Ding Ling and published his story "On the Precipice". In 1957 he was wrongly labelled a Rightist.

In recent years he has published "Our Army Commander", "Tales of Taoranting Park", and "Three Women Soldiers", each of which has won an award. He is now a council member of the Chinese Writers' Association and a member of the standing council of its Beijing branch.

A Land of Wonder and Mystery

Liang Xiaosheng

IT was a deathly silent and boundless swamp, covered the whole year round with dried branches, rotten leaves, and poisonous algae. The surface, dark brown and stagnant, had a deceptively peaceful appearance. Below it was an oozing abyss which contained the decomposing skeletons of bears, hunters' guns and tractors belonging to reclamation teams. It sent out a morbid odour for a hundred *li* and was known as Spirits' Swamp.

When I first arrived in that Great Northern Wilderness, I heard many legends about this Spirits' Swamp: deep in the starless, moonless night one could see across the slumbering wasteland the eerie greenish glow of the will-o'-the-wisps; one could hear bears roar as they were swallowed by the swamp, gunshots fired by hunters for help and the desperate cries of those caught in the mire . . . sometimes one could hear a strange bird's song which sounded just like a sad woman's wailing, "What a pity, what a pity. . . ." But no one had ever seen what kind of bird it was. The local Oroqen people called it the bird which "summons back the spirits". They thought that it was really an incarnation of the God of the Earth and that deep in the night it came to comfort and call back the spirits of people and animals who had died in Spirits' Swamp. And the will-o'-the-wisps were its lanterns.

Spirits' Swamp, like the ferocious nine-headed dragon of Greek myth, forcibly occupied the land behind it, a fertile land of more than ten thousand hectares, and no one dared cross the swamp to reclaim it. The Oroqen people used to call this land the "Devil's Reach". During winter they occasionally crossed it, but they never killed any animals for fear of inescapable punishment by the "Devil".

It was my third winter in the Great Northern Wilderness. A detachment of a dozen or so educated youths had been sent by our reclamation company to Devil's Reach.

As a result of being wrongly sited at the outset, our company was located in a natural depression with fairly limited arable land. If harvest happened to coincide with a rainy season, the combine harvesters got bogged down in the wheat fields like paralysed toads. So we had always had bad harvests and that particular year could not even produce enough for the following year's seeds. We couldn't afford to live off the land, much less send grain to the state. That was why the reclamation regiment decided to disband our company and re-allocate the more than two hundred young people to other companies.

What more profound humiliation could there be than this decision? Many of us burst into tears as we listened to the old company leader's announcement. Li Xiaoyan, the company's deputy instructor, was the first to stand up and indignantly refute the decision.

"The company should not be broken up! We can reclaim Devil's Reach. We ought to have thought of it earlier. We must rebuild our company there. Let Devil's Reach be covered with our reclaimers' footprints for the first time. We'll guarantee the regiment that we'll get a crop the same year we reclaim the land. The following year we'll have our new company base. Take our word for it!"

Though usually we listened indifferently to her ambitious words, this time her rousing speech actually did encourage us and many of us felt the same way.

Finally the regiment cancelled their decision and accepted our guarantee.

Several days later, we set off with two first-rate 54 h.p. tractors decorated with red ribbons and flowers, a newly-made wooden sled trailing behind each for the vast snow-covered wilderness. The whole company had lined up to see us off. Hope, confidence, trust and a silent concern was in their eyes, and each of us felt a strong sense of responsibility. Everyone cried.

The first sled held our food and luggage and we squeezed ourselves into the tent set up on the second.

We sat silently shoulder to shoulder. Beside me my younger sister cuddled a wicker cage which contained a small squirrel. She looked pale, her expression dull, her eyes sad and, like a deaf-mute, said nothing the whole journey. I had no other brothers or sisters. Although I had loved her very much since childhood, I felt a mixture of pity and hatred towards her then because she had recently acquired a bad reputation and I was thoroughly ashamed of her.

Li Xiaoyan, the deputy instructor, sat opposite with the blacksmith, Wang Zhigang, a sturdy man with a tanned, rough complexion, who gave the impression of being powerful, strong and determined. It seemed natural for us to compare him with Othello, and we had nicknamed him the "Moor". He liked to be alone, and had a just and ethical character. He didn't seek the limelight, and had a strong influence over the younger people. I rather envied him for that. It was the deputy instructor who had nominated him specifically to join our detachment. Now I stared with jealousy as Li rested her head on the Moor's broad shoulder to take a nap.

I asked myself why I was attracted to her. Was it her beauty? Certainly she was beautiful, a girl from Shanghai, with a lovely face, white, delicate skin, large, shining eyes, and thin, curved eyebrows. Her face always had an expression of wonder. Her slender figure seemed to confirm what we'd heard, that she had been a good ballet student in Shanghai and that many dance troupes had wanted to recruit her but that she'd refused them all. She had come to the Great Northern Wilderness of her own free will. From the first moment I saw her, I couldn't help being aware of her. But I wasn't usually someone who was easily seduced or overwhelmed by pretty girls. On the contrary, whenever I meet a girl, the more beautiful she is, the more aloof I am. It's one of my maxims — never be a slave of love through indiscretion. Was it her seriousness, her solemnity that enticed me? Not really. I rather preferred girls with enthusiastic, frank and open-minded characters. Sometimes I thought Li's solemn bearing was hypocritical and it disgusted me. It was true she'd sworn not to pay a home visit to Shanghai for three years in order to consolidate her determination to settle in that border area. She also made the suggestion that other girls in the company ought not to wear make-up or colourful clothes. But some of them passed it around that Li still worried about her white, delicate skin and that in summer she stealthily went to the river bank to get a suntan. Unfortunately the sunshine only turned her white skin pink, not the brown she wanted. She also tried to be more masculine, wearing what the boys wore, doing the same manual labour they did. She wanted to change her figure, to adopt the so-called "beauty of the labourer", but she remained slim and graceful. Strong and healthy, she was like a small white birch, erect and tall during those three years in the Great Northern Wilderness. She had not been home once during that time. In the first year she had become the head of the platoon, in the second a Party member, and the third the deputy instructor of the company, a model for the whole regiment, showing others how to strike roots in the frontier reclamation areas.

One summer evening in that third year, right after she was appointed deputy instructor of the company, I suddenly heard someone singing when I was sketching on the river bank.

> Under the bright sky of early spring,
> My eighteen-year-old lover sits on the river bank.

It was a "decadent" song strictly prohibited at the time. Who was singing it? If our deputy instructor heard about it, an "ideological struggle" would inevitably ensue. Whoever it was sang well. Her voice was very sweet. Burning with curiosity, I picked up my home-made drawing board and went quietly along the bank to find out who the singer was. Suddenly I came upon someone sitting on a large, smooth grey stone beneath a reclining willow tree on the opposite bank of the river. It was none other than our deputy instructor!

She was washing her clothes, dangling her bare feet in the water, her trouser legs rolled up above the ankles and her white calves uncovered.

> Under the bright sky of early spring,
> My eighteen-year-old lover waits for his sweetheart,
>   Yinglian. . . .

After scrubbing, kneading and wringing out the clothes, she stood up on the large grey stone and tiptoed cautiously across a group of cobblestones to hang them over some branches. Afraid the cobblestones might hurt her feet, she moved gingerly, with quick light steps, just like the dance of the cygnets in *Swan Lake*. Having spread the clothes across the shrubs, she returned to the river bank with the same steps. She collected a few wild flowers, taking in their scent and placing some in her hair, two on the right and three on the left. Then, squatting in front of the river, she stared for a long time at her own reflection in the water. She was admiring her own beauty! After a while she rose slowly. Then suddenly she jumped up on to the grey stone's smooth surface and, her arms outstretched, made an elegant semi-circle and performed a Mexican folk dance with quick steps.

The drawing board slid from my hands and dropped into the water, causing a slight noise. Alarmed, she stopped dancing and saw me watching her from the opposite side of the river. She appeared stunned, like a bewildered fawn or a startled crane about to take flight.

The river between us, we stared at one another in astonishment.

The first to recover my composure, I jumped into the river to retrieve my drawing board. Feigning a casual manner, I waded through the shallow water to the opposite bank. By then, the wild flowers in her hair had disappeared and the trouser legs had been rolled down.

"You . . . what are you doing here on the river bank?" she asked, intending to gain the upper hand, and with it the psychological initiative. She tried her best to conceal her embarrassment, assuming a relaxed manner as much as she could. She became again a solemn, reserved young woman in the presence of a young man, a deputy instructor with the requisite dignity. But she hadn't had enough time to button up her jacket, faded from many washings, and underneath she wore a pink shirt, short and tight, with a V-neck through which I caught a glimpse of a white neck and bosom, round white shoulders and even the cleavage of her heaving breasts. Immediately I averted my eyes and felt my heart racing with excitement. I flushed, feeling an inexplicable kind of shame, guilty about debasing her and myself as well, though I could swear to heaven that I didn't, even for a moment, desire her. I didn't even feel the instinctive response which ordinarily occurs when a young man meets an attractive girl, the passion which originated with Adam and Eve.

She was so very sensitive. As my eyes took her in, she immediately covered her jacket flap and turned round. When she turned back again I saw the old familiar deputy instructor, jacket buttoned right up, and feet burrowed deep into the sand to hide the fact that she had no shoes on.

I felt humiliated by her behaviour and tried to find words to break the awkward silence, but ended by blurting out something very foolish, "You're . . . so beautiful!"

"What!" Her face blushed like a crimson cloud. My sudden appearance had caused her problems, placing her in an impossibly awkward position.

"What I . . . I meant is that you danced beautifully. If I'm not mistaken, it was a Mexican folk dance, wasn't it?"

"Mexican dance? Don't make fun of me. I was just doing the radio limbering-up exercises for middle school students."

"Does that mean you're going to deny you were singing as well?"

"Singing a song? Why should I deny it? I did sing a song." In addition to her feigned puzzlement, she now added one more thing, an artificial directness. She began singing:

> Near the Qinghe River, on Tigerhead Hill,
> Is situated Dazhai Production Brigade. . . .

After singing two lines she said to me, "That's the song you heard me singing."

The blush had receded and she had completely recovered her normal complexion.

I felt that she had made a fool of me and treated me as though I was blind and deaf. I couldn't stand any more such insults. Suppressing my anger with great effort I said coldly, "No, that wasn't the song I heard. You sang: 'My eighteen-year-old lover waits for his sweetheart, Yinglian'!"

"Eighteen-year-old lover? His sweetheart Yinglian? I've never even heard of such a song. Don't talk nonsense!" She raised her slender eyebrows with a surprised and astonished expression, as if I had called her a thief.

So many hypocritical changes of expression had taken place on that lovely face.

I had nothing more to say, and just looked at her in astonishment. To me she looked like the Sphinx, with her lion's body and human face, only the Sphinx was more honest. As I remember, even the Sphinx said the same thing to everyone: If you fail to solve my riddle, then I will devour you. But the Sphinx was less shameless than this deputy instructor, since ultimately she jumped down from the rocks and died when Oedipus correctly answered the riddle. The deputy instructor wanted me, a normal person of sound mind, to believe myself to be an idiot, a daydreamer, talking in my sleep.

"You hypocrite!" Indignantly I turned around and abruptly strode off.

"Wait!"

I halted without turning around, but I could sense her anxiety.

"You . . . are you going to report me to the company leader? . . ." she murmured, with an imploring tone.

Still with my back to her, I softened and shook my head. After walking a distance I could not help looking back. She remained standing beside the river like a statue, motionless. . . .

I never told anyone else about the incident.

I couldn't be that mean.

But from then on, whenever she made her speeches she would become uneasy when our eyes met. I regretted that and felt sorry for her.

Not long after that I got a telegram saying that my mother was seriously ill, but I was unable to get permission from the company leader to return home. The reason was clear, since I was the combine harvester **driver** and it was then harvest season. Actually I knew that the company leader didn't believe the telegram was genuine. That was another reason he didn't approve my request. He had been deceived several times by phoney telegrams which parents or their children sent in order to arrange a reunion. Some of them even invented the death of a parent. As a consequence, the company leader had become an empiricist. It was no use pleading with him to let me go, nor would any kind of explanation help. But I couldn't remain indifferent to the telegram. My father had died early and my mother, a worker in a small factory, had brought up my younger sister and I through all kinds of difficulties and hardships. It had not been easy for her, and only I understood how she had put her heart and soul into looking after us. Now my younger sister and I had come to this Great Northern Wilderness and left her at home alone. She was a woman of strong character and would never use deceitful measures even though she was yearning to see us.

I decided I had to return immediately to see her.

That day I stealthily left the company. . . .

My mother! This woman who had tasted to the full the bitterness of life! She was so unyielding, so concerned for her children. She knew she was dying but she only cabled us that she was "very sick" instead of "mortally ill". She didn't want to alarm us with such frightening words.

During my mother's last five days I lived with her and gave her as much care and love as I could to thank her for bringing us into this world and helping us to grow up. I did this not only for myself but also for my younger sister who was unable to return.

Five days, only five days! No matter how I expressed

my love or took care of my mother during those five days it was only a symbolic compensation. How can a mother's love and concern for her children ever be compensated?

My mother's last words were, "Look after your sister. You're all the family she has."

Numbed by grief, I went back to the company.

The day I returned, on the instruction of the company leader, the Youth League branch held a meeting to discuss what disciplinary action should be taken over my desertion. Before the meeting, someone had disclosed that I was certain to be expelled from the League. The meeting itself was purely a formality and I would be used as an example to warn the others.

I myself was totally indifferent to whatever punishment I had to have.

The meeting was conducted by the deputy instructor. I thought she would certainly use the opportunity to take her revenge and I was determined to keep my mouth shut and listen to her long criticism of me.

At first she asked me to say something about my mistake.

I looked down and muttered, "My mother . . . died . . . three days ago. . . ." Finishing this sentence, I put my head in my hands and felt everyone's eyes focussed on me.

For an instant, it seemed that everyone at the meeting was holding their breath. Suffocated by the sudden silence, even the air seemed unnaturally still. Following this pause, the deputy instructor said in a low but clear voice, "The meeting is over. . . ."

She was the first to leave.

As I passed by the company office, I heard the deputy

instructor and the company leader arguing fiercely. I was surprised, since the deputy instructor was used to carrying out the company leader's instructions. Wondering what they were wrangling over, I stopped to listen.

"I am the head of this company. Don't I have the right to punish a subordinate?" It was the angry voice of the company leader with his heavy Sichuan accent.

"I am the Youth League branch secretary. Punishing League members is the duty of the League branch." The deputy instructor's voice was raised too.

"All you're doing is making excuses for a deserter!"

"A deserter? Did he desert the battlefield? Did he cross to the other side of the Heilong River? Do you know that his mother died? Three days after her death he came back. . . ."

"Oh, his mother died, did she!?"

"Company leader, I am an educated youth too, with an elderly father and mother. They're longing to see me. I'd go back home this very minute if I hadn't taken an oath. But I can't. I don't agree that he should be expelled from the League. Company leader, please, put yourself in his position and think it over!"

I heard her start to cry. As I stood outside the company office, tears welled up in my eyes too.

I felt thoroughly grateful to her. Not because she had defended me, but because she had said, "I am an educated youth too. . . ."

All of my misconceptions and prejudices about her were erased by this sentence and I felt I would go through hell for her.

Hearing this I knew she was a good person with a noble character and a sympathetic heart. Nevertheless, two days later this same person told me something which hit me like a bolt of lightning.

That day, while helping me to turf out the weeds in a long stretch of ground, she asked, "After work would you mind coming with me?" It was the second time in three years that she had talked to me. The first had been the encounter by the river not long ago. This time her sullen and serious expression seemed to omen some misfortune.

As we shouldered our hoes and lined up to return, she said to me in front of everyone else, "Please wait. Let's go together." The others looked at both of us with curious expressions.

After they had moved off a distance, she looked me in the eye, and said, "Without consulting you, I've arranged to have your younger sister transferred to our company."

"Why? What's happened? Tell me!"

"When you were home. . . ."

"Tell me!"

"She had an abortion. . . ."

Shocked I felt my body swaying and nearly fell. She steadied me with her hands.

I roughly pushed her aside, shouting, "You're lying!"

She staggered backward. Eyes wide with fear, she uttered two words, "It's true!"

I felt suddenly as if I was glued to the ground. I wanted to shout out but it was as if there was something stuffed down my throat and I couldn't. The only sound coming from my voice was a hoarse moan. My vision blurred and she became indistinct.

Like someone crazed, I raced towards the tent.

I wept through the whole of that night, biting the quilt

corner to avoid disturbing my soundly sleeping room-mates. I remembered my mother's last wish, but before I could carry it out, my younger sister had acted scandalously. Now she was to be transferred to my company so she could be under my wing. Never! With the right of an elder brother, I would punish her severely, on behalf of my dead mother.

The next day I was called to the office by the deputy instructor and there met my younger sister. On seeing her, I sprang at her like a leopard, took her hair and forcefully hit her head against the earthen wall.

"Stop!" I heard the deputy instructor's shout. She dashed forward trying hard to loosen my frenzied grip.

"Get away!" I roared at her.

I tormented my younger sister as though I was tormenting myself. My hysteria seemed to relieve the pain.

Suddenly, I received a sharp slap on the face.

I released my grip.

The second slap was much harder.

The two slaps had sobered me up and unconsciously I stepped back, feeling my burning cheek.

My younger sister didn't utter a single word, nor moan, shout or plead. Her dishevelled hair covered a pallid face bathed in tears, and her large eyes were full of humiliation.

Her face drained of colour, the deputy instructor held my younger sister tightly and stared at me, determined to fight if necessary.

"You bloody animal!"

That was the first time I ever heard her use bad language.

From that day on I was in love with her.

Now she was sitting opposite. As the covered, tractor-drawn sled slogged on through the whirling snow, we were chilled by the northwesterly wind. It carried snow-flakes into the tent through an open flap which no one wanted to draw. We looked at the white world outside, the white land, the white mountains, the white river, the white forests. The blizzard violently pursued us, like millions of maddened galloping wild oxen.

After silently looking round at everyone, the deputy instructor then said, almost to herself, "Should we have someone tell a story? Or perhaps sing a song together?"

There was no response to her suggestion. Everyone was exhausted.

Her eyes fell on me.

I cleared my throat and began to sing *The Reclaimers' Song*:

> Every reclaimer has a sun in his heart,
> One hand holds a gun, the other a pickaxe.

No one joined in and so naturally I halted after the first two lines of the song.

Just then, the Moor started to whistle. He wasn't a good singer, but he could whistle quite tunefully. What surprised me though was that he was whistling the famous Russian folk song *Troika*. He wasn't at all afraid of the deputy instructor's interference. His whistling had an enchanting quality, like a clarinet or a trumpet. His lyrical, rhythmic melody produced in us a sense of sadness, of deep melancholy.

Someone started humming quietly, then another and a third, gradually converging into a chorus.

My younger sister looked up, stared uneasily and

then, lowering her head again, heaved a long sigh. I felt sorry for her.

I gazed across at the deputy instructor's face, guessing that she would immediately put a stop to this sentimental song. But she remained indifferent. Her head was still resting on the Moor's shoulder. Her eyes closed, she pretended to be falling asleep, but I noticed her hand covertly beating time.

I felt that my pride was hurt and bit my lower lip. The song continued:

> The Volga is covered with ice and snow,
> The Troika is driving over the icy river.
> Someone is singing a melancholy song,
> The singer is. . . .

Night fell unobtrusively and the merciless blizzard stopped its howling. Maybe it surrendered itself or maybe, with our tractors driving at full throttle, we left it behind in that silent wilderness.

Now we were enclosed by the chill darkness, a huge natural tent flap.

2

Travelling like the migrant Oroqen people, we drove swiftly across the vast snowy plateau for two days and two nights. When we looked at the map, we were convinced that we had arrived at the snow-and-ice covered Spirits' Swamp. A solemn wilderness dawn was just breaking.

Spirits' Swamp! It was not as dreadful as the legends made out. Perhaps it was in hibernation and its true ferocious appearance was hidden deep beneath the snow. It seemed as if the largest lake in the world lay frozen in front of us. Devil's Reach — it looked so flat we could hardly believe that it extended only as far as the remote horizon.

"Hey! Devil King, where are you? Show yourself!" shouted one of our companions.

But the "Devil" did not appear.

Suddenly the Moor pointed to something in the distance, "Look!" A round wooden stake with a notch cut into it stood at an angle.

Curious, we walked over to have a look. The deputy instructor brushed the snow from the stake and we saw a wooden tablet with something carved on its rough surface. Most of the words had been eroded by wind and rain, but some poor handwriting was still faintly visible: ". . . died here. . . ."

Each of us shuddered.

"There's another one over there!" My younger sister had discovered a similar evil omen. She was the first to walk back to the tractor.

The deputy instructor said softly, "Let's go back. Don't disturb their rest."

If someone asks me what the hardest and bitterest work of all in the Great Northern Wilderness is, I'll answer "reclamation".

And if someone asks me what work in the Great Northern Wilderness I feel most proud of, my answer will also be "reclamation".

Because we were eager to discover the best sources of water and timber, nearly every part of Devil's Reach was covered with our footprints. We finally discovered a stream — not marked on the map — which was the only clean water source. We named it the "Wanderer" since it had been wandering across the flat wasteland for countless years before we discovered it and set up a tent next to it.

When the snow melted, our gleaming ploughs sank into the bosom of Devil's Reach. Who but a reclaimer could experience the joy of ploughing the first plot of virgin land by tractor? There were many wolves on this flat land. In threes and fours they swaggered along behind the tractors, preying on field rats startled by the ploughing, and at night they would howl around our tent. The hardship of this work had transformed all the young men in the detachment into saints. All of us, including my younger sister and the deputy instructor, lived in the same large tent. Their small "world" was separated from ours by a hanging blanket, behind which existed a sacred, forbidden place.

One night, I suddenly woke and could not hear the usual night shift tractor roaring outside the tent. I immediately sprang to my feet and, without thinking, barged into the "forbidden place" to shake the deputy instructor awake.

"What do you want?"

"The Moor is out ploughing, but the tractor has stopped!"

With the tractor silent for such a long time, there must be something wrong with the Moor. Everyone in the tent got up. Just as we were all about to run out, the Moor suddenly appeared at the entrance, his hands gripping the two front paws of an old wolf which was clinging to his back. The animal was still half alive, its mouth wide open, its two back paws gripping either side of his waist.

"It's still alive! Quick! Hit it!" shouted the Moor.

We immediately took up sticks and clubs and beat the large grey animal to death.

The Moor flung himself on a pallet, gasping for breath. After a long pause he told us, "The steel cable on the big plough broke and I was changing it when that damned thing came at me and got me round the shoulders with its claws. . . ." His face and hands were cut and bloodstained, his clothes in tatters. Frowning, he took off his padded jacket. His sweatshirt and skin had also been clawed.

The deputy instructor ordered my younger sister, "Quick, get the first-aid kit!"

Just then we suddenly realized that the deputy instructor, feet bare, was wearing only her underclothes. She had just become aware of it herself and felt uneasy at our stares. But she remained calm, and said coolly, "What are you looking at? Haven't you got any thing better to do? Go to bed again, all of you!" Submissively, one after another, people went to bed and buried themselves in their quilts once again. But I remained, holding the lantern above the Moor's head.

It was the first time the deputy instructor had ever given me such a tender look. Without saying a word, she took the first-aid kit from my sister and carefully bandaged the Moor's wounds. . . .

My younger sister was the "minister of domestic affairs" of the detachment and did all our washing and cooking. The frozen vegetables brought from the company had all been eaten and no edible wild herbs could be found in such a cold winter, so she did her best to make different kinds of food for us with the remaining two bags of flour.

If I had joined this reclamation work because of the deputy instructor, then my younger sister had come to Devil's Reach because of me. I was her only family member. If I went to the ends of the earth she would go with me. Although I had treated her cruelly, she still wanted my protection and shelter. On the surface, I still appeared indifferent towards her, but in truth I had already whole-heartedly forgiven her.

Only those who are guilty of monstrous crimes do not forgive others. And after all, she was my younger sister, my only sister.

I was duty-bound to take care of her. Both before and after the scandal occurred, had I carried out my responsibilities as an elder brother? No, I hadn't. The first day we arrived in the Great Northern Wilderness, she had become fascinated by deer, and had asked if we could work at the deer farm together. But I had refused. I thought her fragility and wilfulness would cause me endless trouble and worry. Instead I had looked after my own affairs and shirked my duties as an elder brother. After her mistake, which had left her open to public censure, my first thought was that she had tarnished my reputation. I had detested her without feeling the slightest ounce of pity or sympathy for her. . . .

Now, in countless sleepless nights on Devil's Reach, I gradually realized my true nature. I had to confess to myself what a selfish brother, what a mean coward I was.

One day, when just the two of us were alone in the tent, I called over to her with a soft voice, "Sister!"

She was kneading flour on the chopping board. Hearing me calling, she raised her head and looked at me with a frightened expression, tears welling up in her eyes.

"Younger sister, are you still angry with me?" I moved to her side.

Tears, large tears trickled down her pallid face on to the dough she was kneading.

"Younger sister...." My voice was hoarse.

Turning around and throwing herself into my arms, she hugged me with flour-covered hands and sobbed.

After a long while she stopped. The first thing she asked me was, "Is mum better?"

It was as though I had been stabbed in the heart.

Oh, mother! If only you had heard what your daughter was saying, you would cry too.

May you not hear, and have no more worries about your children. But I wish that somehow you could know what your daughter had said, because she was the one who loved you most.

I hadn't the courage to tell my sister that our mother was dead. I worried about her delicate feelings and the fragile heart which wouldn't be able to bear such a shock.

I answered in a gentle voice, "She's not sick. She's been missing us terribly. When I told her that we were both alright, she felt better."

A wan smile appeared at the corners of her mouth, a pained and anguished smile. It was the first time she had smiled for several days.

"Tell me who the young man is. I want to teach him a lesson."

My sister firmly shook her head.

"Do you . . . love . . . him?"

Silent, she nodded.

"He. . . . How about him? Does he love you?"

Another silent nod.

I stared at her. The angelic expression on her face was obviously a reflection of her true feelings. I felt lost.

Suddenly she asked, "Elder brother, do you love her?"

"Who? . . ."

"The deputy instructor!"

"Where have you heard such nonsense?"

"I discovered it for myself. She likes you a lot too."

"Really!?" I grabbed her tightly by the arm.

"Yes!"

"But she likes the Moor!"

"She trusts him and so do I. He's worthy of our trust. Any girl would trust someone like him. But you're the one she's fond of. She told me that you have an artistic nature. She also knows that you're in love with her. . . ." Suddenly she stopped talking.

Almost at the same time, both of us saw the deputy instructor standing by the entrance to the tent. She had obviously overheard our conversation.

"*Aiya*! I must go and collect the clothes I left drying by the river." Finding an excuse, I fled from the tent, racing wildly across the flat land. Devil's Reach seemed to be the most beautiful place in the whole world.

That day after eating our evening meal we all gathered together in the tent to tell stories, something we did quite often to amuse ourselves. We told all sorts of stories: fairy stories, ghost stories, horror stories, humorous stories. . . . Each of us, including the deputy instructor, freed of the company's fetters, seemed to have come into our own in Devil's Reach.

The deputy instructor told us a tale from the *Odyssey*, of how the great Odysseus, returning to his homeland of Ithaca after attacking Troy, was detained by a headwind in an isolated island with his companions. She told us how the residents of the island presented them with a magic plant, common on the island, which was so delicious that upon eating it a person would forget all of their troubles. Odysseus and his companions forgot their homeland, their parents, their brothers, sisters, wives and friends when they ate this plant and so they stayed on the island for the rest of their days. . . .

To my surprise, the deputy instructor told this story in such a natural, unexaggerated manner that we were all moved by the depth of feeling she expressed.

She finished her story and left us all deep in thought. Only my younger sister heaved a long sigh, and said to herself, "I'd like to get a lot of those magic plants."

The deputy instructor sat next to the Moor, her head resting against his shoulder as usual. The flames from the big stove cast a red glow across her face. As the light flickered over her pretty features, an expression of longing and sadness appeared before my eyes.

I inevitably felt a deep sympathy for her. Had she not been restrained by the oath she had made three years earlier, she could have visited her family. Three years! She must have missed her parents and friends more than any of us.

I opened my board and said, "Don't move, Moor, I want to draw both of you." Actually I really only wanted to draw the deputy instructor, so beautiful was she, but I dared not openly say so. However, the Moor thought that I was publicly mocking him, something he could not endure. It was obvious that he had misunderstood.

When the deputy instructor subconsciously moved her head away from his shoulder, he clutched her hand and stared at me coldly, "Don't move! Let him draw. Don't disappoint him!" There was a hint of challenge in his intonation. The deputy instructor obediently leaned her head against his shoulder again and looked at me with a faint smile.

Without saying anything more I began to sketch. I was determined that the drawing would be meticulous, would really convey her beauty. So I looked up at her and drew several strokes, took another look, and drew several more. Never had I worked so carefully on a sketch. Finally I finished it and intentionally broke my pencil lead on the very last stroke.

"I'm sorry, I haven't done it very well." I handed it over to the deputy instructor.

Everyone gathered around admiring the sketch.

"Not bad! It looks just like her!"

"Ah! That's really quite a talent you've got. Why have you kept it a secret from us? Will you draw me one day?"

"*Aiya*, you've only drawn me!" The deputy instructor threw a glance at the Moor.

"I'm sorry. My pencil broke." I flushed slightly.

The deputy instuctor took the sketch and looked at it carefully for a while and then said, "May I have it?"

"Certainly. You can keep it if you like."

"I'll look after it." She looked down. As she did, the Moor stood up and slipped out of the tent. From that day on he was much more reticent.

Everything in life can be passed on except love.

I would persist in my pursuit of her, never give up my love for her, never love another, never. . . .

The first spring rain came.

The soil of the reclamation fields, dark and rich, was like a baby greedily sucking Mother Nature's milk. People often compare spring to a gorgeously dressed young maiden, but it was travelling over Devil's Reach more like a solemn woman, walking slowly and with measured paces. Carrying her uniquely soft dye with her, she turned the world green.

One day the deputy instructor fainted by the banks of the Wanderer. She was ill and did not come to for two days. While in a coma, she kept mumbling, "Wheat seeds, wheat seeds." None of the medicines in our first-aid kit could reduce her temperature. On the third day she came to, called my sister to her bedside and asked, "How much food is left now?"

"Only a little," answered my sister.

The deputy instructor looked about with an expression of deep concern, and said with a smile, "My dear friends, on behalf of the company I want to thank all of you. I am going to suggest that the Party branch records your merits. Now, except for one or two of us, everyone should return to the company and give them a hand moving here. This must be finished before the ice on Spirits' Swamp melts!" She gently took my sister's hand, "You have to stay with me, otherwise I'll feel lonely."

"I want to."

"I'll stay too," I said.

The Moor looked over at the deputy instructor. "I'd like to stay as well, if you agree."

She nodded her approval.

Now only the four of us remained on Devil's Reach. One day, a second . . . four days passed. The company still had not arrived. A company of more than two hundred people on the move would inevitably mean many difficulties. But, within those four days, Spirits' Swamp had completely melted. Our trusted friend the Wanderer River had betrayed us and collaborated against us with the Spirits' Swamp. When my sister and I went out on the fourth day, we were stunned by the change in the environment: in one night, the clear, meandering Wanderer had somewhere become a rushing current, turbid and muddy, like a wild galloping horse with hairpin turns and whirlpools, lumps of snow and ice, withered branches and broken trees. The river had overflowed and poured water across the swamp. Spirits' Swamp was now a vast expanse of water.

My sister was worried. "If the company doesn't arrive today, we won't have anything to eat."

The Moor and I shot her a glance but said nothing. What we were most worried about was how the company would cross the swamp.

Without saying anything more, my sister went back into the tent, and the Moor and I followed. She sat on a pallet beside the deputy instructor, who was still in a coma, and tears filled her eyes. Catching sight of us, she quickly wiped them away, picked up a sickle and a small basket and said, "I'm going out to dig some wild herbs."

It was almost noon when suddenly we heard my sister calling out from a distance, "Brother, brother, quick, come here!"

The Moor and I immediately jumped to our feet and ran out of the tent where we saw my sister, like a small terrier, chasing after a weak roe deer. Tossing her sickle, she hit its rear leg and it fell. She sprang at it, but failed to hold it. Struggling free, the deer ran towards the swamp. My younger sister was on its heels. At the edge of the swamp it stopped for a moment, as if looking back at her, then jumped and fled, limping.

"Stop!"

"Sister!"

The Moor and I shouted at her.

My younger sister was at the very edge of the swamp, pacing up and down. She finally came to a halt and looked at the deer with its mired feet. After a slight hesitation, she made a first cautious step into the Spirits' Swamp.

"Come back! It's dangerous...." shouted the Moor as we ran towards her.

She turned round to look at us and then waved her hand as if to say, "Leave me alone...."

When the Moor and I reached the edge of the swamp, she had already caught the deer. Struggling with the small animal, she suddenly sank deep into the mire. Before we could even think what to do, all we could see was her small hand repeatedly grasping the air. In an instant, both my sister and the deer had completely disappeared from sight.

"Keep away...." Her last words in this world still echo in my ears.

"Sister...." I shouted and raced recklessly towards the swamp.

With his strong arms the Moor grabbed me from behind. I struggled against him and then lost consciousness.

When I recovered I found myself lying in the tent, the image of my younger sister's tiny hand appearing repeatedly before my eyes. My mother's last wish rang again in my ears and tears welled up. I struggled to get up and saw the Moor standing still outside the tent. His tall figure was silhouetted clearly against the pale moon. The eerie song of a bird rang out over the swamp and sent cold shivers down my spine. Perhaps the bird was calling back my younger sister's soul. I wasn't superstitious, but the thought suddenly flashed across my mind. I stared at the Moor and blazed with hatred towards him. Had he not restrained me, I believed I would certainly have been able to save my younger sister. I was consumed with guilt over her death.

I stood up and staggered out of the tent. When the Moor heard my footsteps, he turned slowly round, his eyes wide open, and stared at me in astonishment. Maybe he knew I was enraged, for he instinctively stepped back.

I abruptly raised my fist.

"You...." Stunned, he stepped back again.

"I hate you!" I growled, clenching my teeth.

He fixed his eyes on me and said in a low, deep voice, "If it's because of your sister, then I have the right to defend myself. Do you think I have the heart of a devil? Don't you think I'm upset about your sister's death? If I could change places with her, I'd willingly be caught in that swamp myself. If it's because of her...." he threw a glance at the tent, "then go ahead and hit me! So long as I'm still alive, and she's not your wife, I have the right to love her."

His words made me shiver. As though paying condolences to my younger sister, I lowered my head. A silence reigned over the night. The flat wilderness was quiet and sullen, and even the song of the eerie bird who called back lost souls had died away.

The Moor slowly turned and walked away into the darkness. Soon his figure was lost in the hollow black night.

'What are you two quarrelling about?"

I looked over my shoulder to see the deputy instructor standing by the tent. In the past four days she had become so weak that, had she let go of her grip on the tent flap, she would most certainly have collapsed.

After a long silence two words fell from my lips, "The wolf. . . ."

"Wolf? . . ." Scrutinizing my expression, she asked, "You're hiding something from me. Where's the Moor? Where is your sister? Where have they gone? Tell me! What's happened?"

"My sister . . . died in the swamp. . . ." I couldn't hold back my sorrow any longer and covered my face with my hands, sobbing aloud.

On hearing this, she uttered only a short "Oh!" and fainted, as if she'd suddenly received a heavy blow.

The Moor had not returned even though it was now deep into the night. Where could he have gone? Would he come back and share the same tent with me again? Had he met with some mishap? If he had any kind of accident I would be responsible. . . .

I was plunged into confusion, and waited anxiously for his safe return, feeling the dark night move on its long course. I took care of the still-unconscious deputy instructor. It was the first time in the unlimited vastness of that flat wilderness that I experienced such dreadful loneliness. The whole night long I could not fall asleep.

At dawn I heard the hurried clatter of hoofs in the distance and ran out of the tent to find the Moor dismounting from a horse.

"Where did you get the horse?" I said in a friendly manner, trying to put aside all of the unpleasantness between us.

"Several days ago, I found a branch with a trail marker cut into it and knew there must be some Oroqen hunters nearby. I found them yesterday and borrowed it from them. How is the deputy instructor?"

"Still unconscious."

"The Oroqen hunters told me that maybe she has haemorrhagic fever."

"Haemorrhagic fever?!" I froze. I had once heard of someone dying of that like a leaf ripped down by the autumn wind.

"Take this horse and escort the deputy instructor back to the company right now," ordered the Moor. "You must go back the way we came and you will probably meet up with our company and be able to save her."

"No, I'll stay here and you take her."

"I'm too heavy. If I try and take her, the horse will certainly collapse halfway there. It's already exhausted. The two of you go together. If you head westward fifty *li* you can cut around Spirits' Swamp, and go due west beside it!"

To continue arguing with him would have been hypocritical.

The Moor tied the unconscious deputy instructor to my back and then helped me mount.

"Take the gun!"

"You keep it."

"No, you should take it. You need to be prepared for any eventuality." He fastened the gun to the saddle, reined the horse around and then gave the animal a strong punch on its rump.

The horse neighed and raced westward at full gallop.

Although the westward route was thirty *li* less than the eastward one, we had to cross a vast grassland. We were fortunate in having a well-bred Oroqen hunter, a short and compact animal, not handsome but able to bear hardships and stand up to gruelling work. It really is the hunters' friend, the camel of the wilderness.

Having passed the Spirits' Swamp I continued urging the horse on. It seemed to understand what I wanted, and galloped on without slackening. After travelling nearly thirty *li* I felt my cotton-padded trousers drenched by the animal's sweat. Suddenly it snorted several times and began to stagger. It tried to continue with all its strength, but its forelegs buckled. As soon as I dismounted, it instantly inclined to one side, stretched out its neck, and collapsed.

The horse's belly rose and fell, warm air spurting from its nostrils, its mouth dribbling white foam. Before lying down, the intelligent animal had paused to prevent its full weight crushing down on its rider's leg and had looked at me almost apologetically with its clear eyes.

"Put me down! Put me down! Where are we? What are we doing here? Where are you taking me?"

The deputy instructor had come to, and struggled against the rope tying her to me.

I untied the rope and gently put her down on the

ground, her head and shoulders leaning against my chest.

"I'm taking you to meet the company. You're seriously ill."

She murmured, "Am I going to die? Is that it?"

I felt upset hearing my beloved say such words and replied in a loud voice, "No, of course not!"

She forced a smile, "I'm not afraid of death. Really. Don't you remember the lines in our oath to settle in the wilderness: 'It's not necessary to be buried in our home village, everywhere in the wilderness is our home.' The only thing I regret is that in a few months I would have been able to visit my parents. I really miss them. They're longing for my visit, nearly going crazy over it. I've written them a letter promising to go after the autumn harvest here, but now...."

I sobbed, my tears falling on her face.

"Don't cry." She gently took my hand. "If I do die, please bury me beside Spirits' Swamp and let me keep your younger sister company. She was a good girl. My only request is that on my grave tablet, I would like the word 'reclaimer' carved together with my name...." Large tears gradually filled the corners of her eyes.

I held her tightly and sobbed loudly and bitterly.

"Look, what's that? It's like that magic fruit in the legend. Would you break off a branch for me, please?" Her large, beautiful eyes were fixed on something nearby.

Following her line of vision, I saw a cluster of purplish-red azaleas in bud. I helped her to lean against the saddle and went over to break off the branch. She was dead when I returned.

She and the Oroqen horse had stopped breathing at the same time.

Beneath me I felt the ground spinning; above, the blue sky turned black.

Wiping my eyes and pinning the azaleas to her chest, I knelt down and kissed her pale lips for a long time. I think that had she been alive, she would not have blamed me.

Carrying her body on my back, I walked on.

I saw the company caravan appear on the distant horizon.

The whole company expressed sorrow at the death of the deputy instructor. Everyone cried.

. . . . . .

When the company caravan, the carts, sleds, tractors and trucks drew near the swamp, it was already dusk. Someone found a cotton-padded hat stuck on a wooden pole temporarily used as a grave marker. I went ahead and removed the hat. It was the Moor's dog-skin hat. A slip of paper inside read: "I've discovered a way through Spirits' Swamp and have marked it with twigs. A *li* east of here. . . ."

That night the whole company passed safely across the swamp leaving behind only the carts which might get stuck. But nowhere could we find the Moor.

The next morning, beside the Wanderer we discovered bloody strips of the Moor's clothing, a big axe and three dead wolves. . . . There had been a fierce fight between him and the wolves. We imagined how he had fallen after having fought with all his might against them.

During those sorrowful days we began to seed Devil's Reach.

In accordance with their last wishes, we buried the deputy instructor by Spirits' Swamp. From Camel Mountain, a hundred miles away, we transported a huge grey stone which the old mason in our company chiselled into a grave tablet and on which he carved the words: "In memory of reclaimers Li Xiaoyan, Wang Zhigang, Liang Shanshan, our beloved comrades. . . ."

On Camel Mountain we felled more than a thousand pine trees to make a road across Spirits' Swamp along the markers placed by the Moor, and named it "Reclaimers' Road". The following year several other companies came to settle on Devil's Reach.

At last we conquered Spirits' Swamp.

One silent dusk when I visited the reclaimers' graves I saw a stranger standing there and found a bunch of azaleas on the tablet. Azaleas had been my sister's favourite flower.

In an instant, I understood that the stranger was the young man who had been in love with her.

From the expression on his face, I could see that he would never leave Devil's Reach.

We exchanged a glance and he turned and walked slowly away.

I didn't stop him to ask his name, nor even think to ask where he came from. . . .

He was one of our generation — that was all I needed to know.

We had experienced the blizzards of the Great Northern Wilderness, the hardships and the joy of reclaiming this land of wonder and mystery. From then on, no matter what the difficulties were, whether we stayed or whether we left, nothing could produce fear in us or make us surrender.... The Great Northern Wilderness!

Translated by Shen Zhen

Liang Xiaosheng, born in Harbin in 1949, spent eight years working on land reclamation projects in China's northeast. He subsequently became a reporter on a local paper and in 1975 entered the Chinese language department of Fudan University in Shanghai. After graduation he was appointed to work as an editor at Beijing Film Studio. In recent years, he has published more than 34 short stories. "A Land of Wonder and Mystery" won an award in 1983.

当 代 优 秀 小 说 选

熊 猫 丛 书

★

《中国文学》雜誌社出版

（中国北京百万庄路24号）

外文印刷厂印刷

中国国际书店发行

1984年（36开）第1版

编号：（英）2—916—22

00190

10—E—1754P